MY FIANCÉ'S BROTHER

BOOK 1: THE NAVY SEAL SERIES

ODETTE STONE

~

My Fiancé's Brother, The Navy SEAL Series, Book 1

Copyright © 2017 by Odette Stone

www.odettestone.com

First edition, May 2017

To Colleen Hammermaster.

When no one believed in me, you did. Thank you.

CHAPTER ONE

I STARED AT MYSELF IN THE GRIMY GLASS DOOR OF THE SUBWAY TRAIN, trying to avoid the crush of jostling people that pressed against my back. I looked less like a bride-to-be, and more like a college waif with my red hair pulled into a ponytail and my blue eyes devoid of make-up. I had gotten caught up in my book and when I realized how late it was, I had to run just to get out the door, let alone bother with makeup.

The train peeled into my station before jerking hard to a stop, throwing the person behind me against my back. The crowd spilled around me into the underground station once the doors were open. I staggered onto the street above after running up two flights of stairs and passed panhandlers, food trucks that sizzled with the smell of hot grease and overflowing garbage cans. I let out a breath of relief when I reached my destination, the Paper Pelican.

The store was quiet with only the clerk standing at the counter. I glanced at my watch. I was a bit early, and Matt generally was a bit late. I spend an inordinate amount of time browsing through the aisle, trying to look like an avid shopper.

Where was Matt? I checked my phone. No messages. I debated on what to do. He hated it when I called him out for being late, but the store was only open for another 30 minutes. I had deliberately picked this store for our wedding invitations, because it was two blocks away from his office. I decided, with a bit of trepidation, to send him a text.

Me: I'm just at the Paper Pelican. Are you on your way?

Matt: Got busy. Sorry. You're on your own.

A headache pinched at the base of my neck. This was the second time that Matt had stood me up at the Paper Pelican. He didn't seem to realize that I felt paralyzed with indecision about everything that involved our wedding. I needed guidance and input from him. I couldn't seem to organize a single detail, and our wedding loomed a mere twelve weeks away. Maybe I could bring him some invitation samples to dinner.

Me: Where do you want to meet for dinner?

Another long pause before he responded.

Matt: Stuck in a meeting. Will be home late.

He always did this. Why didn't he care about our wedding? We had so many things to cover, and he refused to help. Didn't he realize that I needed his help? Looking towards the counter, I felt sick.

Why hadn't I hired a wedding planner? Oh right, because Matt had convinced me that we'd have a lot of fun planning this wedding together. I took a deep breath. I could do this. I just needed to be decisive. I squared my shoulders and walked up to the front counter. The clerk looked annoyed. We both knew she wanted to start closing the store.

"I'd like to order some wedding invitations."

She grabbed an order sheet and then stood poised with a pen. "Do you have a wedding palette color?"

"Uh. Not yet."

"Do you know how many invitations you need?"

I took a deep breath. Matt still hadn't given me his guest list. "Perhaps between 50 and 200?"

"Do you prefer a reply card and envelope or a reply postcard?"

"I'm not sure."

"Do you know what kind of printing you like?"

A wave of heat washed over my body. "What are my options?"

"Letterpress, engraving, embossing, thermography, and flat printing."

These choices were impossible. This was precisely why I needed Matt here. What did he like? What did he want?

"I don't know."

"Do you know what kind of paper you want?"

My hands curled so tight that my nails dug into my palms. "Not yet."

"Do you have any idea what you want your invitations to look like?"

This was a mistake. "I should go."

She eyed the clock. "Okay. Would you like any samples?"

"I'll come back."

"Have a good night."

I STOOD OUTSIDE THE STORE AND SCRUBBED MY FACE. THREE MONTHS UNTIL the wedding. I had no idea how we would get everything planned in time. Matt was working late, but he needed to eat, right? I could go to his office, wait until his meeting was finished and then we could order take out. He worked long hours as a lawyer. He could afford to spend half an hour with me. With renewed determination, I walked towards his office building. I stood across the street and waited for the light to change. I saw him walk with purpose down the steps.

I raised my hand and waved. "Matt!"

The roar of the street drowned out my voice.

He walked towards a cab. I watched as a woman got out of the cab. I couldn't see her face, but she had long beautiful brown hair. He smiled and kissed her on the cheek before they both climbed back into the cab.

I stood in complete shock. The light turned green, and people streamed around me. Had that really been Matt? Who was the woman?

I swallowed hard and crossed the street, feeling my heart beat in my chest. She was probably just a client. Matt was working a business dinner. My granny used to warn me not to borrow trouble with my imagination. She used to tell me that I needed to take life as it was and stop worrying about things I had no control over.

It took me 15 minutes before I managed to find a cab.

"Where to lady?"

I gave him my address and sank back into the worn seat and stared unseeing out the dirty window. How likely was it that he would kiss a female client on the cheek? If I confronted Matt about this, he would tell me that I was being insecure. I sighed.

"That's quite the sigh," the driver said, "Tough day?"

Our eyes met in the review mirror.

"I just saw my fiancé get into a cab with another woman."

He gave me another glance. "What spooked you?"

"Pardon me?"

"What's making you nervous?"

I toed a dirty Kleenex on the floor with my sneaker. "He kissed her on the cheek. He stood me up and said he was busy working and then I saw him smiling at her and he kissed her on the cheek."

"What kind of kiss?"

I blinked. "Uh."

"Was it a sexy kiss or more that French thing on both cheeks? Maybe he was trying to be sophisticated."

My mind replayed what I saw. Matt had put his hand on her upper arm. He had smiled at her face. And when he leaned in and kissed her, he had lingered. It had felt intimate.

"He lingered."

The cab driver shook his head. "You know, in my line of work, I've seen it all. Trust your gut. If you saw something you didn't like, it's probably ten times worse than you're imagining."

"Matt would never cheat on me."

"That's what they all say." He eyeballed me in the mirror. "You look too young to get married. Are you even out of high school?"

I sighed. "Yeah, I'm 24."

"Well, you look too young to be getting married. You should be out there, having fun," he advised. "Trust me. After you get married, the kids come. And after they arrive, your whole world changes."

"I guess." Not wanting to admit that I couldn't wait to have a baby. All my friends had important careers. I felt slightly ashamed that my only goal was to get married and start a family.

The cab driver spoke to me. I looked up and realized that he had pulled up in front of my loft. I dug through my bag to find some cash.

"You sure this is the right place?" he peered through the windshield around the area. It was the most up and coming neighborhood. Still mostly industrial, there were a handful of condos and lofts in the area.

"Yeah, this is my building."

Matt had convinced me to buy a loft here. He had promised me that he'd help me with the renovations. He had been too busy, and the vast majority had fallen on my shoulders. I had been hopeless dealing with the decisions and the contractors, and without telling Matt, I had hired a decorator to take over the project and see it to completion. To this day, Matt still believed that I had managed to convert the old building into the loft.

"You should be careful out here. They haven't caught the throat slayer yet."

I shuddered. "Who is the throat slayer?"

"Some serial killer creep who has been killing women. They say he chokes them to death."

My heart tripped. "I'm sure he isn't out here."

The cabbie looked over his shoulder at me. "Just be careful, kid."

CHAPTER TWO

I jerked awake. My entire body felt tense with fear, but I had no idea why. I lifted my head, my ears straining. Something had woken me. Another noise from downstairs made my heart race. *Where was my phone?* With shaking limbs, I stood at my closed door and listened. Someone was downstairs and it wasn't Matt. I had gotten up earlier in an attempt to talk to him about the wedding invitations, but he'd already been half out the door. I had returned to bed and now I was a sitting duck in my bedroom while some intruder rooted around downstairs.

My need to hide overwhelmed me. Instead, I looked around for a weapon. My golf clubs. I gingerly pulled out my seven iron. In bare feet, I eased my bedroom door open. I peered over the glass balcony that overlooked the central living area of the loft. I couldn't see anyone. Had I imagined those noises? I could see my cell phone charging on the counter. Never again. I would never leave my cell phone downstairs again.

I slowly made my way towards the stairs, keeping my back pressed up against the wall. Everything was silent below. I crept down the open curved stairs. Nothing. My imagination played tricks on me. I let out a deep breath. I needed to get a grip. My therapist used to tell me that my fear was simply my false expectations appearing real. A catchy acronym to remind me that my fear of an intruder was irrational.

Heart pounded in my throat, I walked towards the large industrial sliding door to ensure that Matt had set the alarm. My foot connected with something solid and I barely caught my balance as I tripped over it.

Recovering, I turned around to stare at the huge black canvas duffle bag. The toilet flushed behind me from the half bath. I froze and my mind raced. I needed to hide.

I don't remember moving. Suddenly, I was flattened against the wall in the front walk-in closet. My breath sounded harsh. My heart raced to the point that I feared I would pass out. My vision blurred with tears.

I strained to listen. I could hear taps running and then the bathroom door opened. Footsteps. Then nothing. Holding my breath, I peered around the corner. In front of his duffle bag, a massive man crouched on his haunches. He had unzipped it and was rifling through it. Was that his *kill kit?*

My body shook. My stomach clenched rock hard. White knuckles gripped the club over my shoulder. I needed to get one clean shot to his head. Then I could run. I crept up behind him. I saw a gun. With a mangled cry, I swung my club as hard as I could. My club connected with air.

Now I was flat on my back with my club pressed against my neck. The monster was on top of me. Pinning me to the floor. I caught a glimpse of a shocked expression and green eyes and then everything faded to black.

I WAS ON MY BACK. I OPENED MY EYES AND TOOK IN THE HIGH LIVING ROOM ceiling from the couch. Someone had pulled a couch throw over me. Images crashed through me. The intruder. A gun. Being flipped onto the floor.

With a cry, I half sat up. The intruder sat in the wingback chair across from me. He stared at me without expression. The pain that compressed my chest was so intense, so all-consuming, I had to look to see if I had a knife sticking out of my chest. No blood. No knife. Just fear that was so real I could taste it.

The man who broke into my loft looked like an intense terminator Robo-cop. All muscles and scariness. Would he torture me like my parents had been tortured or would he kill me quickly? I didn't care about the money. I already decided I would give him whatever he wanted. I just didn't want to die.

"You passed out," his voice was deep and rough. "Drink some tea."

My eyes flicked to a steaming mug on the coffee table. None of this was making sense.

"You made tea?"

He didn't answer. He just sat there dwarfing my favorite chair. Black army boots. Tree trunk legs were clad in army fatigues. Herculean arms crossed over a powerful chest. A thick neck. Stubble that was almost a full beard. A strong jaw and brow. Eyes wide and green. Messy dark blond hair.

I worked to remember what my self-defense class taught me. Keep them talking. Humanize yourself. Refer to your friends and family. Talk about yourself as a person. And whatever you do, *never* ask them what they're going to do to you.

"Are you going to kill me?"

A shocked expression flitted across his face. He leaned forward, resting his arms on his knees. "Matt didn't tell you."

"What does Matt have to do with this?" My voice shook. How did he know Matt? Had Matt hired him?

"Matt invited me to stay here."

I stared back blankly as I tried to connect the dots. He wasn't here to kill me. He knew Matt. Matt invited him to stay with us.

"What?"

"You obviously didn't know about this. I should go."

He stood up. He was so big he was a man tree.

"Who are you?" Still feeling woozy, I threw the blanket off my body and struggled to a sitting position.

"My name is Jackson." He moved with grace towards his bag.

Jackson? This was Jackson? Matt's childhood friend? I tried to remember what Matt had told me about Jackson but the stories were few and far between.

I stood up on wobbling legs. "You were friends with Matt when you were kids, right?"

"Is that what he told you?"

I had no idea what that meant. His massive frame crouched over his duffle bag while he rearranged something. My shock was fading, and now I realized that I had just tried to kill Matt's friend.

"Matt invited you to stay here?"

He didn't look up at me. "Yes ma'am, sorry to have scared you."

I shut my eyes. Matt had invited this behemoth man to come and stay with us. I had no idea why he would do that, but Matt must have his reasons.

"You can't leave."

He didn't respond. He just zipped up the bag, stood up, and swung the huge bag over his shoulder.

Matt always accused me of not being kind to his friends. A couple of weeks ago, after an incredibly awkward dinner with two of his friends, Matt had read me the riot act. He told me I need to be nicer to his friends. He never acknowledged that his friends were rude assholes, but I had promised him that I would try harder. How would I tell Matt that I had chased Jackson off? It wasn't a conversation I wanted to have with Matt.

"You can call me Emily, and this was just a big misunderstanding," I started, desperate to figure out how to fix this. "Just because I almost killed you doesn't mean you're not welcome."

"You didn't even come close to killing me." He glanced at the door. He wanted to leave.

"I almost smashed your skull."

"I was aware of you the moment I came out of the washroom. I just wanted to disarm you without hurting you."

Our eyes met. That part was true. Somehow he had managed to flip me to the floor and cushion my landing at the same time. He hadn't even winded me.

He added. "I didn't think you'd pass out."

Heat crept up my chest, my neck and then my entire face went red hot. I lifted my chin a fraction, unable to meet his eyes. "I was scared."

"You acted pretty brave for being scared."

My eyes collided with his gaze for a millisecond. I swallowed. This was a monumental cluster. How would I explain to Matt that Jackson was here but then he left? I needed him to stay.

"I'd appreciate it if you would let me make you breakfast."

He held himself still for a long moment. "Unnecessary."

He was so unyielding. He reminded me of a solid, powerful and unbending mountain.

Pent-up air wheezed out of my chest. I crossed my arms over my chest, suddenly conscious of the fact that I was wearing only a tank top and a pair of sleeping shorts. "I don't want to tell Matt that I scared you off."

His eyes narrowed. "You aren't scaring me off."

"Could have fooled me."

I never talked like this. I was quiet and unassuming. Why I had chosen the most intimidating man to exert my cheekiness with was beyond me.

His eyes flickered over me. And then in an answer, he dropped the duffle bag on the floor with a heavy thud.

"Just let me get dressed."

Back in my room, I caught sight of my reflection. My long copper red hair stuck up in every direction. I had a big pillow crease on the side of my face. My tank top was so thin the material was practically see through.

I tried to remember what Matt had told me about Jackson. Something about a tree fort and another story about a schoolyard fight? Matt said that they'd grown apart because they were so different.

That was an understatement.

Matt was a young liberal, urban lawyer. He dressed his lanky frame in expensive suits, he could talk about wine for hours, and he had a constant, impatient vibe to him. The fierce man downstairs, with a body like a solid fortress, didn't even seem human. His intensity made him unapproachable. He intimidated me. I could not imagine him and Matt having anything in common.

It baffled me that Matt had invited him to stay with us. For how long? Was Jackson just passing through town?

I squared my shoulders. If Matt wanted his friend to stay with us, I would make him feel as welcome as possible.

CHAPTER THREE

From my vantage point on the stairs, I could see Jackson sitting at the island. His glance up at me was brief, but I immediately felt self-conscious. To compensate, I bustled into the kitchen, and asked in a bright voice, "What would you like for breakfast?"

"You don't have to bother."

"It's no bother," I pulled a pan out of the oven drawer. "Omelet?"

"Anything is fine."

I felt unnerved by his presence. My kitchen was huge, but when he watched me, there wasn't room to breathe. I did my best to ignore him and started to cook. I wracked my brain to think of something to say, but I came up blank. So I just concentrated on what I was doing.

"Do you want some coffee?"

Did my voice sound breathless? I took a few calming breaths.

"Sure."

I looked over my shoulder. "I can do a cappuccino, or a latte and Matt has some coffee syrups."

He didn't answer me, so I walked over to the espresso machine and started reading off the labels. "He has Bourbon Caramel, Brown Sugar Cinnamon, Mojito Mint, and Sweet Heat."

A long pause hung between us, and finally, he asked, "What's Sweet Heat?"

"I'm not sure," I picked up the bottle and read out loud, "fiery heat of ghost peppers with the sweetness of pure cane sugar."

More silence. I glanced over my shoulder. He had no expression. "Just a coffee."

"So an Americano?"

He gave a short nod.

I made him a coffee which he took black. Of course, he did. Then I slid fruit and an omelet in front of him.

"Where's your plate?"

I set a bowl of fruit down. "I'm not much of a breakfast eater."

He waited for me to sit, before he picked up his fork.

We ate in silence. I studied him through my eyelashes. "So where are you visiting from?"

"Virginia."

I wasn't used to a man giving me so little to work with during a conversation. "Are you just up for a visit?"

"I'm doing a three-month outpatient program at the hospital."

I eyed him. There didn't seem to be anything physically wrong with him. "I hope everything is okay."

He didn't respond.

"That means you'll be here for our wedding."

Green eyes flickered over my face and then dropped to the ring on my left hand. "Matt didn't tell me he was engaged."

I could not reconcile Matt with this man. Matt's friends were smooth and eloquent. They liked to talk about fine wines and the Met. Jackson's silence made him unique.

He stood up and picked up his plate.

"I'll do those," I protested.

He ignored me. I watched in bemusement as he ran the water and then found the soap from beneath the sink. He washed the pan and the three other items in the sink, before picking up a dishtowel and drying them off. He even wiped the length of my countertops. I had never seen Matt willingly volunteer to help with dishes. This guy, who looked like he could kill with his bare hands, quietly tidied up.

"Thank you."

He nodded and looked towards the door. I knew he wanted to leave. I stood up. "Why don't I show you your room?"

He turned his attention back to me. Again, I couldn't read the expression on his face.

"I mean it. I'm not letting you leave here."

"I don't want to put you out."

I stood up next to his giant frame. "If you leave, Matt is going to ask me why. And I don't want to have that conversation."

The best I got from him was a nod.

He grabbed his duffle bag and then I led him up the steps. I was nervous, and when I get nervous, I babble.

"This is Matt's room. This is my room. Both our rooms have bathrooms. This is the laundry room. Please help yourself. I'm sorry, but your room doesn't have a bathroom attached. There's one in the hall here. And this'll be your room."

I pushed open the door and shut my eyes in shame. There was a partially deflated air mattress lying on the floor, an old dresser and a vacuum cleaner in the middle of the room. His eyes looked around the room. "This is fine."

"Ha," I said, my face red. "Obviously, I'll get a bed in here."

"I don't need a bed. I can sleep anywhere."

"Well, you can't sleep on the hardwood."

"This is fine."

My eyebrows went up. "I'll get you a bed."

Even if it meant I had to drag my own bed into this room.

"You two have separate rooms."

My face burst into heat. The first comment he volunteered in over an hour was about my sex life?

I lifted my chin a notch. "I'm saving myself for marriage."

"People still do that?"

I forced myself to meet his gaze. There was an expression of faint curiosity on his face. So Mr. Stone Face had some emotion within him. "You seem surprised."

"Why?"

"Why what?"

"Why are you saving yourself?"

My mouth dropped open. No one was this blunt. Especially about something so delicate. I could offer him a pat answer, but I decided to be honest.

"It wasn't a conscious choice but it just happened."

My face felt hot.

"Are you religious?"

"Not particularly."

"How long have you and Matt been together?"

"About a year."

He stood and stared at me.

"Okay," I said. My voice firm. "I'll let you unpack."

I pushed the vacuum cleaner towards the door.

"I don't think something like that just happens."

I went completely still. "Excuse me?"

"It's definitely a choice."

My face was on fire. I glanced back at him. A slow smile crossed his face. Good *grief*. That smile changed his whole face. He was stunning looking. Magnificent. Something dark fluttered in my belly. In my throat, my breath hitched. I worked to yank my gaze away from his.

Out of breath, I beelined it to my bedroom. He gives me one smile and my entire body tingles?

From my bedroom, I called Matt. No answer.

I texted him.

Me: Your friend Jackson arrived. Did you invite him to stay here?

No response. Well that was just perfect. Typical of Matt to drop a bomb and pull a disappearing act. I put my hands on my warm face. My overreaction to Jackson was probably just a fall out response to the stress of this morning. I had an inordinate fear of home invasions. This morning had triggered a lot of repressed fear.

I sucked in a big breath and worked to remember what my therapist told me.

I needed to focus on the now.

Now, I need to find a bed for the guest room. I walked downstairs with my iPad. My mysterious guest was not in sight.

After a series of phone calls, I realized that beds are not bought and delivered on the same day. In fact, beds take a couple of weeks to be ordered and delivered. Finally, I found one factory warehouse store that did have new mattresses and frames ready to go, but I'd need to pick up the bed myself. Renting a truck would not be an issue, but I didn't know how to drive a truck in the city. Anything bigger than my mini put me at risk of side-swiping other cars. Not to mention I had no idea how I'd unload a bed and drag it upstairs. Maybe if I could unload it off the truck in the garage downstairs, Matt and Jackson could bring it up tonight.

I SENSED JACKSON COMING DOWN THE STAIRS BEHIND ME.

I twisted in my seat to look at him. "Do you know how to drive a truck?"

"I have a truck. What do you need?"

"I need to pick up your bed."

"From where?"

"The store."

A beat passed. "I don't have to stay here. Emily."

My stupid heart fluttered at the sound of him saying my name. He was right. He didn't have to stay here. In fact, it didn't make any sense that this stranger would become an extended guest. But for reasons I could not explain, I wanted to make him stay.

Perhaps it was the sense that he was hell-bent on leaving. I got the distinct impression he despised imposing. Especially on strangers. The man seemed resolute on being self-contained. He was not some freeloader who walked into a place and made himself at home. He didn't want to be here. Which made me want to welcome him and make him feel at home.

"Why don't you want to stay here?"

Green eyes squinted at me. He spread his big hands out wide to stretch and then relaxed them. "Let's go."

I grabbed my bag and then headed downstairs. His truck was big and black and looked exactly like the kind of vehicle this man would drive. I didn't want to drive with him because *we might have to talk.*

In a cowardly act, with my head bent over my phone, I gave him the address. He didn't seem bothered by the fact that I wanted to take my own car.

"See you there!"

He responded with another intense look and then he was gone.

CHAPTER FOUR

THE BED STORE HAD A SHOWROOM FULL OF BEDS. JACKSON PROWLED AROUND while I listened to a salesperson talk about foam density and interconnected coils. I sat down on a few mattresses but I had no idea what Jackson's preference was when it came to mattresses.

"Jackson."

He walked towards us. His movement added to his tough demeanor. I tried to pinpoint why he seemed so dangerous, but I couldn't put my finger on it.

"What kind of bed do you like?"

His inscrutable expression took in the sales guy, me and the bed.

I tried again. "Do you like soft beds? Hard beds? A mattress with lots of spring?"

My face burst into heat. Something about a springy bed sounded provocative to my ears. He contemplated my red face.

Finally, he answered. "It doesn't matter."

The salesperson interjected, "The best way to figure out what you like is to test drive the beds."

An insane vision of Jackson and I rolling around on the bed came to mind. Another wave of heat washed over me. I refrained from fanning my face.

Jackson looked towards the door. He may want to bolt, but there was no way I was choosing his bed. The least he could do was tell me what he liked.

"Well, better get testing then," I said, waving my hand towards the bed. I sat down on the bed and then lay back. "This one seems a bit too hard for my taste, but you tell me."

His face was almost a scowl, but he moved to the other side of the bed. The mattress depressed beside me. I turned my head. He was lying on his back, staring up at the ceiling. This was the last place he wanted to be.

"What do you think?" It was strangely intimate to be lying next to him. Which made me nervous.

"Too hard."

I scrambled up to a sitting position. "We need a softer bed."

The salesperson beamed. "There is a memory foam mattress right over here."

I lay down on the next bed.

"I don't know. This one feels a bit too spongy."

Jackson stood next to the bed. I patted the bed. With a look of resignation, he lay down beside me. "Yup."

"How about this one over here," the salesperson pointed at the next bed. "This is a nice pillow top."

The bed felt soft. I sighed with comfort. I felt the bed move as Jackson lay down beside me. "What do you think?"

"Not bad."

I smiled at the ceiling. "Do you think you could sleep on this bed?"

"Yep."

Anticipating a sale, the hovering salesperson said, "Are you a side sleeper or do you prefer to sleep on your back?"

"I sleep on my side," I said. The salesperson waited for Jackson to answer.

I turned my head. "And you?"

"My back."

"I have the perfect pillows for you both." The salesperson rushed away.

I studied Jackson's profile. He had such strong features. My friends would go bananas over this man. I could hint that he was a serial killer and they would still be scrambling over each other to get to him.

"Here we are," the salesperson handed me a pillow. "This is specially designed for the side sleeper."

I tucked it under my head and rolled over on my side towards Jackson. The salesperson held out a pillow towards Jackson. "This is for the back sleeper."

I held my breath, wondering if he'd swat the pillow away. With a sigh, he tucked it under his head.

The salesperson walked a discrete distance away.

I lay curled up on my side. Even clothed and in a public store, it was strangely intimate to be lying next to this man in a bed. I felt dwarfed by his presence. We were two opposite ends of a spectrum. Next to my petite frame, he was massive in size.

He glanced at me and our gazes locked.

I broke the silence. "Usually when I meet Matt's friends, they bore me to death with their insights on their favorite wine,"

"What are you saying?" he murmured, his eyes never leaving mine.

"Attempted murder and bed shopping is a lot more fun."

His smile sucker punched me. My breath caught in my throat. No one had the right to be that attractive.

"Were you attacked before?"

His words shocked me. "Excuse me?"

"Right before you fainted, you said, not again."

A wave of pain flashed through my body. I hated talking about my parents. "My parents died when I was 15."

That wasn't a great explanation, but it was the best he was getting from me.

"Okay." His eyes studied me.

"It was a bad situation."

"I'm sorry I scared you."

My breath let out of my lungs in a rush. "That's okay."

We looked at each other. I swallowed and then the words blurted out of me. "They were killed by a home invader."

He winced. "Were you there?"

"Yes."

In two short conversations, this man had somehow persuaded me to confess my virginity and my most traumatic life event. I had no idea how he managed to do that, but it was intimidating as hell.

"So what do you two think?" the salesperson asked from the foot of the bed.

I shot off the bed. "We'll take it."

I ENDED UP BUYING THE BED, THE FRAME, AND LINENS. I WATCHED AS Jackson and the sales guy loaded everything into the back of the truck. Jackson moved with ease. He didn't seem injured. What treatment was he receiving at the hospital? Did he have some disease? What kind of medical treatment was he getting? He appeared fit and healthy. There was no visible injury.

Back at the loft, I inwardly fretted about how we would get the mattress upstairs, but Jackson easily carried everything up.

"I stuck your sheets in the wash," I said from the doorway of his bedroom.

Jackson was on the floor of his room, putting the bed frame together.

"Thanks."

"Do you need any help?"

"I'm good."

I hovered. Part of me wanted to bolt, the other part of me wanted to stay.

"How did you two meet?" His question came out of nowhere.

"Me and Matt?" I frowned. "He came into the art gallery that I work at."

"Did he ask you out?"

"No. But we ran into each other at a party about a month later and he asked me out."

"When did you get engaged?"

"Just after Christmas."

"And you started dating a year ago?"

I lifted my chin. "Yes."

"Did you buy this place together?"

"Kind of."

He glanced up at me.

"I bought it. Matt fell in love with it."

"But you don't love it."

Did this man have x-ray eyes into my soul? How could he possibly know that?

"I'm still getting used to this place. I used to live in my granny's place, but I'm sure this is going to be fine."

He gave me a quick glance. As far as looks went, that one was pretty benign, but it still made me feel defensive.

I took an even breath. I had no idea why I was balking at his benevolent responses. He wasn't overly scrutinizing me, yet I still felt judged.

"I thought it was a good idea. Plus Matt said that this place would have great resale value."

"Sure."

"Are you dating anyone?" I deliberately steered the conversation towards him.

A long beat. "No."

"Any kids?"

"No."

"Oh. Well okay." I turned to go. Just as I was about to cross the threshold, he spoke.

"Do you want kids?"

I looked over my shoulder and debated how to answer. I wanted a baby and to be part of a family. The sooner, the better. But this was a huge point of contention between Matt and myself. I wanted to start a family right away. Matt wanted to wait. "I want kids very much."

Green eyes met mine. Studying me.

I couldn't understand his look, and that made me feel awkward. "What about you? Do you want kids?"

He shrugged and turned away. "Probably not a good idea."

I stared at his back. What did that mean? Why did he think he shouldn't have kids? I wanted to press him because it was my innate nature to convince everyone that they needed children, but I refrained. Maybe men didn't typically want children? With a maturity I didn't feel, I changed the subject.

"Come and go as you please. I left a key on the island for you. Will you be here for dinner?"

"You don't have to cook for me."

"I cook every night. It isn't any bother. Just let me know."

"Will Matt be home?"

"Yes." My fingers crossed behind my back. I would do my best to get Matt home for dinner.

"Can I bring anything?"

"No."

"Thanks, Emily."

There he was repeating my name in that deep, gravelly voice. Face aflame, I turned and fled.

CHAPTER FIVE

AFTER JACKSON LEFT, I CREPT INTO HIS ROOM WITH THE WASHED LINEN TO make up his bed. The room still felt empty. I dragged in a small table for a nightstand. Then I added lamps and a throw blanket and I stocked his bathroom with fresh towels, soap, and shampoo.

Matt texted me back.

Matt: Sorry. I forgot to tell you about Jackson.

When was the last time Matt talked to Jackson? What was their relationship? Why had he invited his childhood friend to visit? How long was he staying? I chewed on my lip, debating on what to write.

Me: How long do you think he'll stay?

Matt: I don't know. Maybe a few months?

In disbelief, I stared at my phone. Jackson was going to move in with us for a few months? I took a few deep breaths. It'd be fine. This would be fine. Matt would come home tonight, and he'd explain everything to me.

Me: Okay. I'm going to make dinner for us all tonight. Will you be home?

Matt: Sure

∿

A FEW HOURS LATER, DINNER WAS ALMOST READY, AND THERE WAS NO SIGN of either Jackson or Matt. Not wanting to eat dinner alone with our guest, I pressure texted Matt.

Me: Are you on your way home?
Matt: I'm leaving in 5 minutes.

A knock sounded on the door.

"Come in." My voice echoed across the loft.

Jackson wore a baseball cap and a t-shirt that looked damp in places. In his big hand, he carried a small paper bag. His glance took in the entirety of the loft and the stairs. He was looking for Matt. He stopped on the other side of the island. His eyes observed the simmering pots on the stove behind me, but he didn't speak.

"No formality required. You don't have to knock."

His response was deadpan. "I thought it'd be safer."

At my expense, the man had cracked a joke. It took me a moment, but I started to laugh.

"Is Matt here?"

"He texted that he's leaving the office in a few minutes."

He put the bag down and pushed it towards me.

"Oh." My breath hitched in my throat. I opened the bag, and the most beautiful scent wafted out. Inside was a delicate little blue ceramic pot with a perfect jasmine plant inside. I buried my face into the tiny white flowers. "I love the smell of jasmine."

He cleared his throat and avoided my gaze.

"Thank you so much," I said. "That's so thoughtful."

"Would you mind if I took a quick shower? I was working out."

"Of course. Please make yourself at home."

He took the stairs three at a time. All power and smooth movements. I watched as he walked along the long hallway. When he got to his room, he turned on the light and stood there, taking in my homey touches. My heart thumped in my chest. Despite his wary nature, something was driving me to make him feel welcome.

Why did I care if he was comfortable here?

I rushed around to put the final touches on the roast chicken meal. Without warning, Jackson now stood next to the island. I jerked when I saw him. Usually, I could hear Matt coming from a mile away. This guy was a Ninja. His messy hair was wet and he exuded a fresh, clean scent.

"Thanks for fixing up my room." His eye contact was steady.

I wanted to, but I couldn't hold his gaze. "You're welcome. Just let me text Matt real quick and see where he's at."

Me: Dinner is ready

Matt: Almost done. Go ahead without me. I'll get there asap.

I took a deep calming breath. This was fine. Matt frequently ran late, but he knew about Jackson. He'd be home for dinner.

"Matt's running late. Let's start. He should be here soon."

He gave a short nod and helped me carry food to the table.

"Please sit," I gestured to a seat.

The lone burning candle in the center of the table had felt like a festive gesture before, but now it felt like a cheap seduction ploy.

"This looks good," he spoke.

"Would you like some wine?"

"Just water."

"We have beer."

Long pause. Thinking. "Water's good."

We sat down and I passed him dish after dish, marveling at the sheer amount of food he put on his plate.

For a few moments, we ate in silence.

"This is good."

"Thank you."

The silence hung heavy between us.

I racked my brain to make conversation. "So, what do you do in Virginia?"

"I'm in the navy."

My friend Julie was going to have a shit fit. She loved military men. "Are you a sailor?"

"Navy SEAL."

I had an amusing vision of a group of men walking around with baby seals on their t-shirts. Maybe they specialized in marine wildlife? Or seals? Did the navy have an animal conservation group as part of their regime? Maybe they trained seals to work with them? I looked at the huge man across from me, trying to imagine him talking to a baby seal. The image was kind of cute. "What does that entail?"

"We perform combat missions in sea, air, and land."

I blinked at the words combat mission. Another less fun vision of a seal with a bomb strapped to its slick little body crossed my mind. They did that in World War II. They used to strap bombs to dogs and send them over to the enemy to blow up their tanks, and the dogs blew up with them. Who even came up with something so cruel? I was so upset when I saw that on the history channel that I cried.

"With seals? You do combat with seals?"

A peculiar look crossed his face. "SEAL is an acronym for sea, air, and land."

"So you don't work with seals?" I needed confirmation. I couldn't like this man if he hurt seals.

He stared at me for a long moment and then shook his head. His chin dropped to his chest, and I realized that he was shaking with laughter. He looked back up at me, his whole face changed as he laughed. "I'm so sorry. I shouldn't laugh."

"Sorry. I don't like the military or anything to do with fighting. No offense."

He smiled at me. "No offense taken."

I cleared my throat and tried to be serious again. "Doesn't navy meant boats and water?"

"We specialize. We're part of the navy, but we also engage in the water, in the air, and on land."

"You fly a plane?"

"No. I jump out of them."

"Oh." I had a vision of him running and leaping out the back of a plane. The thought made my heart want to stop.

"That sounds scary."

"It's a rush."

I did not understand this mentality. There were two kinds of people in this world. The ones who did all the adrenaline seeking adventures like rock climbing and sky-diving and then there was the other group of people that stood on the ground with their hands over their mouths, watching in horror. I was definitely in the second group. The less adrenaline I had rushing through my body, the better.

"How can you even make yourself jump out of a plane? Doesn't that go against everything your mind is telling you?"

"We learn to control our responses to things like fear and pain."

I had no idea what he meant by that. "How can anyone control their body's response to that?"

"We're trained to become comfortable in uncomfortable situations."

This morning I had been so scared I had passed out. My fear had overtaken my body.

"So I guess you don't faint when you get scared."

"No."

Our eyes met over the table.

"I've never fainted before."

"I've never had anyone faint in my arms before."

My face got hot. I was breaking records today for the number of times I could blush.

"So, what do you do?" He broke the tension between us.

I hated this question. People got so judgy about careers. It was an automatic way to size someone up. I had dreams, even if I didn't have a big fancy career like some of my friends. Besides, I liked what I did. "I work part-time in an art gallery."

"Are you a painter?"

Surprise rippled through me. Most people asked me which art gallery. And then they wanted to know what I did for the art gallery. Was I a curator or a collections manager? Did I do marketing and fundraising? No one ever wanted to hear that I was just an assistant. And they never asked me if I was one of the artists.

"I like to paint but just in my spare time. At the gallery, I help sell the work of real artists."

"Did you paint the paintings in the loft?"

I felt embarrassed to admit that the art on the walls was my own. "Yes."

"You seem like a real artist to me."

No one since my grandma had ever called me a real artist. This man could have no idea how much his words had just impacted me. I shook my head. "No. I just do that for fun."

Green eyes studied me.

"Would you like some more food?"

"No. I'm good."

We finished our meal in silence. It wasn't awkward, but it wasn't entirely comfortable either.

He stood up. "I'll do the dishes."

I stood up too, picking up my plate. "No. That's fine."

He took my plate from my hand. "You cooked. I'll clean."

"Let me put the food away."

I carried my wine glass into the open kitchen.

Now we were both in the space behind the island. Every time I turned around, he was within touching distance. I had a distinct desire to flee and had to focus on putting the food away while he loaded the dishwasher. He filled the sink with soapy water and started to wash. He gave me a look when I picked up a tea towel.

"I know where everything goes. It'll just be faster if I help."

In silence, we washed and dried dishes together. I tried to think of something to talk about, but I could only focus on how big he was next to me. I was used to my routine. I didn't know how to share my space with a stranger. My shy, inner self seemed to come out in force in his presence.

He drained the sink as I put the last dish away. I handed him the dish towel so he could dry his hands.

"Thank you for dinner." He sounded sincere, but his expression was unreadable.

"You're welcome. I'm sorry that Matt wasn't here."

"Does he frequently work this late?"

I gave a little smile. "Yeah, he does. There's no break for a junior lawyer. They try and work them to death."

I watched as he folded the tea towel perfectly, before hanging it on the towel rack.

He didn't respond. He redefined a man of few words. Any less talking and the guy could qualify as a selective mute.

I took a deep breath. "I'm heading up to bed to do some reading. I want to tell you that Matt will be home soon, but I think we both know that he could be a few hours yet."

He nodded.

I started walking upstairs but looked down at him when he began to speak.

"When Matt invited me, I had no idea that he lived with you. Nor did he mention that this was your place. I thought I was just crashing at Matt's."

I smiled at him. "Consider yourself lucky. Matt's bachelor pad was, in my opinion, uninhabitable at the best of times."

I took a few more steps and stumbled. Bachelor pad. My face burned. Maybe this sailor wanted to have more space to pursue women. I stopped walking, grasping the railing tight. I turned and looked down at him, shocked that he was watching me.

I tried to find the right words. "If you…uh…have a date that goes well you can bring her home. I don't want to cramp your style…or anything… with stuff like that."

He stared up at me, his angular face without expression.

I blushed. An awkward pause hung between us, which galvanized me into filling the silence. "So, don't worry about me. I would be…uh…happy for you."

I was so red. I got up four more steps when he spoke. "What do you think that is?"

His words stopped me in my tracks.

"What?"

"You said that you didn't want to cramp my style. What do you think my style is?"

With my heart in my throat, I looked over the railing down at him. His gaze was so intense. What did I think his style was when it came to women? They would be beautiful, sexy and a hell of a lot more experienced than me.

"I think your style is probably sophisticated and experienced."

Great. I sounded like a 90-year-old pensioner. I took two more steps.

"You would be surprised at what my style is," he said, his voice so quiet I almost didn't hear him.

I had no idea what he meant by that. I gave him one last wild glance before I concentrated on getting up the stairs and into my bedroom.

I stood looking around my room, unsure why I felt so caught off balance. It made no sense that I was working so hard to make this man feel so welcome when he made me feel so uncomfortable. Pressing my hands to my warm cheeks, I focused on getting ready for bed.

CHAPTER SIX

I GLANCED AT THE SLIM CARTIER WATCH ON MY WRIST. IF I DIDN'T HURRY, I was going to be late for my shift at the gallery. I stared at my reflection in the mirror and smoothed down the houndstooth pencil skirt. My hair hung in a thick curtain over my shoulders. I had taken undue care with my makeup. I had no idea why I was fussing so much with my appearance today.

I stared at my reflection. That was a lie. The reason why I fussed had everything to do with our new houseguest. Sometimes when you're around someone that impresses you, you don't want to slink around in your baggies with your hair in a ponytail. You want to feel like your best self.

My high heels clattered on the hardwood of the stairs. At the bottom, I stood and stared at the island, a light-hearted feeling tickled in my chest. A bowl of perfectly sliced fruit and a glass of orange juice awaited my arrival. My heart contracted at the unexpected gesture. Someone had prepared my breakfast for me.

I slid onto the bar stool and hesitated as movement on the garden patio caught my eye. Jackson, clad only in runners and a pair of shorts, squatted deeply. My eyes drifted over muscular thighs and a taut ass. Sweat glistened on his golden skin. He moved to pump out endless pushups. The thick and corded muscles of his arms contracted each time he lowered himself with perfect form. My fork hovered over my bowl as I worked to look away.

I swallowed hard forcing myself to concentrate on my breakfast. Matt had arrived home long after I had gone to bed and I still hadn't talked to him about our new houseguest. The two men could not be more different. Why were they still in contact with each other? Why had Matt asked Jackson to stay here? For three months? Was this man really going to live with us for three months?

My betraying gaze pulled back to the patio. He performed some crazy hard jump lunge thing that involved a pushup. Didn't old acquaintances get together for a casual beer and a promise to do it again in the next five years? How did you go from never seeing someone to inviting them to live with you for three months? And why had Jackson agreed? What was the deal between Matt and Jackson? There was more to that story, but until I talked to Matt, I had no idea.

I stood and dumped my empty dishes into the sink. If I didn't leave for work now, I would be late. Without saying anything to the huge man on the patio, I grabbed my bag and walked downstairs.

I sat in my mini, begging it to behave. "Please baby, please don't do this to me."

No matter how many times I turned the key, my mini just ground away in a wha-wha-wha sound that never turned over the engine. I put my head on my steering wheel and took a deep breath. I was going to be so freaking late.

A knock sounded on the window next to me. I turned and blinked at a six-pack that would make Arnold Schwarzenegger envious. I rolled down my window.

"Having some car troubles?" Jackson sounded out of breath.

"She's pretty fussy. I meant to get her to the mechanic."

"Huh." His hands were on his hips. "Why didn't you?"

The man was blunt. I peered up at his face. "Matt told me I'd get ripped off at the garage and said that he wanted to take my car in for me."

"Try again."

I turned the key.

He listened. "That could be anything. Your alternator, your fuel, your starter."

"So nothing you can fix with a piece of string and some chewing gum?"

"Are you comparing me to McGyver?"

"If the shoe fits."

His lips twitched as he studied my car. "You need a ride to work?"

My thoughts tumbled. I needed a ride, but I didn't want to impose. "Aren't you working out?"

"Just warming up. Haven't got to the fun stuff yet."

If that was the warm-up, I hated to know what the work out entailed. I internally debated. I could call a cab, but it could be 30 minutes before one showed up here. "Okay. I would appreciate it."

"Let me grab my keys."

He disappeared upstairs and reappeared a couple of minutes later wearing a green t-shirt that said US NAVY across the front and a pair of jeans. He walked me to the passenger side of his truck and opened the door for me. Embarrassed by his chivalry, I moved to step up into the truck. My tight pencil skirt impeded my ability to lift my leg high enough to get in.

"Need some help there?" He sounded amused.

Why was this happening to me? So much for looking sophisticated and mature.

I spun and almost bumped into his chest. His big frame blocked me in. "I'm just going to go change."

"Hang on." His hands grasped my waist, and I squeaked as he lifted me onto the seat like I was a five-pound bag of sugar. No effort required on his part. Our eyes met, and then he winked at me before shutting the passenger door. The man winked at me! I sat there trying to breathe like normal. Suddenly I had that very familiar feeling of tingling butterflies in my stomach.

No no no no.

Don't even go there. This is Matt's friend. He may be hotter than Hades but do not get fluttery around the man. He's in the flutter-free zone.

He climbed into the driver seat beside me.

"So where to?"

"In Soho. Do you know where that is?"

He turned the key, and loud music blasted through the speakers. Matt didn't listen to loud music. He only listened to non-digitally recorded classical music. Matt said that digitally recording music destroyed real art. The music that was blasting now was big and about as un-classical as you could get.

"I think I can figure it out," he said over the music.

He drove like a bat out of hell. Before I could get my seatbelt on, he had backed up at about a hundred miles an hour. I was shocked and desperately trying to put my belt on as he shifted through all the gears as he tore up the street. I braced myself as he brought the vehicle to full speed. Now we wildly fishtailed on the gravel road around a bendy corner. I held onto the ceiling strap as we flew over a bump and I swear the entire vehicle took on air.

"Holy shit!" I breathed as we took another corner and he swerved expertly to deliberately hit a large puddle. Water poured over the windshield, momentarily blinding us.

I looked at him in part horror and part amazement. He seemed indifferent to the fact that he was driving his truck like we were in a life or death car chase.

"So do you like working at the gallery?" he asked mildly, as we wove around a bus and then around the corner. No one I knew drove as he did.

I was breathless. I couldn't tell if I was terrified or excited or both. "I love it. I know it's only part-time, but what people don't realize is that this is my dream job. I would pay to work there."

He threw a glance my way making me feel self-conscious. My skirt was riding too high up my legs. I discretely tried to yank my skirt down over my thighs.

My hand reflexively hit the dash even though my seatbelt held me back, as he slammed on the brakes due to a group of pedestrians that crossed the road and we came to a complete stop. We didn't speak. We didn't move. I was acutely aware of him beside me. His clean scent filled my nostrils. His long fingers slowly, impatiently tapped on the steering wheel as we waited for the last of the crowd to cross the street.

"What people?"

I chewed on my lip. Damn. Why was I always inadvertently disclosing details about myself? "Some people think I need a real job."

"Who?"

I didn't answer right away which made him turn to look at me, taking in my heels and my skirt that seemed determined to climb up my legs. "Just people."

We watched in silence as one last person jogged across the road. "Fuck em."

"What?" my voice faltered. I watched as his muscular forearm negotiated that stick shift like he owned it. Again we accelerated to an alarming speed.

He looked over at me. "People can mind their own fucking business. Do what you want."

My eyes were wide. First of all, shouldn't he be keeping his eyes on the road? And secondly, no one I knew talked like this. The last person who had given me this kind of advice, sans the f-word, had been my granny.

"You remind me of my grandmother," I blurted out.

His eyebrows went up a fraction. "That's a first."

"That isn't what I meant."

Jackson laughed and looked over at me. "No. I like it."

My stomach flopped. The guy had great teeth. And again with that smile. Did he know that his smile changed his face, morphing him from a good-looking man into a heart-breaking sex god? *Sheesh.* I forced myself to look out the front windshield.

"She was just always telling me that life was short. That I shouldn't pay attention to what other people think."

"She's right."

"That's easier said than done." I turned my head to look out the passenger window. I didn't recognize the feeling in my gut. It was part loneliness and fascination. When was the last time someone had encouraged me to stand up for myself? Jackson felt like dangerous territory. He made me miss my granny.

We pulled up in front of the gallery in record time. I was early, mostly in part to his Indy 500 skills.

"Can I have your car keys?"

I stared at him.

"I want to take a closer look at your car. Maybe I can fix it."

I fumbled in my purse and handed them to him without question. "I can take my car to the garage."

He ignored my protests. "What time are you done?"

I shook my head. "Oh, I can take a cab home."

"You're hosting my sorry ass. The least I can do is pick you up."

"4 PM."

Without another word, he swung out of the truck. By the time I had my seatbelt off, he was opening my door.

"I can do it."

He took my hand, and I scrambled off the seat, hovering for a moment on the edge. I probably should have just jumped but I'm a chicken, and I hesitated. He gave a half laugh and reached up and plucked me off my two-foot ledge before setting me down on quivering legs. His fresh scent invaded my senses.

"Thank you for the drive to work." I tend to get formal when I'm nervous. "It was enjoyable."

It was enjoyable? Who even talked like that? I swear to God my granny sometimes channeled through my body just to mess with me.

A half smile played on his lips as he looked at me with a mixture of curiosity and bafflement. "You're welcome."

I straightened my shoulders and nodded. "Have a nice day."

And without looking back, face on fire, I walked into the gallery.

CHAPTER SEVEN

I walked straight to the back and pulled out my phone to call my friend Beth. She was the only one who knew me.

Beth answered after one ring. "Yo."

"I'm freaking out."

"Do tell."

"We have a new houseguest who's an old friend of Matt's."

"Matt has friends?"

There wasn't a lot of love lost between Beth and Matt.

"Ha, funny, Beth. The new houseguest is staying with us for three months."

"WTF! That's such a dick move on Matt's part. He doesn't help you plan the wedding but decides to add a houseguest to the mix?"

"I was caught off guard."

"So is this guy as douchy as the rest of Matt's posse?"

A fair question, since most of Matt's friends were complete nightmares at the best of times.

"Even worse. He's…attractive."

I could hear Beth thinking. "Like how attractive?"

I winced. "Remember the crush I had on the hockey player in the second-year of university?"

"Now that guy was stupidly hot. No one could blame you for that. Even I drooled a bit when I saw him."

"It's possible this guy is hotter than the hockey player."

"Shut up. Impossible."

I scrunched up my face. "You know my thing about big, athletic guys. I get all weird."

"What kind of weird? Like the need to rip your clothes off kind of weird, because I'll stand behind you on that one."

"Beth! Remember how bad my crushes were?"

"Mmmm…..I was there. If anything you were committed. No one could fault you on that."

"I obsessed over the hockey player for almost a year before I had a conversation with him."

"Oh my God, I forgot that you got up the balls to speak to him once."

"Those crushes were endless fodder for my therapist. They were deemed unhealthy."

"What did your therapist know? I'm pretty sure she wore orthotics."

I laughed again. "I can feel it."

"What?"

"These butterflies inside of me. The dry mouth. The pitching of my stomach. I can't carry on a normal conversation."

"Aw, are you developing a crush?"

"Beth. He's my houseguest. He's living with me. I can't be crushing. I'm engaged."

"Sweetie, I love my man, but if you knew the number of times I had fantasies about Kurt Browning, you would be stunned."

Beth harbored her own little crush on a particular aging Canadian figure skater. "Isn't Kurt getting a bit long in the tooth?"

"First of all, he's perfect, and secondly, the heart wants what the heart wants."

"So talk to me when Kurt Browning moves into your guest bedroom."

She started laughing. "I can't argue that logic. I would be a mess. A complete wreck."

"Look I'm not saying that I have full-blown, hockey player passion, but I can feel it starting, and I can't go there. I love Matt."

"Look, show me a cross-section of a hundred thousand women across America, and I would bet every single one of them has a little secret hanky spanky in her pocket for some guy, whether it is the mailman or the Chinese food delivery kid. It's normal."

"Really?"

"You gonna act on it?"

"No!"

"Well, then just accept that by getting married to Matt this is going to be one of the first of many happy fantasies for you in your marriage."

"Beth," I moaned, laughing.

"Besides hot guy would be lucky to get someone like you to crush on him from afar. You kind of missed your calling as a stalker."

"Beth!"

We were both laughing when we hung up.

~

IT ALARMED ME HOW MANY TIMES JACKSON POPPED INTO MY HEAD DURING the day. I talked to people, I helped set up an exhibition, and I stepped out for a sandwich with my co-worker, but intense flashbacks of Jackson's warm hands on my hips kept coming back to me. I needed to gain a level of control over myself. I vowed to stop thinking about him.

This was just an old pattern of mine rearing its head. My therapist used to tell me that the only reason why I had these monster crushes versus actually having a real live relationship with a guy was that it was safe. I could live in a fantasy world about them where everything was perfect and I never actually had to deal with the realities of a relationship. It was all fantasy, and she had repeatedly challenged me on that fact. Didn't I want truth more than fantasy? Fantasies were safe. And I had a lot of control in my head.

But who is to say that reality is better? I mean, Matt was real. He was real life. And that came along with a lot more issues than my fantasies. Like the hockey player had ever told me he was too busy working. Hockey player never forgot to call, and he never got too busy. He had been the perfect boyfriend in my mind while he lasted.

I took a deep breath. Matt may not be perfect, but he was my fiancé. This is where I should be putting my attention. Just because there were a few bumps along the way was no excuse to start daydreaming about someone else. Matt was everything I wanted in a husband. We were going to get married, and everything was going to be great. I would have my family. Besides there was nothing safe about Jackson and any extracurricular thoughts about him were wildly inappropriate.

MATT CALLED AN HOUR BEFORE MY SHIFT WAS OVER.

"Matt," I said, stepping into an empty office.

"So you met the infamous Jackson."

I pressed the phone to my ear, my voice low. "Why didn't you tell me that you invited him to stay with us?"

"It slipped my mind," his voice instantly traced with defensiveness.

"It's fine," I said hastily. Matt hated criticism. "I was just caught off guard."

"He's not going to be a bother."

"I know," I rushed. "I just…I mean, you never really mentioned him."

Silence crackled between us. "Jackson grew up with me."

That confused me. "What do you mean? He's a childhood friend, right?"

"No, I mean, he lived with my family."

I blinked in shock. Matt had always maintained that he was an only child. He had regaled countless stories about his family life, but he had never mentioned Jackson before. "What? For how long?"

"For about 11 years. On and off."

"What? You never told me this!"

"Just…" Matt paused. I could hear the strain in his voice. "Jackson is welcome to stay with us for as long as he needs to."

"Of course. Can you tell me…"

Matt cut me off. "I don't want to get into it right now, okay?"

"Okay."

More silence between us.

"Will you be home for dinner?"

"Yes, Emily. I'll be home for dinner." His tone sounded annoyed. Cutting.

I rolled my eyes. "Okay. See you then."

He disconnected the line.

I stood there for a long moment. Thinking. What exactly was going on here? Why was Matt so agitated? What did he mean that he and Jackson grew up together? None of this was making any sense. How could I date Matt an entire year and never know that someone else grew up with his family? In his home? Is that what he had told me? This whole thing was weird. I needed to know more.

AT THE END OF MY SHIFT, WHEN I WALKED OUT OF THE GALLERY, MY HEART hitched when I saw the big black truck. Jackson moved with grace. A baseball hat adorned his head, pulled low over his eyes. Without speaking, we walked to the passenger side. He opened the door for me. The man had the most incredible forearms.

"I can do it," I lied, knowing full well that it would take a miracle to step up that far in this skirt.

He ignored me. His big hands wrapped around my hips. My body went completely still while my heart hammered. He easily lifted me up onto the seat.

I sounded breathless. "I'm never wearing this skirt again."

"That would be a shame," he teased, a smile on his lips.

I fumbled with my seatbelt. His flirtations meant nothing. He probably flirted as easy as he breathed. I wasn't going to make a big deal about it. I remember that fateful day in university. I had been late for class and racing around the corner. I had slammed into a warm wall. Huge hands had grabbed me by the shoulders, and I could still remember that slow-motion moment of looking up and seeing the hockey player. His name was Seth, and he had the most beautiful eyes. I had walked around in a daze for weeks after that. Replaying the feeling of his hands on my arms.

Yep. My therapist might have had a point on the unhealthy part of my crushes. She used to tell me that no good came from living in make-belief.

Jackson started the truck. And even though I had mentally prepared myself for his driving, I was breathless within seconds. I stole a glance at him. He had changed into a navy t-shirt and jeans. His longish hair stuck out in tuffs from beneath his baseball cap. The man was sexy. Crush or not, I would give him that. And he probably knew that about himself. He emanated his big manly pheromones. I bet women within miles of him were lifting up their heads and sniffing the air like wild animals catching the scent of their prey. But even if he was near me, it gave me no license to indulge in any of my little fantasies. I had paid good money for therapy, and we had all moved well past the crushing stage of my life when I started dating Matt.

"How was your shift?" Jackson's question pulled me out of my thoughts.

Green eyes looked at me when I didn't answer.

Think. Use your words.

"We're showcasing some new artists this month. They're so grateful and enthusiastic that it makes it a lot of fun."

"Do you ever think you'd want to show off your paintings?"

A snort escaped out of my nose. The thought was absurd. "No. I mean, my art isn't even real art."

"Did some asshole tell you that?"

I startled and looked over at him. He was giving me an intense look. Like he was willing to have a word with someone if they did tell me that. "No. I mean, I've never tried."

"Why not?"

"I don't know."

"How do you know you're not good enough if you don't try?"

"I just know."

"Sounds like bullshit to me."

My mouth dropped open. No one ever talked to me like that. How could I tell him that I feared rejection? I was happy with the dream of being an artist. What held me back was the fear of losing that dream when the art world rejected my work. It would take away one of my greatest joys. "I'm happy helping other artists."

"I don't buy it."

My eyes widened. I had no response to that. "It's complicated."

"I can help you load up your paintings and carry them to your work."

The thought of Jackson carrying my art into the gallery and demanding they hang them up almost made me laugh. "I can't."

He glanced over at me. "It's up to you."

"I'll think about it," I lied.

WE PULLED UP TO A STOP IN FRONT OF THE LOFT. I YANKED OPEN THE DOOR and leaped out, not caring if I ripped the back seam out of my skirt. I had no intention of letting him touch me again. This guy, unlike all my other crushes, wasn't even remotely safe.

I stopped short. "Where's my car?"

"I pushed it into the garage." He walked forward and pulled on the chain to open the door. I walked into the space that was Matt's parking spot. The engine of my car lay in several pieces on the floor of the garage on a tarp.

My eyes widened.

"Sorry about this," he said. "I got carried away."

I stood there in shock. My car had undergone an automotive autopsy, and now all its important little pieces were lying on the floor. How had this happened? A car bomb was the only thing that would've taken this car apart more efficiently. I worked to find the words to make him feel better. "That's okay. I'm pretty sure we can find someone to put it back together."

Maybe. Maybe if I found a genius mechanic and paid him triple the rate he might be able to put it back together. But at this point it was doubtful.

He laughed. "I can put it back together. Your alternator failed. The part isn't going to be in until next week."

My heart tripped. Jackson had pulled my engine apart and had plans to fix it. "You can put my car back together?"

"Yes."

I thought for a long moment. "You're fixing my car?"

"Hope that's okay. I was bored."

I remained tongue-tied. No one had ever done something like this for me. "Thank-you."

He crossed his arms. "Any reason why you don't park in the garage?"

"Matt parks his car inside because his car is more valuable."

"But you have an entire bay here. You could get at least two more cars in here."

I pointed at the massive tractor tire that was lying in front of the other door. "That's in the way."

"The tire?"

"Yeah."

He tugged on his ear. "Why didn't you just move it?"

"Well, Matt ordered it because he was going to use it as part of his work out regime, but after it got dropped off, it was too heavy to move. Matt tried."

He frowned. "Matt tried to move it?"

"It's the latest rage. I guess you're supposed to flip the tire as part of a workout. But that tire weighs over 600 pounds." I informed him. "It's way too heavy for one person."

"Where do you want it?"

I cringed when I recalled Matt's attempts to flip this tire. He had grunted and groaned and swore to no avail. I intended to call someone to take it away but had never gotten around to it. Jackson was a big man, one of the biggest men I had ever met in my life, but I was reasonably sure he wouldn't be able to budge it.

"It's no big deal to park outside."

He walked over to the tire, crouched beside it and with seemingly minimal effort, flipped the tire. My mouth dropped open. He repeatedly flipped it further into the garage, before resting it up against the wall. He wasn't even out of breath.

He walked back to where I stood. "Mind if I use that to work out?"

I envisioned him wearing only his runners and his shorts, flipping that tire. His muscular body would be covered in sweat. My mouth flooded with moisture. I swallowed hard. I opened my lips to speak. Our eyes met. He watched me with interest.

I snapped my mouth shut and nodded.

Fearing he could see my thoughts, without saying another word, I turned and headed for the stairs.

CHAPTER EIGHT

"I'm home," Matt announced his arrival. I looked up from the stove. Matt walked across the loft, into the kitchen and kissed me hard on the lips.

"Something smells amazing in here."

Jackson appeared at the top of the stairs. Matt stood back, and the two men stared at each other. Jackson lightly jogged down the stairs.

"Buddy, it's been a long time," Matt said, grinning, even though his voice sounded strained.

"Too long."

"How long has it been?"

Jackson glanced at me. "Dan's wedding?"

Matt frowned with a smile. "Can't be. That wedding was over four years ago."

Jackson shrugged. "Good to see you."

They shook hands and continued to stare at each other.

"Likewise." Matt nodded, his grin wide. Too wide. "Shit man. You're a brick shit house. What the hell are they feeding you in the navy anyway?"

"Nothing good."

They both had variations of smiles on their faces. The air crackled with unexplained tension.

"Have you tried any of Emily's cooking yet?"

Jackson's gaze, wide and green, trapped mine. "She can cook."

I flushed.

Matt stepped back and pointed at Jackson. "I'm just going to change. Grab some beers."

He pounded up the stairs and then his bedroom door shut.

The silence settled between us. He stood on the other side of the island studying me.

I walked to the fridge and set two cans of beer on the island between us. I took a deep breath. "Well, Matt's finally home."

"Yes."

I couldn't quite decipher the energy he was giving off. If I wasn't mistaken, he was even more on guard than when it was just the two of us.

"Matt said that you used to live together."

He cracked open a beer. "I used to live with Matt's family."

I held my breath. "Matt just mentioned that to me today, but he didn't say why."

Green eyes held my gaze with intense honesty. "Matt's dad used to arrest Ted for being drunk and disorderly. And more often than not, I ended up at Matt's house."

My eyes widened. "Oh."

He picked up his beer and took a long drink.

I hesitated over my question. "Ted is your dad?"

"Ted is the man I lived with after my mom died."

Questions flowed through my mind. When did Jackson's mom die? How old was Jackson when she passed on? Who was Ted? Did Ted have legal guardianship over Jackson? If he wasn't Jackson's birth father, then who was? I stood there looking up at him unsure what to ask next.

He swallowed and pinned me with his gaze. "It was a long time ago."

His tone said the conversation was over. I stood there and watched him take another sip of his beer while I tried to keep the sympathy from showing on my face. I had a feeling that Jackson didn't want anyone feeling sorry for him.

∼

MATT POUNDED DOWN THE STAIRS. WORDS FLOWED FROM HIM BEFORE HE even hit the bottom step. He grabbed his beer, tasted something from the stove, kissed my neck and checked his phone. I secretly referred to Matt as a tornado in a bottle. His energy was explosive. He never slowed down. I watched as he fired questions at Jackson, talked about work and scrolled through his phone to show Jackson something. Matt moved a hundred miles a minute. Jackson revealed his intensity through his quiet demeanor and his stoic strength. Matt noticed nothing and Jackson observed everything.

"Time to eat," I said, carrying the last of the food to the table.

They communicated like old friends, but their differences were stark. Matt talked nonstop. Jackson listened more than he spoke. Matt looked short and lanky. Jackson appeared to have DNA from some mythical Adonis. Matt appeared younger with his combed-back blond hair and a clean-shaven face. Jackson's overgrown hair and stubble added years, giving him the appearance of being older. I needed to stop comparing these two men. I disliked where my thoughts were going.

I abruptly stood up. Both men glanced up at me.

Matt gave me a smirk. "You okay?"

I looked down at my plate. It was still half full. "Yes."

"You're as nervous as a cat," he said, grabbing my hand and pulling me back down. "Relax."

I sat down and picked up my fork. They continued to talk. It was hard to believe these two guys had grown up together. What was the story? I was dying to get Matt alone so that I could pump him for information.

Finally, they were done eating.

I shot up again and started to pick up their plates.

"I'll do dishes." Jackson's voice was low.

No. That was a bad idea. I needed some space. To think and clear my head. "Don't even think about it. You two should sit outside. It is a beautiful night."

Matt stood up. "That's a great idea."

I carried plates into the kitchen. Matt followed me and grabbed a beer out of the fridge. "Great dinner, babe."

I smiled, looking up at his face. Matt ignored my expression and walked out to the patio. Matt's brush off made me flush. Jackson observed all from where he sat.

I wiped my hands on my skirt. "Would you like another beer?"

"No thanks."

"When he hits five beers, shut him down. The last time he had six beers, he tried to take off his shirt at a work party."

He smiled a smile that I felt down in my toes. "Still a lightweight?"

Seriously. This man needed to stop smiling at me. "Still a lightweight."

"Come join us. I can do the dishes later."

Who was this man? I decided that him being in the kitchen with me was more than a bad idea. I shook my head. "I think you two need man time."

"What exactly is man time?"

"When you talk about women and sports and other secret topics that women don't know about."

His eyebrows moved up in amusement, but he obeyed and followed Matt onto the patio.

I WASHED THE DISHES, UNABLE TO STOP MYSELF FROM LOOKING OUTSIDE. Matt moved up and down from his chair. He regaled big stories with big gestures. I recognized this Matt. He wanted to impress. Jackson reclined in his chair, his long legs crossed in front of him, playing audience to Matt. As if sensing my gaze, Jackson turned his head and looked directly at me. I flushed and spun around, embarrassed that he caught me staring. Still, I lingered. I wiped a counter that was already clean. I swept a floor that had no crumbs. I wanted to walk out onto that patio, but I held myself back.

Enough. I needed to stop. Since he had arrived, Jackson had pushed his way into my thoughts far more than was acceptable. Yes, he was stupidly hot and extremely manly with his big muscles and broad shoulders, but it wasn't even that. It was the way he talked to me. When I spoke, he listened. He paid attention. He encouraged me.

Matt had become so busy at work and was so absent. It was normal to feel flattered that someone was noticing me as a human being. Right? Matt and I had a great relationship. Everyone said so. When we first started dating, he had been so attentive and fun. So life had gotten in the way a bit. He was rarely around. He seemed to work all the time. And did I need him hanging off my every word? That wasn't a realistic expectation of a relationship, was it?

I loved Matt. He was everything I needed. He had a respectable job. He enjoyed some of the same things I did. We rarely fought. Did it matter that sometimes it seemed like we were two roommates leading different lives? Things would become different after we got married. Matt was going to be my husband. And we would have a wonderful marriage. I had everything I wanted and needed right here.

It was irresponsible to get distracted by this intense stranger who stared at me with those knowing green eyes. Just because he talked to me and seemed to see me, didn't mean anything. That was just who he was. He was an intense person. You couldn't misread someone's intensity as interest. So, maybe he made my stomach flutter a bit. Anyone who still had a pulse would get a fluttery stomach around him. I was mature, and I could admit that he was attractive. So what if he made me a bit nervous when he was around. That was normal. He would make anyone nervous.

But that didn't mean I needed to read into anything. I wasn't a college student anymore that daydreamed about hot men. I was the fiancée of a lawyer. And now, I just needed to refocus my energy on the wedding and Matt. Without looking back, I forced myself to climb the steps to my room.

TO TRY AND GET MY MIND OFF EVERYTHING, I FORCED MYSELF TO READ IN bed. A soft tap sounded on my door. Matt poked his head in, giving me a grin.

"You look snug."

"Hey."

"How are you?" He sat down at the end of my bed.

"Good. Glad you got home for dinner."

"Thanks for making Jackson feel so welcome."

I blinked, remembering the golf club incident. "Are you joking?"

"He told me you bought the bed and fixed up his room. That was nice of you."

My lips parted. I marveled that Jackson had not told Matt about the warm welcome he received when he showed up. "Any friend of yours is welcome."

Matt studied me. "Are you sure?"

"He can stay here as long as he wants." I lied. The sooner the man left, the better. I decided that maybe Matt having asshole friends was far preferable to nice attractive ones.

"Has Jackson told you what treatment he's getting at the hospital?"

I shook my head.

"Me neither."

We stared at each other. Didn't Matt think it was weird that he had invited someone into our home that he barely seemed to know anymore? A man who apparently wasn't entirely comfortable here and who made Matt feel the same way. The whole situation baffled me.

"Is everything okay between you and Jackson?"

He shrugged. I expected him to blow off my question. It threw me when he was honest. "Things have been pretty shit between Jackson and me since my dad passed away."

"I'm still really confused as to how Jackson became part of your life."

His eyes slid up to my face before shifting away. "One day, I woke up and Jackson was sleeping in my top bunk. He was my dad's charity case. There's more to the story, but that's the gist of it."

"You're kidding. How old were you?"

"About seven."

"And your mom was okay with this?"

"She knew it was important to my dad."

I blinked at the bitter tone in Matt's voice.

"I've never heard this story," I said. "Were you friends?"

"Yeah. We used to be good friends."

Matt was holding back. "How old were you when he stopped staying at your place?"

"He lived on and off with us until he left to join the navy."

"So he was part of your family for most of your life."

Matt looked down at his hands. "It was complicated. My dad invited him to be part of the family."

"Were you okay with it?"

"Sometimes it was fun. Lots of the time, he felt like a brother. He was completely wild."

"Was he a bad kid?"

"No, he wasn't a bad kid, but trouble always seemed to find him. I remember one lunch hour, these older kids came over and started to pick on us. There was six or seven of them and the two of us. I was ready to bolt, but Jackson just stood his ground. I took one hit to the face, and I ran screaming to the lunch lady, but he didn't run. He took them all on. They messed him up so bad he was in the hospital overnight with a bruised kidney, but when the teachers got there to break up the fight, it took two teachers just to subdue him. He was tougher than anyone I knew."

"Oh, my gosh."

"A bunch of kids got suspended over that fight, but that's just who Jackson was. He had no fear. He would take anyone on. He was wild that way."

"So, what happened?"

"What?" He avoided my gaze.

"Did you guys have a falling out?"

His shoulders twitched. "We're just really different."

There was way more to this than Matt was letting on. "Does your mom still keep in touch with him?"

Matt looked at me sharply. "Wow, someone is interested."

My eyes widened. "This guy grew up with you, and I have never even heard about him. Of course, I'm curious."

"It isn't a big deal."

"Okay."

He cleared his throat. "Can you keep your eye on him for me?"

"What?"

"I had to twist his arm to stay here, but you know what my work schedule is like. We need time to work on some stuff."

"Having me keep my eye on him isn't going to fix your past with him."

"I know, but I need you to buy me some time. I don't want him to take off."

I studied the chipped clear polish on my nails. "I don't think I'm the one that Jackson wants to hang out with."

"Getting him to fix your car was a brilliant idea."

"I didn't ask him to do that."

"I know, but maybe ask him for help on things. Make him feel useful."

That felt manipulative. "Matt, no. Jackson seems like a great guy, but I'm not going to impose on him."

"At least spend some time with him."

"We have nothing in common. Forcing him to hang out with me might drive him out of here quicker than if I just left him alone."

"Please. It means a lot to me. Keep him busy."

"Matt, you need to come home for dinner more. More than once a week. I get the sense that if Jackson feels like you're blowing him off, nothing will get him to stay."

"You're right. I'll try. Honest."

We eyeballed each other. The cosmos laughed at my expense. I wanted to avoid Jackson, not spend more time with him. I needed to be more careful. Schoolgirl fantasies aside, flirting with anything Jackson was just a terrible idea.

"Where is he now?"

"I think he's downstairs working on your car."

I nodded.

"Hey, did you see that he moved that tire?"

"I noticed."

He leaned forward, his eyes wide. "Tell me the truth. Did he use his truck to move that thing?"

The lie rolled off my tongue. "I have no idea."

"I guarantee he used his truck."

CHAPTER NINE

I walked into the kitchen. Jackson stood and stared at the espresso machine. I could do this. I could be the playful fun sister-in-law that made him feel welcome.

"You have to press a few buttons to make it work. They haven't installed an eye retina scan on espresso machines yet."

He turned, giving me an amused look. "Whatever happened to just a regular coffee maker?"

"I meant to buy one. The espresso machine takes forever when we have a dinner party. Do you want a latte?"

"Just a regular coffee."

"I can make it for you."

"If you can make me a coffee, I'll make you breakfast."

"Deal."

We worked together in silence.

"What are your plans today?" I asked.

"Just work out. You?"

"I need to run some errands," I said. Then I paused. My car was in pieces.

"Let me take you."

I avoided his glance. "I can take a cab."

"Let me take you."

I chewed on my lip. Thinking about how Matt asked me to keep him busy. "I have to do wedding stuff. Trust me. You're going to hate this."

"I think I can handle it."

WE STOPPED FIRST AT THE PAPER PELICAN. JACKSON NOSED AROUND THE small shop. I stood at the counter, a shaky hand on my forehead, while the clerk droned on about grades of paper, type of font and messages. I stared unseeing at the dozens of examples before me. A familiar sense of panic washed over me. I don't know why I had thought it was a good idea to bring a witness to my meltdown. I still had no clue on how to proceed.

"You okay?" Jackson asked from just over my shoulder.

I shook my head. "I can't seem to make a decision which just makes me even more anxious."

I glanced over at the door and debated just dropping everything again and running.

He moved beside me. "You want some help?"

"Suggestions are welcome."

He looked up at the clerk. "What do you suggest we focus on first?"

"Pick your paper first. Then your design," she said.

"Are these all your paper samples?"

"Yes."

He spread them out on the counter.

"Okay, Emily. Focus just on the color. Anything you don't like?"

I pointed at four. "I don't like these."

"Good," he pushed those away. "What about texture?"

I bit my lip. "I like this texture."

The clerk said, "That's the linen. It comes in these four colors."

She pointed at four sheets of paper.

"Anything jumping out at you?" His voice sounded so calm and soothing.

I sighed. "I don't like the green or the blue."

He removed those. "So we are down to pink...and..." he squinted, "and another pink."

The clerk chimed in. "This is sugar egg pink, and this one is pink innocence."

Jackson leaned in. His low voice rumbled in my ear. "My vote is on pink innocence."

I blushed as I fought to keep a ridiculous smile off my face. I pointed to pink innocence. "We'll go with that one."

The clerk wrote it down on her paper. "Now what about the font?" She took out a sample card. "These are our most popular fonts."

Jackson leaned his arms on the counter and studied the sheet. "I can't even read these two fonts."

He was right. "Agreed."

"Which one is easiest to read?" He glanced up at my face.

We both, at the same time, pointed to the font on the top left.

Jackson looked up at me. "Is this the one?"

"Yes."

"This wedding stuff is easy," he teased.

I rolled my eyes, but something released in my chest. We were doing this.

"What about messages?" the clerk prompted.

"Show us your samples."

She pulled out five sheets. He leaned over and read them. I stood there and studied his dark blond hair, noticing the way it curled around his ear. It looked so soft and thick. My fingers itched to touch it.

"Any thoughts?" Jackson turned and glanced up at me.

I squirmed. I had no idea. "What are your thoughts?"

"These two samples mention the parents in the invitation."

Out of four parents, only one remained. "Not those."

"And this one writes out the date and time in word format. I never liked that."

"Me neither."

He pointed at a sample. "This one is to the point, which is my style. Date, time, location. Simple."

This is what I had wanted Matt to do with me. Jackson offered pragmatic and logical advice.

"It's my style too."

He pointed at the sample and said to the clerk. "She's the one."

The clerk wrote that on her sheet. "We have all your other details. The last thing we need is how many invitations you need?"

I shrugged. "I have no idea."

"Do you know how many guests you're inviting?"

"The less, the better," I said under my breath.

Jackson turned, his open curiosity filled his expression.

"Let's go with 150 invitations. Too many are better than not enough."

WE STARTED TO WALK TOWARDS THE TRUCK. RELIEF COURSED THROUGH MY veins. One task removed from my gigantic list. I wanted to high five the world.

"Jackson, that was amazing. How did you do that?"

"It's all about elimination."

"I've been stressing about the invitations for months. Every time I have walked in that store, I just walk out overwhelmed."

"Seriously?"

"I can't seem to decide anything."

"Why do you think that is?"

We started to cross the street. Why was I paralyzed about my wedding instead of being filled with excitement and joy? When we first got engaged, Matt and I had been so excited. We talked about what we wanted our wedding to look like. I had floated around on cloud nine for weeks. But those talks never materialized into anything more. And now Matt seemed so disinterested.

"I just thought it'd be easier. You know? To make decisions. It's supposed to be our big day."

"You should get Matt to help you."

I looked up. A car roared towards me. It was too close. I couldn't move. I shut my eyes, bracing for impact. Strong arms lifted me and spun me around. My back hit something hard. My breath knocked out of me in a soft umph. I opened my eyes. Jackson's long length pinned me against the side of the truck.

My breath sputtered out of me in short little gasps.

Warm fingers touched my head, my neck, my shoulders.

"Are you hurt?"

Dazed, I stared up at him.

He repeated his question. "Are you okay? Did I hurt you?"

I could not seem to catch my breath. "You saved me."

My back was against his truck. His hard warmth seeped into me. My mouth dried up.

"Are you hurt?" I worked to speak.

"I'm fine. You sure I didn't hurt you? I yanked you pretty rough."

"I froze."

"You did." He opened the passenger door. I scrambled in and sat staring straight ahead. My heart was still thumping, but I was pretty sure it was from his proximity not from the near miss.

"You need help?"

I looked at him stupidly. What was he asking me?

"Here, let me help you." He reached in and pulled the seatbelt over me, his head bent over me as he fastened the belt. I caught the fresh, clean scent of his hair. I worked to bring oxygen into my lungs. His nearness trapped my breath.

He straightened. Our eyes met. I compulsively worked my throat, unable to tear my gaze from his. His jaw tightened, and then he shut the door.

A few moments later, he climbed in beside me, acting like nothing was wrong. "Where to next?"

SIDE BY SIDE, WE FACED THE VAST ARRAY OF COFFEE MAKERS IN THE LARGE department store. Endless choices intimidated me.

"Who's idea was this?" he asked.

"Yours, I think."

"Process of elimination?"

"Yup."

"Single cup or pot."

"Pot."

He walked up the aisle and then came back. "We've got 4 cups, 6 cups, 8 cups and 12 cups."

"Let's go with 8 cups."

"What color?"

"Black or silver."

"Do you want simple or gadgets."

"Definitely lots of gadgets."

He studied our choices and then tapped on two coffee makers. "Okay, you have eliminated it down to these two. This one has a built-in bean grinder."

"Sold."

He looked amused. "You haven't even heard about the other one's features."

"I want the grinder. What do you want?"

"The built-in grinder is alright."

"That's the one."

"Shit," he looked at the price. "No way. This coffee maker is over $300."

I shrugged. "The average person spends $5 on coffee a day which is over $1800 a year. What's the guarantee on that?"

He checked the box. "Lifetime."

"Need I say more?"

I watched as he picked up the box and we walked to stand at the cashier line up. He pulled his wallet out of his jeans.

"No," I said.

"You admitted it was my idea."

"My coffee grinder, hands off."

He leaned forward. "You work part-time. Let me help."

"My dad heavily invested in this unknown company called Microsoft in the 80s," I said. "And because of his foresight, I can drink a lot of coffee."

His eyes widened. "You telling me you're rich."

"Grossly so."

"Like how rich?"

"Bill Gates used to send my dad a birthday card."

"No shit."

"My Dad was a financial genius. He liquidated at it's highest point, and now I just live on the interest, but I would give every penny back if it meant my dad was still here."

He dropped his gaze to my face. "I bet."

"My granny was no slouch in the financial department either," I said with misery in my voice. This was the moment I dreaded. Once people realized how much more I had than they did, things got weird. Resentment reared up. Or worse, people started to suck up.

"Well shit, you should have told me sooner."

My eyes flew to his face. "Why?"

A smile played on his lips. "I would have gone for the $500 one that had the timer and the grinder."

I laughed in relief. We stood there smiling at each other.

"People get weird about that stuff," I admitted.

He stood there for a long moment staring off at some distant point. It was almost as if he didn't hear. Just when I thought the conversation was dead, he said, "The money?"

"Yeah."

He looked me in the eye. "Fuck em."

"Is that your life motto?"

"Pretty much."

"Does it work?"

"Most of the time."

I sighed. "It must be nice not to care what anyone thinks."

"I still care about the opinions of a few."

My eyes went wide. I wanted more than anything to ask whose opinion he cared about, but at that moment the clerk greeted me with a big smile.

CHAPTER TEN

We walked through the mall. A voice squealed from behind me.

"Emily?"

I spun around to see my friend, Julie, standing there. She looked gorgeous with her cute green jacket and windswept dark hair.

"Julie," I smiled as we hugged. "So good to see you."

"You too," her eyes were wide on Jackson's face. "Oh, my gosh. What are the odds?"

"Julie, this is Jackson. He's a family friend who's staying with us until the wedding. Jackson, this is Julie, one of my friends from university."

I watched as they shook hands.

"Pleased to meet you," Jackson's voice rumbled low.

Julie's eyes fluttered. "The pleasure is all mine."

She turned back to me, her eyes wide. She was sending me a message I'd recognized. She wanted me to be her wing woman. "Sweetie, it has been way too long. Seriously. Come now, we need to get together."

I glanced up at Jackson who had zero expression on his face. "I know, I'm so sorry, this wedding has been taking up all my time."

A complete lie unless you counted stressing about something and not taking action as good reason for being busy.

"I still can't believe you're getting married before me, how's that even possible?" She shook her head with a teasing smile. "How's the wedding planning going?"

I sighed. "Slowly. We ordered the invitations today."

"We?" She raised her eyebrows.

"Jackson helped."

She smiled up at him. "You don't look like a typical wedding planner."

"Jackson introduced me to the process of elimination. It's very effective."

"I can't wait to see what you both chose." Her laugh sounded louder than normal. "Are you bringing a plus one to the wedding, Jackson?"

I blinked at her brazen approach. Julie had no fear when it came to men.

"Not currently attached."

She beamed at Jackson and then turned to me. "The four of us should get together for dinner."

The last thing I wanted was to spend the evening watching Julie bust moves on Jackson. I nodded. "Okay. Should I make a reservation somewhere?"

"Why don't you cook for us? Not all of us are swimming in money like you."

I had no idea why she said that. When we ate out together, Julie never paid because I always picked up the bill. "Okay. I don't mind cooking."

"Perfect, I'll bring the wine."

Julie bestowed Jackson with a beautiful smile and tossed her brunette hair over her shoulder. "How long are you in town for?"

He glanced at my face. "Twelve weeks."

"Are you here on vacation?"

"Something like that."

"Well, I can't wait to hear more about this something," she flirted, batting her eyelashes. I gritted my teeth together. I recognized Julie's signature moves. They usually didn't bother me, but today annoyance tickled my skin.

My voice sounded thick to my ears. "Great. How about Saturday night?"

Jackson glanced down at me. I feared he was reading my flaky tone.

"Perfect." She beamed another megawatt smile towards Jackson.

"Great," I repeated, struggling to keep the displeasure out of my voice. "How about 7 PM?"

"Love it," She had eyes only for Jackson.

"Well, we should be going," I hedged. "I've taken up enough of Jackson's time today."

"Okay." She cooed as she pulled me into another hug. Her voice changed as she whispered in my ear. "If you tell anyone else about him, I'll seriously kill you. He's mine, okay?"

I pulled back and worked to keep the shock off my face. "Uh, okay."

"Bye." Her eyes clung to Jackson before she turned and sashayed off.

JACKSON AND I CONTINUED TO WALK THROUGH THE MALL, THIS TIME IN silence. I fumed over Julie's last comment. That exchange had pissed me off. She wasn't allowed to call dibs on Jackson just because she saw him first. I bristled at her assumptions. She always did this. She found someone she liked and declared her feelings to the world so that no one else could make a move. But did that ever stop her when someone else liked a guy? I remember actively hiding my crushes from her in University because the moment she found out whom I liked, it seemed like she inevitably found a way to date the guy. She would give me a sympathetic look and say, "It just happened. We couldn't help ourselves." Julie was never to be trusted when it came to men. I didn't tell her Matt's name or introduce them when we first started to date. It wasn't until we got engaged that I let them meet.

What did it matter to me that she wanted to get her little man claws into Jackson? Was it any of my business?

"You okay?" Jackson asked. I worked to keep pace with his long easy strides.

"Yes, why?" I huffed. Julie gobbled up men like they were going out of style. Matt called her a man-eater.

"Is she a close friend of yours?"

Air puffed out of my lungs. "Yes."

"She upset you."

I refused to look up at him. "They teach you to read minds in the Navy SEAL program?"

"You've adjusted the zip on your jacket four times, your lips are moving, but you're not speaking. They teach us how to read body language, and I would say that you're seriously agitated."

I stopped walking, and he turned and stopped too.

"I hate you right now," I said without feeling.

He half-smiled. "I like to fix stuff."

"Like my car?"

"And other stuff."

"I'm unfixable," I said. A hollowness carved out my chest. I hated my emotional response to the idea of Julie and Jackson. It occurred to me that I was a terrible partner to Matt. I allowed myself to notice how thick Jackson's forearms were and how soft his hair looked which was the ultimate betrayal. I deserved my misery.

"Come on," he said. "We need something to cheer you up."

"I'm un-cheerable."

He laughed. "I love the drama queen act. And I would kill to know what just happened."

"Nothing."

I started walking. He matched his gait to mine.

"So is this a setup?"

Again, my teeth started to grind. "Why would you say that?"

"Just a question."

"Julie's sophisticated, and she's single."

My words hung between us.

"Okay."

I worked not to grab the coffee maker from his hands and toss it on the ground. "Okay."

We walked again in silence.

"Kind of a lot of pressure, don't you think?" he asked. A smile teased his voice.

"Totally," I said. "I thought so too."

"Do you think I can handle it?"

"I think it is rude of me to make you try."

"Huh."

"An intimate dinner party is too much." My mind whirled.

"You think?"

"So I think I should have a party instead. I'll invite a lot of people."

My eyes locked on his face. An enigmatic expression reflected back on me. "Okay."

"Okay."

We walked outside to the truck. He put the coffee maker in the back behind my seat and then turned around and looked at me, blocking my path into the truck. "So, is that what upset you?"

I stared up at him. My heart pumped in my chest. "What?"

"The fact that Julie wanted you to set me up with her?"

"No!" I sputtered, unable to think of a quick response. I avoided his gaze. I envisioned her slender arms wrapped around that thick neck. My stomach burned. I wanted to rage when I imagined him leading her up to his guest room for an overnight stay. My emotional response was disturbing. This was Jackson, my fiancé's childhood friend. Desperation stabbed me, as I drowned in these swirling dark feelings. Shame flooded me too.

"So you would be okay if I dated your friend?" He brought me out of my thoughts.

My gaze clashed with his. His words stabbed my heart. I imagined her tall and willowy body snuggled up to his massively strong frame. Ringing sounded in my ears.

"You can do what you want."

He hesitated. "I can't always do what I want."

I struggled to keep my breath even. He regarded me with his green gaze, making me feel like he could read everything I was feeling. I felt naked and exposed. I needed to remember that I was engaged. I loved someone else. I had this monstrous thing growing inside of me, spinning me out of control. I hated it.

My voice wavered. "Me either."

He reached out. Big hands wrapped around my waist and then I was being lifted onto the passenger seat. My breath slammed into my lungs.

"You don't have to do that anymore. I'm not wearing a skirt."

He looked at me. "I just like how little you feel."

Then he shut the door.

CHAPTER ELEVEN

In the coming week, Jackson and I fell into a comfortable routine. He woke up early to work out. When I came downstairs, he had already made me breakfast.

I would work at the gallery or spend the mornings painting, while he worked on my car or disappeared to one of his standing appointments at the hospital. He never talked about his treatments. I was worried that something was seriously wrong with him, but I refused to ask. He was fiercely private about it, often not even telling me where he was going.

After lunch, we always ran some sort of errand together. With my car still in pieces, he acted as my chauffeur, and I used him shamelessly in helping me plan my wedding. Jackson was decisive, pragmatic and extremely good at coaxing decisions out of me.

Despite the fact that he was stupidly good looking, he was a lot of fun. He teased me into making decisions. We talked about safe subjects like art and travel. He told me almost nothing about himself, but we found our rhythm. He was nice, and for the first time in a long time, I didn't feel lonely. It didn't matter when Matt didn't come home for dinner because Jackson was there. Sometimes we watched TV together. Sometimes he worked on my car, and I sat on the steps and hung out. It was easy, and he kept his flirting to a minimum. Sometimes he teased me, which made me blush, but mostly he was pretty good about just treating me like a kid sister. Although Jackson was sincere, he wasn't very forthcoming about himself. Despite his apparent reluctance to share, I did my best to ferret information out of him.

ONE NIGHT, WE STOOD IN THE KITCHEN COOKING DINNER TOGETHER.

"So, Matt told me about a fight you were in during elementary school."

He glanced over at me and then focused his attention back to the salad he was making. "Sounds like me."

"You don't remember? Matt said you took on all these older boys, and you didn't back down, and you ended up in the hospital with a bruised kidney."

He momentarily stopped chopping. "Not sure."

"How can you not remember this?"

"Ted and I shared many visits to the hospital, so it doesn't stand out."

"Matt said there were half a dozen boys and they were all bigger than you, but you refused to back down."

A smile traced on his mouth. "Yup, then that was me."

I turned to face him and crossed my arms. "Why do you do that?"

"Do what?"

"Not back down. Matt said he ran to the lunch lady, but even though you were outnumbered, you stayed to fight."

He glanced at me, his expression one of curiosity. His question was genuine. "Why would I back down?"

"Because you could get hurt!"

"That isn't a reason to back down from a fight."

"Why fight at all?"

"I never start fights. I just finish them."

I stood there thinking for a long moment. "Why did you have so many visits to the hospital?"

He continued to chop his tomato without speaking. I waited. Finally, he rewarded me with an answer. "Ted was a drunk. Either he was getting hurt, or he was hurting me. Hospitals were avoided, but sometimes they were necessary."

I tried to hide my dismay at his words. Ted had hurt Jackson. This was the reason that Jackson had spent time with Matt's family. The man he lived with had beaten him. And Matt's parents had saved him.

"How were you hurt?"

His face concentrated as he remembered. "Broken leg, broken sternum, broken arms, broken collarbone…but only when he could catch me."

I froze. "And when he did?"

"He just punched, but when he kicked, that's when my bones got broken."

I covered my mouth with my hand. "Jackson."

How did a person's soul survive such a travesty? Is this where his will to fight back came from? His determination to protect others? My heart ached for the little boy who was alone with an abusive alcoholic man who rained down on him with his fists and kicks, hurting him to the point that his bones broke. The images I conjured in my mind were almost bringing me to tears. How alone he must have felt. The fear and pain he must have endured ripped at my heart.

He moved to put the salad in the fridge. "Did Matt say he was coming home tonight?"

"How did the doctors not know about this?"

He started to walk out of the kitchen. "They knew. They called the cops."

I followed. "Matt's dad."

"Yup." His voice remained even. "I'm going to go work on the car."

I flung myself at his broad back, awkwardly wrapping my arms around him from behind. He stopped walking, and I tightened my arms around his solid waist.

"What's going on?" he sounded amused.

I lay my face against the middle of his warm back. "I'm sorry."

I felt him laugh. "For what?"

"That Ted hurt you."

I felt his entire body go still. We stood there for a long moment, the side of my face pressed against the warmth of his back. I tried to inject light and happiness from my body into his. As if to heal his childhood wounds. To try and take away some of that pain.

I began to step back, but his hand reached up and pressed my hands into his stomach, preventing me from moving. I sighed and sank back into our hug. I matched my breath to his and concentrated on pushing all my positive energy into his body through his back. It might sound stupid, but I like to think that stuff like that worked. His hand remained on mine, trapping me against him.

Moments ticked by and we stood sharing our awkward hug. He made no motion to remove me. I squeezed him even harder. As if I could squeeze the pain out of him. My mom had taught me the value of hugs. She used to say that there was precious little in this world that a decent hug couldn't fix.

I heard a car door slam and then the sound of Matt's feet pounding up the stairs. I began to step back, and this time Jackson let me. I moved with haste back to the kitchen and bent over the island, staring unseeingly at my phone. All in an attempt to hide the emotion that I knew was fraying my expression.

"Hey," Matt said. "How was your day?"

"Pretty good and you?"

Matt strode into the kitchen. "Good. Em, I can't stay for dinner. I have to take some clients to a game."

I glanced up. "Okay."

"I just came home to change."

"Do you want me to save you a plate?" To my own ears, my voice sounded wooden.

"Nah. I'll eat at the game."

I glanced behind me. Jackson had disappeared. A moment later I heard his truck roar to a start.

Matt left in a whirlwind, barely affording me a second glance. I waited until 8 PM to eat dinner, but Jackson didn't return. I sat at the island, turning over the thought of Jackson in my mind. I was still trying to put the crumbs of information together that I could garner from Matt and Jackson.

Jackson had lived alone with Ted, a man who was not even his father.

His mother had died. So where was his birth father? Why had Ted, a man obviously not interested in loving or caring for a small child, continued to keep Jackson in his life only so that he could abuse him?

And what about all the trips to the hospital? A seven-year-old who was at the mercy of a violent drunk was an impossible situation to imagine. I could not wash away the image of a small boy wary and alert, hiding and running from a drunk and menacing man intent on causing pain. Why hadn't the authorities protected him?

Matt's father had been a police officer and had taken Jackson into his home, but apparently not full time. Why hadn't he called social services? Why had the system failed Jackson as a boy, to the point that he was riddled with broken limbs and probably unimaginable emotional scars? The whole situation made me so angry on Jackson's behalf. I wanted answers, but the past was something that both Matt and Jackson preferred not to talk about. I had a weird feeling that they needed to talk about their history, to bridge the issue that hindered them now.

These days, Matt was almost never home. He avoided Jackson and myself like the plague. Jackson seemed more patient about the entire thing. His energy was very neutral when Matt did show up, but there was not a lot of warmth between the two of them. They were both on their guard and were excruciatingly distant and polite with each other. Matt had adamantly expressed to me that he did not want Jackson to leave and Jackson continued to stay which told me they both wanted to mend whatever had come between them. I got the sense neither of them knew how to fix it, so we were left in this uncomfortable impasse.

I sighed and dumped my half-eaten plate in the sink. The fact that Jackson took off indicated to me that maybe my hug had been a little bit too much. Yet he hadn't wanted me to let go. The man was complicated.

I sat downstairs until 11 PM reading the same page in my book over and over again, but neither Jackson nor Matt came home. Finally, defeated, I went to bed.

CHAPTER TWELVE

"Why did I think that a party was a good idea?" I wailed from the kitchen. Fifty people were about to descend into my space in a matter of hours. I hated parties. I knew no greater punishment than to host a party.

Jackson stood shirtless at the door, drinking from a water bottle. The man liked to grind his body through the most intense, insane workouts imaginable and this afternoon was no different. Did people even realize that a body that looked photoshopped was the result of ruthless determination and constant work? No wonder the dad bod was coming back in style.

"I think you wanted me to have more selection than just Julie."

I pointed a knife at him. "After this, you and your sex life are completely on your own. You're the last person that needs help in that department."

He grinned. "Tell me what to do."

"I don't know."

"Where's your list?"

"What makes you think I have a list?"

"You have an entire binder for your wedding. You're the queen of lists. Cough it up." He grabbed his t-shirt from the back of the chair and pulled it on. I worked to not watch.

I grabbed my notebook and stared unseeing at my scrawl. I suppressed a deep shiver when he came around and leaned over me.

"Clean back rooms," he read.

"That says bathrooms."

He leaned closer, so close I could feel the heat off his body. "You get an F in handwriting."

"I'm left-handed."

"Why do left-handed people always use that excuse for messy writing?"

"It's not an excuse. It's a fact."

"Is that why your car is so messy? Because you're left-handed?"

I started to laugh. "Life is too short to be a neat freak."

"You do realize that the average messy person wastes more time looking for stuff than a neat freak spends tidying up."

"You can't just make stuff up and act like it's a fact."

He grinned. "It's a scientific study. Look it up."

"I don't have time. I'm too busy looking for things."

We stood there smiling at each other.

"Okay, I'll do the bathrooms."

I snorted. "Please."

His gaze held mine. I noticed flicks of gold in his green eyes. "You think a sailor doesn't know how to clean?"

"I'm sure you can clean. But I can't ask you to clean the bathrooms."

"I'm on it."

Jackson vacuumed, dusted, set up chairs and cleaned the bathrooms to a state I'd never seen them before. I cooked a tremendous amount of appetizers. He stepped out to get ice while I changed. I worked to create ambiance with lights, candles, and music while he showered.

I almost choked on my wine, when he came downstairs after his shower. A black, short-sleeved buttoned shirt showed off his arms, and his jeans hugged his butt. I struggled not to stare. His sex appeal rocked off the charts. I envisioned my worldly, ultra-hip New York girlfriend's reactions as they laid their eyes on him.

"What's left?" He interrupted my thoughts.

"I think we're pretty much done."

He looked around. "Looks good."

"Thanks for your help. I couldn't have done this without you."

His eyes tracked to my mouth. "All this effort to get me laid."

"Yeah." I inwardly winced.

My heart fluttered when a smile slowly spread across his face.

"What's so funny?"

"You just get this look on your face when we talk about my sex life."

"Your sex life is none of my business."

"How old are you?"

"24. How old are you?"

"29." His eyes traced my face. "So what made you want to abstain from all things in the bedroom?"

My mouth dropped open. "Are you serious?"

He nodded. Completely serious. "Yeah."

My breath stuck in my ribs. "It took a few years to recover from losing my parents. My grandma was pretty liberal, but she was old-fashioned when it came to boys."

"What about when you went to college?"

I lifted my hands. "It isn't like guys were beating down my bedroom door. I had crushes on guys."

"What kind of guys?" his eyes narrowed.

"I seemed to gravitate towards big, athletic guys. At parties, I was the shy redhead, who stared at them from across the room. And I was incapable of talking to a single one of them. I would watch them go home with my friends."

"You're killing me."

"They never saw me. Not when there was someone like Julie in the room."

"She's average."

If he thought someone like Julie was average, I couldn't imagine the caliber of women he dated. "She's a catch."

He crossed his thick arms. "So, if the hunky quarterback had found the balls to put the moves on you, would he have been able to have you?"

My mind raced, uncertain of my answer. "I don't know."

"Matt doesn't protest your vow of celibacy?"

I rubbed my forehead. Matt rarely attempted to touch me. Since we had become engaged, I had hoped we would fool around a bit more, but he seemed uninterested in taking things further. "He seems okay with it."

Jackson tilted his head and paused. "He's either an idiot or he's a better guy than me."

My head jerked up. "What? Why do you say that?"

"I don't think I would be okay with it."

My heart bounced in my chest. "What about all your navy trained self-discipline?"

"SEALs have discipline, but they thrive on challenges. If you and I were engaged, I wouldn't pay attention to any of this waiting-for-marriage bullshit."

My eyes widened in shock. The thought of being engaged to Jackson did weird things to my stomach. Something forbidden hung between us. Decadent, sinful images flashed wildly before my eyes. I imagined him crawling up the bed, laughing with that smile, teasing me, kissing my neck. My entire body reacted to his statement.

"You can't say that."

"I just did."

He watched my face with interest.

"All of my friends are going to go bananas over you, but to be honest, you scare me."

The intensity of his stare whipped shivers up my spine. "You're the one who scares me."

I struggled to bring air into my lungs. Why did I scare him? How was that even possible? "I thought you didn't feel fear."

"I feel it. I just manage it."

Our eyes stayed locked.

"Hello?" A voice intruded from the door.

I tore myself away from his gaze. Julie walked in, carrying two bottles of wine.

"Hi," I scrambled towards her, part grateful and part resentful for the interruption.

We hugged.

She peeked around me. "Hi, Jackson."

He raised his hand and waved.

She looked back at me, and a smile stuck on her face. She whispered through her smile. "I thought I told you that I wanted it to be a quiet evening?"

I had texted Julie a couple of days ago, telling her that we had upgraded the dinner to a party.

I cleared my throat. "I thought it would be a good chance for Jackson to meet people."

"I wanted him to myself," she hissed. "You have everything. Why couldn't you help me out on this one thing?"

I glanced back at Jackson who watched our whispery exchange from the kitchen. "More alcohol and more chances to flirt than a boring old dinner."

She pushed her arm into mine. "Good point. I forgive you."

She spoke in a normal voice. "Where's Matt?"

We walked to the island, and I checked my watch. "He should be home soon."

She shifted her attention to Jackson. "Hi, Jackson. How are you?"

"Good, how are you?"

His friendly smile stunned Julie into an uncustomary silence. Her arm squeezed mine tight in response. Geez, he needed to keep that thing on a leash. Yup. I sensed a feeding frenzy in our near future.

"So what brings you to New York, Jackson?" Julie vibrated with energy.

I uncorked the wine and poured Julie a glass.

"I'm stateside for a few months."

"Stateside? Are you in the military?"

"The Navy."

Her mouth dropped open. "Like a real sailor?"

"Navy SEAL."

Her hands danced to her chest. "Oh, my God."

I looked down at her wine and decided to take a big sip before passing it to her.

"Julie has a thing for guys in uniforms." I paused, thoughtful. "And guns."

"Emily doesn't lie." Julie batted her eyelashes like she had something in both eyes. I inwardly sighed. Julie's behavior was reminiscent of our University days. But this time, I would not be at the party alone. This time I was engaged.

I stepped away and dialed Matt's number.

A female voice purred. "Hello?"

I looked at the face of my phone. I confirmed that I had dialed Matt's number. "Is Matt there?"

"Sure. One moment."

The phone fumbled and then Matt's voice was on the line. His voice sounded too whispery. "Hey."

I swallowed an awful feeling down my throat and let it sink into my stomach. "Who was that?"

"That was Katherine. We're all working overtime on this brief, and there must be ten cell phones on the boardroom table. I think she just thought my cell was hers."

"There are other people there?"

A short laugh punched out of him. "Of course. Honestly, we're up to our eyeballs here."

I placed my hand on my forehead. "Do you know what day it is?"

"It's either Saturday or Sunday. I'm hoping it's Saturday because if it's Sunday, we're fucked."

"Matt," I whispered, looking up. Jackson watched me from across the room. Julie was talking at him, a mile a minute. "The party for Jackson? Remember?"

"Oh crap," he said. "Emily."

"We have over 50 people arriving here in less than half an hour. You have to come home."

"I'll make it up to you."

"Matt." I heard the pleading tone in my voice.

"Emily. You know I'd be there if I could, but it's just not going to happen. Not this weekend."

"What am I supposed to do?"

"Well Jackson is there, isn't he?"

I focused on the ceiling in despair. Why could Matt never make me his priority? He promised me repeatedly that he would come home, but lately, he was a ghost. He pushed me to spend time with Jackson. My emotions confused me. "He's here. But he isn't my fiancé whom I want to spend time with."

"Have fun for me, okay?"

I remained silent on the phone, my hand pressed against my throat. I suppressed the anger that threatened to bubble out of me. Why could Matt never stick to his word? How would I survive this party on my own? I hated parties. For the hundredth time, I questioned my sanity in planning this event.

Matt sounded short. "Emily, you can't be like this. I have to go."

"Fine."

"Love you."

I sighed and clicked off the phone without replying.

CHAPTER THIRTEEN

TWO HOURS LATER, I STOOD IN MY VERSION OF HELL. MUSIC BLASTED, people talked and laughed. I was just a girl, standing alone, at her party. I sipped my wine. I sighed and looked down at my ring. I thought one benefit of getting engaged and married was so that you had the plus one who gave a fuck about you at parties. My throat tightened as I remembered the throaty female voice that answered his phone. I forced myself to not think about that.

Four women surrounded Jackson. Julie trailed one hand up Jackson's arm and then laughed as she squeezed his bicep. I gulped more wine. My University days flashed in front of my eyes. Friends tripped over themselves to capture Jackson's attention. I predicted that Julie would win. I already envisioned Jackson tugging Julie's hand as he discretely led her upstairs to his room.

Julie waved at me. "Em, come over here."

With great reluctance, I fixed a smile on my lips and walked over.

Julie studied me. "Wow, your lips look fantastic."

I swallowed and avoided looking in Jackson's direction. "Thanks."

"My lips would look that good if I also could afford $40 lipstick," she looked around the group. "But not all of us got so lucky in life."

"Five dollar lipstick from Walgreens." I kept my voice light.

"So we were just bugging Jackson about his workouts." Julie changed the subject.

"Oh."

"He won't tell us about the crazy things he does. He says that he just works out like everyone else."

I stared at her. What was she even talking about? This had to be the most inane conversation I have ever walked into. I took a big sip of my wine.

I evaded making direct eye contact with Jackson.

"Are you going to tell us?" Julie urged. I looked at her. Her eyes burned bright, giving her a somewhat alarming look. She loved the conquest. This persona appeared when you mixed Julie, a hot man, wine and some female competition. No one liked this side of her, mostly because she became a tiny bit scary.

"Tell you what?"

"Tell us about Jackson's workouts. We need to know how he created such a perfect hard body."

A few other women nodded and leaned in. This entire conversation mortified me. Is this how people flirted? It pained me even to listen. Jackson stared at me without expression.

"I apologize for my friends," I said to him. "They're acting like they just broke out of a nunnery."

Jackson looked away. He struggled not to laugh.

Julie's laughter peeled so loud; she almost blew out my eardrum. "Maybe we just haven't met someone of Jackson's caliber."

I hadn't realized that Jackson's party experience might be worse than my own.

Beth squeezed my arm. "Do you mind lending me that soup cookbook you were telling me about?"

I breathed a huge sigh of relief. That was our code for we needed to talk. "Absolutely. Come with me."

We walked away from the group.

Beth leaned into my ear. "Julie's acting crazy tonight. She's barking way out of her league."

I sniffed. "She doesn't seem to think so."

"He's being nice about the fact that she is trying to molest him without ever giving her a single shred of hope that he's interested."

I looked across the room. Jackson listened politely to someone talk. "He's a nice person."

"You didn't lie. I'm confident that he's about a thousand times hotter than the hockey player."

I took a deep breath. "Ever since he arrived, Matt has been missing in action."

"Why?"

"I have no idea. Meanwhile, I'm trying to plan this wedding and Matt is no help. Jackson is a great houseguest but I just…"

Beth's gaze focused on mine. "I get it."

"You do?"

"You're living with a GQ model, and your fiancé has fucked off. Shit gets complicated."

My breath gusted out of me. "I love Matt, but I feel like I haven't seen him, much less talked to him in weeks." I lowered my voice and leaned in. "And Jackson is constantly working out with his shirt off. My car is in pieces, so he's driving me everywhere."

Beth started to laugh. "And this is a problem why?"

I shook my head. "He listens to me when I talk, and he cares about things like my art and my job."

Beth gave me a sympathetic smile. "He's treating you like you wished Matt would treat you."

"Yes!"

"Where is that dick anyways?"

I hesitated. Wanting to confess that another woman had answered his phone, but knew that it would only make Beth angry. "He canceled. He promised me that he would be here, but he bailed at the last minute."

Beth sighed and rubbed my arm. "You do realize you deserve better, right?"

I didn't want to talk about it.

"It's not Matt's fault. He has a crazy job. I just need to get through to the wedding. That's my goal."

Beth and I chatted a bit more, and despite my pleading, she had to leave. She had an early brunch with her family, and she didn't want to show up hung over.

The room felt lonely without her. I glanced around the room. Julie and company were crowding Jackson like a poorly mannered fan club. I stood in the kitchen alone, sipping my third glass of wine. How many parties in my youth had I attended precisely like this? Where my friends were off chasing some guy, and I was left standing, by myself, feeling socially awkward. I looked around the room. It was my party, my place, but no one noticed me. I needed one moment. I needed to clear my head.

I walked upstairs, moved into my bedroom and shut the door. I flopped back onto the bed. The music throbbed from below. Loneliness crashed over me. I sucked in a deep breath. I permitted myself to partake in a three-minute pity party, and then I would head back downstairs.

A soft knock sounded on my door. Before I could answer, Jackson stepped in and shut the door behind him. His size dominated the room. I pushed myself into a sitting position.

"Is everything okay?" my voice sounded raspy.

"I was just about to ask you the same thing."

I blew the bangs off my forehead. "Just taking a breather."

"Where's Matt?"

"Working."

"Seems like that's all he does."

"Agreed."

He frowned and walked over to sit on the bed beside me. "You sure you're okay?"

I nodded, trying to swallow the lump from my throat. His care exacerbated my pity party feelings. "I think I was having some University flashbacks."

His gaze sharpened, but he remained silent.

"I thought I had grown out of standing off to the side and watching my friends flirt with the hottest guy in the room."

I exhaled and pasted a smile on my face.

"Wait," he paused, thinking. "Am I the quarterback?"

"Shut up." My voice was devoid of meaning.

"Em," his quiet voice sounded sincere. "I bet those University guys were dying to come and talk to you, but they didn't have the balls."

I snorted. "Trust me. You had to be there."

He lifted a hand and brushed a strand of hair off my cheek. "I see you standing off to the side. You're so untouchable to the rest of the world, it hurts."

I grabbed his thick wrist, and my eyes drifted shut when I felt his thumb gently brush my cheek.

"I bet they constantly thought about kissing you." His low voice hypnotized me.

I opened my eyes. Green eyes studied my face. His huge hand slide around the back of my neck and then he pulled me close.

My hands fluttered in my lap when his mouth touched mine. He tasted like wine and desire. I moaned, and instantly the kiss deepened. His lips coaxed my mouth, intoxicating me with pleasure. I opened my mouth beneath his while his fingers tangled in my hair. He moved my head, angling it so he could torture my mouth some more with his wicked perfect kiss. My entire body responded. My skin tingled, my body tightened, my heart tumbled. A deep noise rumbled in his chest, and his passion staggered me.

His mouth yanked off mine, and he turned away from me. His breath was harsh. "Oh fuck."

My body violently trembled. My heart was like a feral bird, fluttering with madness in my chest. I could not believe that I had just kissed Jackson. I was a terrible person. I had just cheated on Matt. Matt, who was working late tonight. I couldn't even reconcile what had just happened. What had I done?

"I'm sorry," I bleated.

He tilted his head at me. His look was incredulous. "This was not your fault."

My eyes were wide. I was still in shock. My body still trembled. Guilt crushed my heart. "It kinda is."

I watched as he stood up and walked to the door.

I stared at his broad back, wishing my voice wasn't shaking so hard. "I'm engaged to be married."

His movements stopped. He faced away from me, but he was listening.

"You need to go downstairs and flirt with someone else. I can't do that again. I'm a faithful person."

His body pivoted with control. He looked different. Real emotion moved across his face, a mixture of anger and deep, hot desire.

"Emily."

"Yes?"

"There is only one other person in this world that I have met that is as good as you. You have no responsibility or guilt here. I kissed you. That was me, taking something that wasn't mine to take. It'll never happen again."

He turned around and walked out of the room.

I THINK I WAS IN SHOCK. I COULDN'T EVEN PROCESS WHAT HAD JUST happened. I held my fingers to my lips. I had never been kissed like that before in my life. I worked to recall kissing Matt, but my mind was drawing a blank. Who failed to remember what it was like to kiss their fiancé?

I washed my shaking hands and pulled a hairbrush through my hair. I wanted to crawl into bed and not come out. Instead, I took a deep breath and opened my bedroom door.

Standing in the midst of his she-pack, Jackson lifted his eyes and watched as I slowly walked down the stairs. I momentarily fantasized about turning off the music and kicking everyone out, but instead, I walked into the kitchen, found my wine glass and poured myself another generous glass.

His mouth covered mine.

His teeth nipped my bottom lip.

I moaned into his mouth.

Our kiss flashed in my mind on repeat. I felt my face heat up. It was going to be a long night.

CHAPTER FOURTEEN

An hour later, I stood in the kitchen and pretended to wipe down the counter, because secretly it was the best vantage point to watch Julie and Jackson. Watching Julie flirt with Jackson was painful, but watching Jackson flirt back felt like a knife was going through my heart. The man had charm. I thought Matt was an outstanding flirt, but Jackson took it to a whole other level. They were no longer even interacting with other people at the party. They were huddled together talking. Every time Julie spoke, Jackson leaned down, putting his face near hers, so that only he could hear what she said. Whatever she said was apparently funny, because he laughed. I watched as he gently brushed some of her hair off her shoulder. Something ugly moved in my stomach. How could he flirt like that with her, when only a short while ago he had given me one of the most incredible kisses of my life? Just because his kiss had defined all kisses in my life to date, did not mean that it had meant anything to him. For Jackson, that was probably just another everyday kiss. He had come to my room, and I was having a pity party, so he tried to make me feel better with a pity kiss. I needed to get my act together here and just be happy for them.

Jackson lifted his gaze and green eyes met mine. My face burst into flames. I was staring at them like some creepy forlorn lover. I almost tripped over myself to turn away. This was my doing. Jackson and I had done the unthinkable. I had cheated on Matt. I had kissed Jackson. There was no coming back from that. I needed to focus my attention back to Matt. Jackson needed to concentrate his ridiculous charm and charisma elsewhere, and who better than at Julie, who looked like she was about to self-combust in heat.

Furthermore, I had no business concerning myself with Jackson's love life. And I certainly had no right to let it bother me. I had a wonderful fiancé whom I was going to marry in three short months.

"Matt!" someone yelled over the music. I looked up with relief to see Matt walk in the door, carrying two bottles of wine. I started towards him, and then stopped in my tracks when a beautiful woman walked in behind him. He turned and smiled at her, and then put his hand on her back, ushering her further into the loft.

I watched as he walked through the room, introducing her to our various friends. She was probably just a co-worker that he had brought along. So why did something cold crawl across my skin?

I pasted a big fake-ass smile on my face and walked towards them.

"Hi," I said.

"Hi," Matt smiled, avoiding my eyes. The three of us all stood there. It was awkward.

"Hi Matt," I said again and raised my eyebrows at him. His eyes were bloodshot and red, and he had that look to him. The look that said he had already drunk more than his fair share.

"This is Katherine, one of the partners at my firm." He pointed a wine bottle at me. "And this is…."

He was loaded.

"Emily," I glared daggers at him and stuck my hand out to shake hers. "Pleased to meet you."

"I was getting to your name," Matt enunciated carefully. "Any booze in this place?"

My manners kicked in. I'd deal with Matt later. I asked her, "Can I get you something to drink?"

"I would love a glass of pinot."

As I turned away, I heard her say, "How long do we have to stay here?"

I stood in the kitchen, my hands shaking as I poured the wine. What exactly was going on here? Who was Katherine? Why had she answered Matt's phone? Why was he already drunk? Why hadn't he introduced me as his fiancée? Questions crowded my mind.

How could I possibly jump to conclusions when I had just kissed Jackson. Was I going to turn this situation back around on Matt and make this his fault?

I brought her a glass of wine, and we smiled at each other. Polite and welcoming conversation. I could do it.

Someone shouted from across the room, "Emily."

"Excuse me."

"My girlfriend accidentally knocked over your plant," Ben said with an apologetic face.

I stared down at the tiny jasmine plant that Jackson had given me. It lay mangled on the floor amongst the black soil and the smashed blue ceramic pot. The fragile small plant lying there made me want to cry a little bit.

"I'm so sorry," Ben's girlfriend said with genuine regret in her voice.

"No problem," I sat on my haunches in front of the mess.

A familiar figure appeared beside me with a hand broom and dustpan. "Here let me help."

"Wait," I said, as Jackson moved to start sweeping. "I want to save the plant."

"I don't know if that plant is going to survive the fall," Ben offered his advice. "It looks pretty toast to me."

Annoyance flashed through me. "We can save it."

I picked it up with both hands and then I looked around. "Now what?"

I glanced up at Jackson's bemused expression. "You want to save that?"

"Yes."

"You're different. You know that?"

I lifted my chin. "Can you use your stupid army skills to help me or what?"

A gorgeous smile broke out on his face, and the party faded away from around us. "I think my stupid skills might come in handy."

"You're in charge."

While I cradled the plant at the counter in the kitchen, Jackson rooted through the cupboards looking for a dish. I looked over my shoulder. "That dish."

He looked at the silver bowl in his hand. "I was looking for Tupperware."

I frowned. "Oh no. This plant can't do Tupperware."

He brought the bowl over. "Are you sure? This looks a bit fancy."

"It's perfect," I said, a smile on my face. "My granny bought it for me."

He set it down. "Do you have potting soil?"

"I do actually. In the pantry."

I watched as he poured soil into the bowl, and then I repotted the plant into the sterling silver bowl. Jackson watched as I watered it and then we both stood there looking at the droopy plant.

Julie came over. "What are you guys doing?"

"Someone dumped a plant. We just repotted it."

She peered over my shoulder. "You did not."

I knew the moment she spoke what she was getting at. I attempted to change the subject. "Julie, you want some more wine?"

"That bowl is from fucking Tiffany's. That's the Monteith bowl."

"Ha," I lied. "Not true. I think I got this at a garage sale."

Jackson's eyes met mine.

"Bullshit," Julie sounded indignant. "I know Tiffany. You can't plant that crappy weed in a bowl worth over four thousand dollars. That's sacrilege."

I took a deep breath and then picked up the bowl. "This isn't a crappy weed. This is a friendship plant and I can plant it in whatever bowl I want."

"Must be nice to throw around your money for everyone to see."

"The only reason why this bowl has value is that it was a gift from my granny," my face burned.

"Easy for you to say," her voice was like a whip.

Without looking at either them, I picked up my $6 plant in my $4000 bowl and walked away from both of them.

CHAPTER FIFTEEN

I STOOD IN THE LAUNDRY ROOM AND STARED AT THE PLANT THAT SAT ON THE washer. Why was Julie so obsessed with how much money I had? Why did she have to bring it up every single chance she got? And why did it feel like everything was spinning out of control? I just wanted this party to end and everyone to go home.

I took a deep breath. I just needed to get through tonight. I could process everything later.

I moved back to the living room. Matt was knee deep in the party, joking and laughing uproariously. Katherine stuck to his side like glue.

Swallowing hard, I made my way to his side, and when he saw me, his eyes lit up. "Em, can you please top us up?"

Shame washed over me. Followed immediately by retribution. I had kissed Jackson. Jackson's mouth had been on mine, and I had moaned into his lips. I had wantonly drunk in his kiss like the starved virgin I was. Matt deserved more from me. Now he was entertaining someone from his work, and I was not going to be the insecure fiancé who clung to him.

"Sure," I said with a cheerfulness I did not feel.

∾

THE PARTY RAGED ON. PEOPLE DRANK MORE. THE MUSIC GOT LOUDER. THE laughter became overwhelming. The energy was more intense. I collected dirty glasses. I called cabs for people who were no longer in any condition to drive. I sorted out coats and bags and hugged and kissed everyone on their way out. And the entire time, I drank. I don't know how many glasses of wine I consumed, but the moment my glass was empty, I filled it up again.

I was in the kitchen, trying without success to tie off a bag of garbage but my hands fumbled and struggled with the simple task. Matt appeared in the kitchen.

"Do we have any more of that pinot?"

I stood up and blinked at him. It dawned on me that I would have to come clean about the kiss. The sooner, the better. He was avoiding my gaze.

"Matt," I said carefully. "Can we talk? I have to tell you something."

"Not right now."

"Matt, I have a confession."

Matt's critical gaze roamed over me. Then he looked over his shoulder, his bloodshot eyes narrowed. I followed his gaze to see Jackson towering on the other side of the island. He wore a scowl, and he looked formidable.

Matt looked towards Jackson. "Why do you look so pissed? You're getting lucky tonight, as usual."

"What?" I blinked in confusion. Green eyes shifted to my face and then back to Matt again.

Matt snorted. "Jackson here likes to stroll into any situation, find the hottest chick and then the rest of us get his leftovers."

My mouth dropped open at Matt's crude comment. "Matt!"

"The worst part about it is that it won't mean anything to him."

I now had to tell Matt I had kissed Jackson. I shut my eyes momentarily, and the entire room went off kilter. I grabbed the counter to find my balance.

"You're hammered." Matt looked at me with something close to disgust.

I just needed to get this over with.

"Matt, we need to talk."

He stepped back. "Em, why do you always pick the most inappropriate times to want to talk? You have the worst timing of any person I know."

My mouth dropped open at the barely concealed venom in his tone. Why was he so angry at me? Did he somehow already know that I had kissed Jackson?

Against my will, my hands reached out to grab his arm. He shook me off. My eyes followed him as he walked back into the living room to take his place beside Katherine.

Jackson looked down at me. His expression was unreadable.

"He's mad," my voice sounded sorrowful. "And I haven't even told him yet."

He rubbed the back of his neck.

Why was I always dumping my issues at this man's feet?

I tried to switch gears by asking him, "Did you have fun tonight?"

His expression didn't change.

I swallowed a huge lump in my throat and lied. "I think you and Julie make a nice couple."

"You should go to bed."

"You're scowling."

He looked over his shoulder at Matt and then looked back at me. "I'm going to help you upstairs now."

I carefully stepped, wobbling only slightly. "I can do it myself."

Jackson walked around the island, and before I could react, he scooped me into his strong arms, holding me against his chest. I stared up at his beautiful face as he began to move with ease up the stairs.

"Carrying another person up the stairs is dangerous," I worked to enunciate my words.

He glanced down at me. "I can carry another guy my size on my back."

I blinked, noticing from this angle, just how long his eyelashes were. Was it like firefighters? Did they have to carry someone as part of qualifying for his job? "What distance do you have to carry the other person?"

"It depends."

"On what?"

"If we're five miles away, and he's hurt, that's how far I carry him. If we're ten miles, that's the distance we go."

I frowned at him. "But what if you get tired?"

He pushed into my room. "Getting tired isn't an excuse. You just get the job done."

"I can take it from here," I said. I struggled to lift my head from his chest.

He lay me on the bed and stood over me.

"The room is spinning."

"Keep your eyes open," he moved to the foot of the bed.

His two warm hands were on my ankle. Unable to lift my head, I realized that he was working on the strap of my high heel. I decided to let him since I didn't think I would be able to manage it.

I stared at the ceiling fan. "Do me a favor?"

"What." He pulled off one shoe and moved to my other foot.

"Can you and Julie not be too loud?"

"What?" He sounded harsh.

I lifted my head. "When she comes up here as your sophisticated overnight guest."

"Julie isn't coming upstairs."

I dropped my head back on the pillow. "She would if you asked her."

He sounded pissed. "I won't be asking her."

His breath warmed the skin on my ankle as he worked on my shoe.

"Matt said you were getting lucky."

He tugged my other shoe off. Standing up, he towered over my bed. "I'm going to get you some water and aspirin."

He disappeared out the door. I struggled to sit up. I needed to take my pants off. I unbuttoned them but decided that I could shimmy out of them while lying down. I got them halfway down my hips, but they got stuck.

Jackson reappeared, pausing at the door when he saw me in my state of undress.

"I can't get my pants off," I said, my eyes shut. "Can you help?"

A glass clattered as it got set down on the nightstand.

"I thought Matt was the lightweight."

"Just pull them off."

The bed depressed next to me, so I opened my eyes. He had one knee on the bed, and he looked down at my pants.

"Did you have fun tonight?" I stared at his perfect face.

"It was fine."

"I hated tonight," I said with a sigh. "Tonight was bad."

Green eyes clashed with mine. He held eye contact while his huge hands traced over my bare skin at my waist. A small noise squeaked out of me. I lifted my head and watched as his fingers grabbed the fabric of my pants. He tugged the material down over my hips and down my thighs before pulling them from my body.

"How come tonight was so bad?" His voice sounded very casual.

I lay there, staring up at him. Too drunk to care that he was looking at me in my undies. "Everything was bad."

He grabbed the quilt and pulled it over my body.

"Why?"

My body hurt, but emotionally I needed to talk.

"Just…Matt's co-worker. She answered his cell. And he didn't even tell her that he was my fiancé."

Jackson listened.

My hands fluttered above the quilt. "I know she's an important person, but I'm important too."

"You are."

"It made me feel bad."

"I bet." His expression was solemn.

"And I feel bad about other stuff."

"Like what?"

"You know."

He stood there for a long moment without speaking. "Tell me."

"The kiss," I whispered.

He pinched the bridge of his nose. "I told you, that was not your fault."

I blurted, "I feel bad because I liked it."

He put his hands on his hips and took a deep breath before blowing it out slowly. "Emily, you're going to hurt tomorrow."

"I already hurt."

~

I BOLTED TO THE TOILET. SOMETIME IN THE MIDDLE OF THE NIGHT, I HAD taken off my blouse, and now I shivered in just my bra and panties, as I clung to the toilet bowl, and repeatedly spewed my guts.

"Matt," I called weakly. Then I barfed some more. I flushed the toilet. Acid burned my throat. Tears streaked down my face. "Matt."

The hallway light turned on, and then a figure in the doorway blocked out the light.

"Matt?" I turned my face back into the toilet and retched some more. The night light went on in my bathroom. A soft glow flooded the room.

"No, it's Jackson." Two big hands pulled my hair back, while my body worked to cleanse itself.

"Can you go get him?" I gasped. He walked to the sink, wet a face cloth and crouched down beside me. I struggled to lift my head. He gently wiped my face.

"Where is Matt?" I stammered.

"He left."

My head jerked up. "Where did he go?"

He shrugged. "I think he went out with some of the guys. I don't know."

I wiped my nose. "I feel sick, and I threw up in my hair."

He laughed. "Yeah, I know."

"You don't have to help me," I said, wanting to cry. "This goes way beyond the call of duty."

He stood up, and I heard the shower door open. Water turned on.

"Come on," he said, "You'll feel better after a shower."

I shook my head. "I'll just stay here."

Two hands went under my arms, and he hauled me onto my feet. "In you get."

He pushed me into the walk-in shower. Clad in only my bra and panties, I staggered and clutched the wall, feeling incredibly dizzy.

He stepped in behind me and reached around me to adjust the water temperature. He pushed me to stand beneath the warm water. I shut my eyes and let the water pour over me. His big hands slicked my hair back off my face.

"Turn around," he said.

I faced him, my eyes still shut. Strong hands shampooed my hair before tilting my head to rinse. I dropped my forehead, leaning it against his chest. Strong arms wrapped around me. I sighed as I leaned against his warm, hard chest.

"Do you feel better?" he asked.

I nodded.

"Come on," he took my hand and led me out of the shower. I shivered, my arms crossed over myself. He wrapped a big towel around my shoulders and started to rub me dry. I trembled with cold.

I stared at him in a fog. He was dripping wet. Rivulets of water ran down his huge chest. His drawstring fleece shorts were soaked and clung to his body.

"Aren't you cold?"

"This isn't cold," his face was a mask of concentration as he rubbed first one arm dry and then the other. He turned me around, and roughly rubbed the towel over my back. Down one leg and then the other. Then the towel wrapped around my back.

He disappeared into my bedroom and came back with a t-shirt and a pair of dry panties. "Can you manage this?"

I nodded and waited for him to leave. On shaking legs, I pulled on the dry clothes. I brushed my teeth but was unable to look at my reflection in the mirror. I wondered how much Jackson hated his life right now?

I staggered to my bed and looked down in horror.

CHAPTER SIXTEEN

Jackson reappeared at the doorway of my bedroom. He had pulled on sweats, a t-shirt, and a worn baseball cap.

My voice sounded sad. "I barfed on my quilt."

He walked over to stand beside me. "Just a little bit."

Tears choked me. "Why isn't Matt here?"

He rubbed the back of his neck. "I don't know."

He reached down to my bed and started stripping the duvet cover off the bed and then removed all the sheets from my bed. I was still a bit drunk. He carried the linen out of the room, and I heard the door of the washing machine slam shut.

He walked back into the room. "Do you think you're going to be sick again?"

"No. Sorry." I covered my face. "I'm so sorry."

"Emily."

I sat on my bed. "Which guys did Matt go with?"

"I don't know."

"Did he say when he was going to be back?"

"No."

"What time is it?"

"Just after 0400."

"Don't you think he should be back by now?"

"I don't know."

I nodded. "Okay."

He crouched in front of me, his concerned face looking up at me. My smile trembled on my lips. "Thanks for your help. I can do the rest. You should go get some sleep."

"I don't need much sleep."

I swallowed. "How come?"

"It's my job. When we are engaged, sometimes we are up for 48 hours straight."

"What does engaged mean?"

"When we're fighting."

I pulled in a deep, shuddery breath. "Do you have to shoot at people?"

He lifted his hat on and off his head, and then he squinted up at me. "Sometimes."

"Oh," I swallowed thinking. "I think your job sounds awful."

His laugh was short and low. "Do you want to wait downstairs? I'm sure Mattie will be home soon."

"Okay."

He stood and offered me a hand. We walked downstairs. I stopped when I was on the second last step. The entire place was spotless. Everything gleamed. Clean wine glasses hung on the wine rack. Everything was in order. It looked like a showroom.

I stared at him. "Did you do this?"

"Come on," he tugged on my hand. "Let's get you on the couch."

I sat, and he grabbed a blanket and pulled it over me. "Lie down."

I looked up at him. "Will you sit with me?"

He paused for such a long moment, I was sure he would say no, but then he nodded. "Sure."

He sat on one end, and I lay on the length of the couch, my knees up, and my feet next to his thigh.

He looked over at me. "Do you want some water?"

I shook my head. "Thanks for sitting with me."

A smile ghosted across his face. "That's what friends do."

I shifted my legs. My feet were cold. I burrowed them under his thighs.

He looked at me. I snatched my feet back up. "My feet are cold."

He grabbed my feet and pulled them onto his lap. He wrapped one warm hand around my foot.

"They are cold." He wrapped his other hand around my other foot.

"Your hands are better than socks."

Another smile tugged at his mouth.

I stared at him. "Why did you clean everything up?"

He shrugged.

My self-loathing reached an all-time high. "I bet you wish you never stayed here."

"Not true."

"Why are you so nice?"

His laughter was harsh. "I'm not nice, Emily. Not even close."

"You're nice to me."

"Go to sleep. You'll feel better if you sleep."

I WAS HALF CONSCIOUS WHEN HE GOT UP OFF THE COUCH.

"I'm just switching the laundry over," he said.

I failed to open my eyes. "Okay."

"COME ON SWEETHEART." HE LIFTED ME AND THEN I WAS SNUGGLED UP against something hard and warm. I curled up, burrowing into the warmth. My head rested on a heater that rose and fell with each breath. I squinted. I was cuddled up against Jackson's chest. My arm drifted up around his waist. I felt warm and so safe.

VOICES WOKE ME UP. I WAS LYING ALONE ON THE COUCH.

"What's she doing down here?" Matt's voice. He sounded annoyed.

Footsteps jogged down the stairs. "She threw up on her bed."

"Oh, well fuck," Matt said. "Serves her right. She was hammered last night."

"What the fuck are you doing, Matt?" Jackson sounded pissed, but his voice was quiet.

A harsh laugh from Matt. "Oh, this is rich."

"That girl is so in love with you. She'll do anything for you. All she wants from you is to spend some time with her."

Matt slurred. "You have no fucking clue what you're talking about."

"I know who you fucking left with. Seriously?"

"Don't fucking start with me."

"You're messing up a good thing here."

"Jackson. You have always been so fucking jealous of me, haven't you?"

"This has nothing to do with me. Open your eyes."

"My eyes are wide open."

"So when your fiancée is sick and calling your name, and you aren't home, and she knows that something is up, but she can't wrap her mind around it."

"Just shut the fuck up, Jackson. God. Don't even start with me."

"I'm trying to prevent a train wreck."

"You want to know what a train wreck is? Cynthia Clymore."

"You're still upset about her? She was your girlfriend, what, when you were fifteen?"

"You fucking stole her from me," Matt's voice escalated about four-decibel levels.

"I didn't steal her. I didn't touch her," Jackson's voice remained calm.

"That isn't what she told me."

"Well, she lied."

"You never wanted me happy. Everything I had you needed to break."

"Come on, man. I'm not the one breaking what you have here."

"Cynthia. My family. You came into my home and stole my family."

"Like I had a choice about coming to your home."

"You could have said no."

"I was seven years old. I arrived there kicking and screaming. I wanted to stay with Ted."

"Bullshit. You wanted my life all to yourself."

"Why the fuck do we have to rehash the same old shit? Huh? I was seven years old, and Ted spent more time in jail than he did at home. Looking back I guess I should have just manned the fuck up and dealt with it."

"Poor you. Always the same crying bullshit."

"Yeah, well I have no idea why I'm here since you're the one who begged me to come here. You so obviously don't want to have anything to do with me."

"You're such a dick. You know that, man? Like everything you do, you just do to spite me."

"Not true. It may come as a complete surprise to you, but I think of you as family. I want the best for you."

"You want my fucking life."

"No, I want you to open your eyes and see what an amazing life you have before you fuck it up."

"I'm not the one who fucked my life up."

My eyes were wide open, and my heart pounded in my chest. I pushed myself to sit up. Matt and Jackson stood nose to nose. Matt shouted his points, but Jackson's voice remained moderate. Matt compared to Jackson looked small, yet he looked like he wanted to tear Jackson apart.

I climbed to my feet. "What's going on?"

Two heads rotated in my direction. Matt tossed up his hands. "I can't deal with any of this shit right now. I have to go."

Matt walked out of the loft. Jackson's hand covered his mouth. He turned and walked away, his hands on his hips.

I dropped the blanket on the floor and walked upstairs. I crawled into my freshly washed bed. I forced my brain to shut off. I was in no shape to even process that right now. I stared into the dark with wide eyes until sleep claimed me.

CHAPTER SEVENTEEN

"POLICE HAVE CONFIRMED THIS MORNING THAT THE UNIDENTIFIED FEMALE BODY *found in an industrial area was a victim of foul play. Unconfirmed reports that this may be the work of the throat slayer, a killer that could be tied to seven other murders of women around the city. Police remind women to be vigilant in their travels, to not trust strangers and to not walk in unpopulated areas alone at night."*

The newscaster's voice pierced my brain. Light streamed into my bedroom. I groaned and made stabbing motions towards my alarm clock radio before I finally succeeded in turning it off.

My head throbbed. As I rolled over, I became alarmed that I might throw up again. Memories bleeped through my mind, like a bad movie. The party. Kissing Jackson. Julie and Jackson flirting. Matt and his coworker. Violent barfing. The fight between Matt and Jackson. Matt leaving. So much anger. So much hurt. I couldn't even process what I had heard last night between the two of them. I couldn't digest it.

I staggered out of bed and into my bathroom. Everything looked pristine. The towels neatly folded on the rack. The toilet looked spotless. I shut my eyes. Jackson at some point had cleaned my bathroom. Matt couldn't care less if I had been sick, but somehow Jackson had found the time to clean my bathroom in the middle of the night? He must have done so when I was lying on the couch downstairs. My behavior last night had been reprehensible. Why was Matt acting so crazy? I couldn't even wrap my mind around the trouble between us. I had kissed Jackson, and only God knew what Matt had been up to. He hadn't come home last night. I knew deep in my heart there was trouble brewing, but I honestly did not want to see the truth.

I showered and walked downstairs. Jackson stood in the kitchen, looking fresh in his t-shirt and jeans. Pulled low over his eyes was his favorite baseball cap. I glanced around the spotless room and noticed his big black duffle bag at the door.

My hands jammed into my armpits. He was leaving too. I lifted my chin and walked to the island. Green eyes looked at me. So serious.

My voice scratched. "Thank you for helping me last night."

He regarded me with an intensity I didn't know how to decipher.

"Did Matt come back yet?" I tried again.

He shook his head. I stared up at his face unable to determine his thoughts. He let nothing show.

"Why are you leaving?" My voice sounded desperate even to my ears.

He looked down at the floor. "I think it's better for you and Matt."

"Who did he leave with last night?"

"That's a conversation you need to have with him."

"Why won't you tell me?"

"You should talk to Matt."

"What was last night about between the two of you?"

"You need to ask him that."

"I'm asking you."

Green eyes met mine. No response. Just blank.

"Do they train you to be like that?" Hurt laced my voice.

"Like what?"

"Not showing how you feel?"

He stared back at me.

"Where will you go?"

Nothing. He inhaled through his nose. Emotionally unresponsive.

Anger bubbled up inside of me. For how stupid everything was. For the fight between him and Matt. For how this man who stood before me made me feel things I didn't want to feel. For the cold fear I felt every time I thought about Matt and me. And for the anxiety that drenched my skin when I thought of Jackson walking out the door. If I could make Jackson stay, I might be able to reverse this curse in my life. However irrational, if Jackson didn't leave, then maybe, somehow, everything else would work out.

"You're not going," I marched to his duffle bag. It made no sense, but I dreaded being alone with Matt. I refused to face what would happen if Matt and I had too much time alone together. Terrible things would happen.

I attempted to pick up the duffle bag but staggered under the weight. I managed to lift it a couple of inches off the ground. I panted with effort.

He appeared beside me.

"What could you possibly have in this bag to make it weigh this much?" I grunted. When it became too heavy, my weak arms unwillingly dropped the bag back on the floor.

"Emily."

"No," I put my hand up. "Don't. Just don't, okay? I'm bringing your bag upstairs, and you can forget about leaving."

"Emily."

He showed no emotion. I clung to the duffle bag handles.

"Why is everyone leaving!" I yelled. "Why does everyone leave me?"

He crouched down on his haunches in front of me and looked up at me. His beautiful features were swimming in my tears. "Who left?"

"Everyone. My mom. My Dad. My granny. Other stupid people. Matt. And now you. No one wants to stay. I just thought if one person stayed here things would work out." Tears poured down my cheeks. "What's wrong with me?"

"Nothing is wrong with you."

"Where is Matt? What's going on with him? Why is he gone all the time?" My voice cracked. "I don't understand this."

I dropped to the floor, wrapped my arms around my knees and put my head down. I lifted my face and looked at him. "But I understand why you want to leave."

"Why is that?"

"Because I'm crazy. And messy. I don't blame you. I want to leave me too."

His eyes were shadowed beneath the brim of his baseball cap, hiding his expression.

The words poured out of me in a torrent. "I tried to kill you, but you still helped me pick wedding invitations. You saved me from getting run over. My stupid friends, even the married ones, all hit on you. And then I kissed you. Right before I barfed on you. You cleaned up after my big stupid party, and no one would blame you for wanting to leave. But you should know that you might be the greatest house guest I have ever had and maybe one of the nicest friends too."

He just crouched there, watching me. No expression.

I hiccuped.

"I'm not leaving because of you. I'm leaving for you."

"If you want to do something for me, then just stay."

A long, sad pause hung between us.

"Sorry. I'm so stupid," I gulped air into my lungs. "Now I'm making it worse. I'm just embarrassing us both."

He lifted his hat up and put it back on his head. "Emily."

A soft knock sounded on the door. Jackson and I looked at each other. The rolling door slid open. Irene, Matt's mom, stood in front of us. She took in my huddled form, and tearful face with Jackson crouched beside me and his duffle bag.

"Oh sorry," she said, "Is this a bad time?"

Jackson stood up and walked over to her. I wiped my face and watched as she presented a cheek for him to kiss.

I scrambled to my feet, and she gave me a look that was hard to read. "I'm so sorry to drop in on you like this. I heard that Jackson was in town."

I shook my head. "Of course. I didn't think. I should have invited you myself."

She looked down at the bag and then up at Jackson. "So are you coming or going?"

Jackson looked at me. His expression was hard to make out.

I wiped my face. "Why don't I make some coffee? Did you drive here?"

"No, I took the train and yes, I would love some coffee."

I started moving to the kitchen. Jackson had set up the new coffee maker, and now it was my turn to stand and stare at it. I had asked for a coffee maker with gadgets.

He appeared behind me. "I can make the coffee."

I sat down at the island while Irene and I looked at each other. I had hoped that Matt's mom and I would become close friends, but she wasn't the warmest woman I had ever met in my life. I vowed to give her another try.

Irene looked at Jackson, "How long are you stateside?"

"Three months."

"Matt told me that you were here."

"I should have called."

Silence hung in the air.

His voice was low, "How's the house?"

"Oh, things are good. I might need to have the shingles replaced this year. My neighbor gave me the name of two contractors."

CHAPTER EIGHTEEN

IRENE STUDIED ME. "HOW ARE YOU?"

I lied. "I'm good."

"How's the wedding planning coming along?"

Another lie. "Good."

Silence descended upon us. She looked around. "Is Matt sleeping?"

"He's at work." I was getting quite good at lying. Lying to myself. Lying to others.

She shook her head. "I have no idea where Matt got his work ethic from. He's the hardest working person I know."

"Lately, he's been working around the clock."

Jackson stood on the side, leaning against the counter, his long legs crossed, his arms folded.

Irene looked back between Jackson and I. "So, I obviously walked in on something here. Want to tell me what's going on?"

Jackson cleared his throat. "Same old shit."

"Did you and Matt fight?"

"Yep."

"Jackson. I know for a fact that Matt wanted you to come and stay with him because he wanted to repair your relationship. Why are you making this so difficult for him? You always do this."

Jackson didn't answer. Shock skidded across my skin. Jackson wasn't the difficult one in this situation. He was probably the only sane one.

She folded her arms. "Matt is trying here. Why can't you make an effort to get along?"

He stared back at her.

She cleared her throat. "I woke up this morning to a very incoherent drunk message from Matt. Half of which I couldn't understand. Jackson, you seemed to have upset him."

More silence while Jackson and I processed that statement.

"It's not your situation to fix," Jackson finally said.

"Ever since Harry's funeral…" her voice trailed off. "I'm asking you to fix this."

He glanced at me. "I think cooler heads might prevail."

She made a little noise. "So you're just going to take off again? That's so typical. We're trying here with you. We've always tried with you."

I was shocked at how biased this woman's view was of this situation. She was holding Jackson entirely responsible for this mess. I couldn't reconcile that Jackson had grown up with this woman. They seemed like two strangers.

"Matt wasn't exactly an angel in this situation," I interjected.

Cold eyes that reminded me of Matt turned on me. "And how's that?"

I swallowed again. "Well, Matt's been pretty distant lately."

"He works so hard."

"Yes. But he hasn't been around to try and fix stuff either."

She sniffed and looked around the loft. She turned back to Jackson. "I'm asking you to stay. For Matt. This is obviously important to him."

I held my breath. His face was devoid of expression, but he nodded. My heart bleated with joy. I didn't care that he was being coerced.

It was like a switch went off inside of her. Now that she had her way, everything was sunny in her life again. It reminded me of Matt. He would have his little temper tantrums about stuff, but as soon as I agreed to give in, I was back in his good books. At the time, I always felt such relief that things were back to normal, I had never stopped to realize how manipulative it was.

Irene chatted gaily about her choir that she attended every Thursday night and asked Jackson advice about shingles. I sipped my coffee while their conversation drifted around me. I stopped listening, so I could think.

Something nasty was going on with Matt. When had he stopped talking to me? I couldn't even remember the last time he had returned one of my texts. We used to text daily. Now it seemed like we hadn't talked in weeks. It had happened so slowly, I had barely noticed, but now it didn't even feel like he was living here, much less in a relationship with me.

Was it supposed to be like this? When we first started dating, he had been fun and sweet. We had cooked together and gone on date nights. Matt never did have a lot of time, but he had always made time for me. When had he stopped doing that? And why did he call his mom in a drunken stupor last night? It didn't make sense.

My head pounded and I felt light-headed. I glanced up. Jackson listened to Irene, but his eyes watched me. He moved to the fridge and took a ginger ale out of the refrigerator. He cracked that open and set it in front of me. Then he peeled a banana and placed it on a plate and shoved that in front of me. I picked up the banana and washed it down with the ginger ale. My stomach heaved dangerously at first, but in a few minutes it settled, and I became less lightheaded.

A few weeks ago, everything in my life had been fine. Not fabulous but pretty okay. Matt had been busy, but at least we were texting on a regular basis. Jackson showed up. Matt accused Jackson of infringing on his life which didn't even make sense, considering Jackson hadn't even existed in our lives up until Matt allegedly begged Jackson to come and stay here. Matt pleaded for my help in keeping Jackson here so he could spend more time with Jackson, but instead, every time there was a situation that he could hang out with Jackson, he invented some excuse to do otherwise.

Jackson and I found a space where I didn't ogle him too severely, and he refrained from flirting with my heart. We laughed together and had a comfortable friendship. Perhaps his scent was more intoxicating than any other person I had ever smelled in my life, but that was beside the point. We kept all of that under control.

Then he kissed me. I blew hot as I remembered his kiss. The way his mouth had moved over mine. The taste of him. The feeling of his big hand on the back of my neck. I had never been kissed before in such a manner. I would probably be remembering that kiss in my dotage.

But it had been a colossal mistake of epic proportions. My face burned as I recalled my over-the-top response in my attempt to keep him here. It didn't get any more mortifying. Nor did it make sense. What could make sense about my frantic desperation to keep him here? I had left the guy utterly speechless. He had no words while he watched me completely lose my shit. Basically, I had begged him to stay.

Irene decided that she'd had enough. "I think I'd like to go back to my hotel now. Jackson, would you mind driving me?"

"Sure."

I stood up. "Would you like to come by for dinner tonight? I'm pretty sure Matt won't be working."

She gave me two air kisses. "That would be lovely, dear."

CHAPTER NINETEEN

I WANDERED AROUND THE LOFT, AT A BIT OF A LOSS AS TO WHAT TO DO. Jackson had cleaned everything to a state of perfection, so I didn't even have to clean. I didn't feel like painting or watching TV. My book didn't hold my interest. I couldn't bring myself to even think about last night.

My phone rang, and I lunged for it. It was Julie. I sighed.

"Hello?"

"Hi, Emily."

"Hey."

"How are you feeling?"

"Hungover. You?"

"Like I want to hang my head over the toilet for the next three days."

I gave a short laugh. "Been there, done that."

A brief pause.

"That was quite the party you had last night."

"I aim to please."

"So what are you and your two boys up to today?"

I looked around the empty loft. "They're both out."

"Is everything okay?"

I stilled as a coldness ran through my body. "Yes. Why?"

Her laugh sounded false. "Oh, no reason."

"Why would you ask that?" My spider senses tingled.

"Just that Matt was pretty wasted last night."

I sat up straight. "You were there? Did you go out with them?"

"Yeah, there were a few of us, and someone had suggested going down to that blues bar on 5th. Matt was all over that."

"Who all went?" I asked, working hard to keep my voice casual.

She laughed. "I don't know. A guy named Dave and Adam, I think."

"Aiden?"

"Yeah. And his girlfriend."

"Wife."

"Whatever. And there was another dude, but I never caught his name."

"How long were you at the pub?"

"I think we left around 2? We shut the place down."

I wanted to, but I couldn't ask her what happened after that. I didn't want to admit that Matt had gone missing for the remainder of the night. "I missed all that."

"I tried to get Jackson to come out with us."

"Why didn't he?"

Her voice accused slightly. "He said you were too drunk to be left alone."

"Oh." Matt obviously had no issue leaving me behind, but Jackson had been concerned about my welfare. Jackson seemed to highlight exactly how Matt failed me as a fiancée. "He could have gone."

"I offered to stay with him," Julie sounded pissed, "But of course he said he would be busy cleaning up and monitoring you."

"Oh." I had no idea what to say about that.

"Only you could manage to get in the way of the hottest sex of my life from a coma state."

"It's not like I asked him to stay."

"Doesn't matter. For some stupid reason, the man feels responsible. Why couldn't you stay sober enough to clean up after your party?"

Defensive. "I didn't mean to get so drunk."

"Next time, think about your actions."

My mind worked in overdrive as I tried to determine what had happened to Matt.

"Whatever." I didn't want to talk about Jackson.

"What's going on between you and Jackson?" her question was direct. I guess we *were* going to have a conversation about Jackson.

"Why?"

"He carried your drunk ass upstairs."

"I don't remember that," I lied. "Are you sure it wasn't Matt?"

A harsh laugh vibrated in my ear. "No. It was Jackson. He just picked you up and carried you off to your bedroom right in front of Matt. He seems super protective of you."

"What did Matt do?"

"Nothing. It was odd. He glanced up and shrugged. I was the one standing at the bottom of the stairs, my mouth hanging open."

I swallowed the fear that was in my throat. "He's the army guy. I think they're all just trained to be like that. It's nothing personal."

"He's in the navy," she corrected. "You never mix up army and navy. You'll royally offend if you do."

"Okay," I said. I wanted to avoid a lecture on her knowledge of military men. Her interest in men in uniform bordered on an obsession.

"So is Jackson going to be around later?"

"Matt's mom is in town. Everyone is going to be here for dinner."

"Oh good. You can make it up to me by inviting me over."

Dinner promised to be an intense family affair, adding Julie to the mix would be like adding fuel to the fire.

"Irene just wants a quiet family night," I lied.

"You owe me," she shot back. "You have to help me."

"From the looks of it, you were doing just fine on your own last night," I said. "If Jackson wants you, he'll come after you."

"You're right. We were doing well last night."

"Okay."

"You don't understand anything. A Navy SEAL is the most elite soldier in the world. To make it to that level, he's the best of the best."

I picked up a magazine and set it down. "You would know."

"Not to mention how hot he is. He gives me shivers. He looks like he would be a machine in bed."

I gasped, and my face burned red hot. "Julie."

"What! The guy looks like he could fuck a girl six ways from Sunday. He's so strong and big, and he could pretty much do anything he wanted as many times as he wanted."

"Oh gosh," I breathed, shutting my eyes on the images she was conjuring up of him. I did not want to imagine his magnificent naked body doing crazy sex things. Because it would be crazy. And intense.

"That man is my Mt. Everest," she declared.

"I don't even know what that means."

"It means, he's the ultimate goal. He's the man I have been waiting for my entire life."

"Well when you set your mind to something, you usually get what you want."

"Damn straight."

"If you could do me a favor and not get your hanky on with him over here? You have your place. Please take all your sex noises elsewhere."

I was joking. But not really.

She laughed. "Okay, I don't want all my screams of ecstasy to shock your virgin ears."

"Thank-you," I said, suddenly exhausted with this conversation.

"So if you're not going to invite me over for dinner, do you mind giving me his number?"

"Why don't I give him yours tonight," I compromised. I wasn't going to inflict more pain on him by subjecting him to Julie's excessive determination.

"Right now. Send it to him right now."

"Julie, have you ever heard about playing hard to get?"

"Nope," she said. "Give it to him. I'll take it from there."

"Fine," I said. "I promise as soon as I hang up I'll text him your number."

"Thanks, gorgeous. I'll talk to you tomorrow."

I walked over to the whiteboard in the kitchen where Jackson had written his cell out in black marker. I shook my head. I would pass on her digits, and he could do what he wanted with that information.

Me: Jackson, it's Emily
Jackson: Hey

Me: Julie asked me for your number. I didn't give it to her, but she asked me to provide you with hers. 718-425-3423

Jackson: Not interested

I stared at my phone for a long time. And reread those two words again and again.

Me: She made me promise to text it to you, so there you go. Sorry to interrupt

Jackson: You're not interrupting

Me: You and Irene's time together

Jackson: I dropped Irene off at her hotel. I'm picking her up later

I stared at the phone. I wasn't expecting a conversation with him over text. Curiosity drove me to keep talking to him.

Me: Why don't you think you're interested in Julie?

Jackson: I don't think she's a good friend to you

What? What did that even mean?

Me: Care to elaborate?

Jackson: No

Me: You must have some reason for saying that

Jackson: I saw enough of who she is to know that I don't want to go on a date with her

Me: I don't know if she is looking for a date...per se

Jackson: I saw enough to know I don't want to fuck her either

Me: Blushing now. Bye!

Jackson: You walked right into that one

Me: I did :-(

Jackson: Haha

Me: What are you doing now?

Jackson: Currently sitting in my truck at a park

Me: Oh

Jackson: Are you okay?

I stared at my phone. Sighing, I decided just to be honest.

Me: I feel embarrassed about yesterday. And for crying and everything

Jackson: You have nothing to be embarrassed about

Me: You're too nice to me

Jackson: I told you. I'm not a nice guy

Me: Funny, you're one of the nicest people I know

I sat there staring at my phone, while moments ticked by.

Jackson: Why did you want me to stay so bad?

I started and stopped at least a dozen responses. Finally, I decided just to be honest.

Me: You make me feel good about myself. Why did you want to leave so bad?

Jackson: You don't want to ask me that

I sat holding the phone to my lips.

Me: I'm sorry you're being forced to stay here

Jackson: No one can force me to do anything

Me: Can I have a redo?

Jackson: What's a redo?

Me: I want to erase the last 24 hours

Jackson: Everything?

I chewed on my lip. I didn't want to erase how he was so helpful before the party or the way he helped me repot my plant. Nor did I want to erase the way he cared for me when I was barfing my guts out.

Me: Well, not everything

Jackson: What do you want to remember?

Me: It's more what I want to forget

Jackson: Tell me

Me: Barfing

Jackson: Consider it forgotten. Anything else you want to erase?

Why was my heart racing? I stared at my phone screen.

Me: I want to erase the fight between you and Matt

Jackson: Me too

Me: I also want to erase my stupid meltdown this morning when you were trying to leave

Jackson: Nope. I don't agree to those terms

Me: What? Why not? That was me at a weak moment

Jackson: I learned something about you

Me: I'm scared to ask what

My hands sweated as I waited for his response. Why did he want to learn about me? I did not understand this man, but I was like a moth drawn to a big flame. I couldn't help myself. I jumped when my phone dinged.

Jackson: I don't erase truth or honesty. Anything else you want to erase?

What was he saying? That my meltdown was me being honest? Being truthful? If that was me being real then that was a scary thing, considering what a hot mess I had been this morning. That's precisely the part of me I wanted to keep hidden from people.

Did I want to erase anything else?

The kiss.

I should tell him that I want to erase the kiss. That should have been on top of the list for things to forget. I should banish that moment from my life, but I couldn't bring myself to erasing that.

Me: No

Another long pause and then my phone dinged again.

Jackson: Me neither

CHAPTER TWENTY

I STARTLED WHEN I HEARD THE LOFT DOOR SLIDE OPEN. I LOOKED UP ACROSS the room. Matt walked in, still wearing the same clothes from the night before. He looked rough. He paused when he saw the black duffle bag on the floor. Slowly he lifted his head and looked up at me. I leveled him with a look.

He slowly walked to the island, tossed his keys on the granite and slid onto a stool across from me. My heart galloped in my chest. I had so much to say and so many questions to ask. Instead, I just looked at him.

"Don't look at me like that," he said.

"Look at you like what?"

"Like you hate my guts."

"I don't hate your guts."

"You should."

"Why should I hate your guts?"

His blue eyes turned and stared at my face. "Because I fooled around with someone last night."

My mouth dropped open. My heart was a sickening thud in my chest. Blood rushed through my ears. I became aware of how shallow my breath was. I stared at him. "Who?"

"Doesn't matter. She doesn't matter."

I brought in air through my nose. "Was it Katherine?"

He stared at me for a long moment. "No, and you need to just to let it go. It didn't mean anything."

My entire body felt cold.

I looked around my loft in a daze. I knew something had been wrong between us, but I hadn't wanted to face it. I had tried to pretend that everything was going to work out.

"I just ordered our wedding invitations," I said, feeling stupid. I had thought that if we could just get to the other side, we would be fine.

He refused to look at me. "I'm sorry."

"You're sorry that I ordered the invitations or you're sorry that you cheated on me?"

"I'm sorry for what I did. I didn't mean to hurt you."

But he had hurt me.

"Now what?" I stared at him. Would he move out? What about dinner? And Jackson? Pain shot through my heart. If Matt left, there would be no reason for Jackson to stay. I couldn't process the thought of both Jackson and Matt leaving me alone in this loft. I would not stay here alone. Thoughts were flying through my mind in no particular order.

He looked down at his hands. "Can we just forget it happened and carry on?"

My entire body went still. Then I put both my hands on my forehead and squeezed my eyes shut. I felt relief. Relief that Matt did not want us to break up.

Jackson flashed through my mind. The way he pushed his hands into my hair and pulled me into the most sinful kiss. The feel of his hot breath on my ankle when he took off my shoes. How he allowed me to curl up with him on the couch.

I felt guilty as I looked at Matt. He might have messed around with some stranger, but I have coveted Jackson, flirted with him and developed a stupid crush. Jackson was Matt's pseudo-brother. What I had done seemed so much worse.

"Em, please. Say something."

I lifted my head. "What does fool around mean?"

He gave me an incredulous look.

"Did you have sex?"

He shook his head.

"I want specifics."

"Emily."

"I need to know the extent of this situation."

"We kissed. And we messed around."

"What does that mean?"

"She went down on me."

My eyes went wide. I had never seen Matt naked. We had never gone below the waist. What he had done was so much worse than what I had done. It was crazy, but as I listened to Matt confessing his sins, it felt like it absolved me from my own.

"Is that it?"

His eyes were on my face. "That's it."

I hesitated. "You still want to get married?"

"Yes."

"Can we have a baby?"

He blinked slowly. "What?"

I licked my lips. "I want a baby within the first year. I want a family."

"How about you get pregnant within the first two years."

I crossed my arms. "The first year."

His eyes narrowed. "And we never speak of this again?"

Would it be this easy? Could I just pretend that Matt hadn't cheated on me and we would get the wedding back on track? I stared at him. By this time, next year, I could have a baby. Then my family would be complete.

"We'll never speak of this again."

We both just sat there. Long moments ticked by.

Finally, he spoke, switching gears. "Is Jackson leaving?"

"Is that what you want?" I looked up.

"No," he couldn't meet my gaze. "It may not seem like it, but I don't want him to leave."

"He was going to, but your mom showed up."

Shock crossed his face. "Where are they?"

"Your mom is at her hotel, and I have no clue where Jackson is. But they're both coming back here for dinner."

Matt shut his eyes and his face crumpled. "Fuck."

"What happened between the two of you?"

He shrugged and refused to meet my eyes.

"Why won't you tell me what happened?"

"It's water under the bridge."

"To move forward, you both need to address this."

He rubbed his face. "I can't talk about it."

"Why not?"

"I can't."

I stared at him for a long time. Why could he not discuss it with me? What had happened between them? Had they committed some crime together and were bound together by some blood pact? I knew that Matt would not budge on the issue.

He stood up, looking stiff and a bit wrecked. "Are we good?"

I nodded.

"Okay, I'm going upstairs to shower."

I watched as he slowly started to walk upstairs.

"Why do you want to be married to me, Matt?"

He glanced over the railing at me. "Because you and I can have a perfect life together. Look at this place. Together we can do it all."

His answer left me completely cold. There it was. We both were getting married for different reasons. Maybe we didn't have the fairy tale marriage, but Matt would give me what I wanted. I would get my husband, and together we would create a little family. And in turn, I would give Matt what he wanted. Money. It's not like we hated each other. Before all this craziness started, we had quite liked each other at one point. He would be a successful lawyer, and I would be a stay-at-home mom. And together, we would each find our version of happiness. Love was messy. With Matt, I was in control. There was no dark jealousy or intense fluttering in my stomach. We were a stable couple together. All those big passionate emotions just de-stabilized everything. Created an imbalance. Marrying Matt was the smart choice. Not everyone could have the perfect love story, but together we could create a happy life together. And right now, that sounded good to me.

I looked around the kitchen. There was no way I could cook tonight. I flipped through our take-out brochures and then decided on Thai food. I called for food and then wiped down an already spotless counter. Why did I feel so bereft? I was going to get what I wanted. I wanted a baby. I wanted a family. Together Matt and I would create our own little perfect family. This is what I needed most in this world. So why did my heart feel so heavy?

CHAPTER TWENTY-ONE

THE LOFT DOOR SLID OPEN. IRENE WALKED IN, AND JACKSON FOLLOWED behind her. Stupid nerves jangled my body the moment I laid eyes on Jackson's big frame. He exuded a solid, unshakable presence that instantly made me feel nervous and safe at the same time. My eyes slid past his direct gaze, and I proceeded to flush hot.

I forced myself to focus on Irene. "How was your afternoon?"

"Decadent," she smiled. "After a walk with Jackson, I went back to the hotel and had a long nap and a swim in the pool."

He was watching me. I could feel it.

"Oh, that sounds lovely," I smiled trying to shut out his presence. I failed to ignore how tall he was, how his baseball cap was pulled so low on his brow, how green his eyes were. I swear his broad shoulders seemed to get bigger every time I saw him. Why was I noticing him again like this? Was it because of the kiss? I needed to get my mind back in the slow lane with this guy.

Footsteps pounded down the stairs and then Matt stood in front of his mom.

"Sweetheart," she beamed, opening her arms. Matt bent down and gave her a long hug.

Matt straightened and Jackson and him eyeballed each other.

"Want a beer?" Matt asked.

"Sure."

Matt went to the fridge and cracked open a couple of cans. "Want to go out on the patio?"

"Yup." Jackson took his proffered beer, and then the two of them walked outside.

"Can I get you a glass of wine?" I asked Irene.

"That would be nice," she made herself comfortable at the island.

I poured her some wine. "I decided to send out for dinner tonight. It should be here in a bit."

I looked outside. Jackson and Matt stood facing each other and seemed to be in a serious conversation. Matt looked agitated as he talked, but Jackson had one hand in his pocket and looked relaxed as he listened.

"It's been like that since they knew each other," Irene said as she glanced over her shoulder. "Matt talks and Jackson listens."

"I didn't realize until recently how integral Jackson has been to your family. Matt never really mentioned him."

She looked carefully down at her wine. "Jackson was more my husband's intention. I would never say this to Jackson's face, but when he came into our family, it came at quite a price to Matt."

That wasn't exactly what I had expected her to say. "Jackson shared with me some of his experiences with Ted and how he came to live with you."

"Jackson never talks about Ted."

"Well, I don't want to exaggerate how much he told me, I'm just trying to figure out what happened."

"I have known Jackson since he was a little boy and not once have we been allowed to talk about Ted. Not once."

I was pretty sure she was exaggerating. "Can you tell me how Jackson came to be part of your life?"

"You know that Matt's dad was a police officer, right?"

I nodded.

"We lived in a small town. Ted was the town drunk. Harry was called to deal with Ted on a regular basis for various reasons, most of them not good. Typically they just stuck Ted in a drunk tank. But that left them with a small child on their hands."

"Jackson."

She nodded. "Night after night, this little kid would sleep in the police waiting room. In the morning, my husband would drive Jackson to school. Harry couldn't take it. One night, he showed up at our house, with Jackson in tow."

"Oh wow."

"Jackson was trembling and dirty. I have never seen a more malnourished looking child in my life. You would think he'd have been grateful. We offered him food and a warm bed and yet he just fought us. You would think that our home and our generosity would have been preferable to a police station waiting room, but he didn't want to be with us."

"He wanted to be with Ted."

She raised one eyebrow. "That he did."

I stole a glance at the patio. As if he could sense me Jackson turned his head and looked at me. I dropped my glance.

"What happened?"

"Ted kept getting drunk. My husband kept bringing Jackson home. And it was like that every single time. The only thing Jackson asked for was to be brought back to Ted. He never cried. He fought. He fought that separation tooth and nail. At age seven, he had more fight in him than two grown men. Harry and I were just trying to be charitable. Then one night, it was like he realized that even if he stayed over, he'd still return to Ted. Harry dropped him off. He walked past me, climbed into his bunk bed and was asleep within two minutes."

I swallowed my pain. My heart ached for that little boy. The little boy that knew only violence and suffering at the hands of the one person he should've been able to trust. And even when they removed him from all that heartache, he just wanted to go back to it.

"What happened to Jackson's real father?"

She shrugged. "Who knows. His mother was quite trashy, and when she died, Ted was the only one left. Ted was his legal guardian."

I tried to phrase my question with tact. "Did anyone think about calling social services?"

"We lived in a small town. Our options were to report Ted and have Jackson shipped off to some foster home in the city. Harry was scared Jackson would get lost in the system." She lifted her shoulder. "We had unofficial custody of Jackson more than half the time. My husband checked up on them frequently."

I could not wrap my mind around the idea that letting a young child face physical abuse had been an option at all.

She saw the look in my eyes. "We did what we could. You should know that. Every time Jackson landed in the hospital, we took him to our house. We tried to adopt Jackson unofficially. He had his own dresser, his own toys, his own clothes. He even had a placemat at our table with his name on it. But once his wounds healed, he started asking to go back to Ted. No amount of convincing could get him to relent. Harry would haul Ted into the station and read him the riot act, and Ted would promise to behave, and the entire cycle would start over. Jackson wanted to go back there. We didn't make him. He asked."

That sounded like a terrible reason to let him go back. I didn't want to say anything, but I questioned their judgment on that one.

Her eyes blinked without emotion. "You don't know Jackson as I do. He has this fierce loyalty. We tried to get Jackson to talk about Ted and some of the accidents that seemed to happen, but Jackson only protected him. Ted was completely off topic. He has been for all these years. He's never once let us talk about Ted. Not once."

"He didn't want Ted to be alone." I murmured to myself. My eyes strayed to Jackson, who laughed at something Matt had just said. He looked relaxed as he leaned back against the railing with a beer casually slung in his hand. His plain navy t-shirt stretched over his hard chest.

"So that's why I find it hard to believe that Jackson would talk about Ted with you," Irene watched my face.

Had Jackson openly talked about Ted with me? Perhaps I had been overly nosy and disrespectful of his boundaries?

"Where is Ted now?"

"Ted fell in the drunk tank and hit his head. He died six days before Jackson's 16th birthday."

I watched as Matt talked grandly, gesturing big. He had Jackson's full attention. Jackson rewarded him with another laugh, making me marvel at his beautiful smile. "When they hang out they seem to get along. As children did they get along?"

"They got along, but as I said before, I think the situation was very hard for Matt. My husband and I fought about that. I saw changes in Matt. I knew he felt threatened and that broke my heart. But Harry insisted that Matt needed to learn that love wasn't exclusive. But growing up in this unconventional situation took its toll on Matt."

My eyes widened in disbelief. Why was she worried about Matt? What about Jackson who was orphaned and frequently hospitalized by the violent drunk? What about the people whose job it was to protect children like Jackson? Why had they looked the other way? My stomach tightened in anger.

"Is that where this animosity started?"

She shook her head. "It started at Harry's funeral. The casket lowered into the ground, and we stood there in prayer. Suddenly, Matt was on top of Jackson. They were rolling around and throwing punches."

My lips parted in shock.

She shook her head. "It took five men to break up that fight. One man to restrain Matt. It took the other four men to hold Jackson back. I thought Jackson was going to kill Matt. It was so horrible. And embarrassing. Jackson took off. Neither Matt nor I heard from him for two years after that."

"What was the fight about?"

"Neither one of them will tell me."

We sat there in silence, lost in our thoughts. She began again. "Matt has expressed that he wants to mend this rift. I only hope that Jackson is man enough to let that happen."

I raised my eyebrows. "From what I have seen, it looks like Jackson wants to mend the rift too."

She sighed. "We'll see."

∽

THE MEAL WAS THE IRENE-AND-MATT SHOW. THEY WERE LIKE TWO OLD lovers catching up. I stopped counting the number of times she reached out and touched his arm. She laughed at all his inside jokes, and they had a lot of them. Matt held center stage and Irene played his faithful audience. Jackson and I sat silently listening. Matt and Irene had eyes for only each other. They hung onto each other's words. They talked about things only they knew. My experience at private schools helped me realize that they were excluding us from their conversation. I looked at Jackson who listened with a benign look on his face. He didn't try to participate, but he didn't seem annoyed either. A dark thought crossed my mind. Had it been like this when he was a child?

I sighed and pushed my noodles over my plate. I was still trying to wrap myself around how bizarre the last 24 hours had been.

Matt had cheated on me. I was still waiting for the shock and the horror to crash over me and send me into another spiraling mess. Some chick had put her mouth around him, and that probably wasn't the worst of it. It was alarming that I felt nothing over this fact. Shouldn't I be feeling some measure of anger or pain? Shouldn't that bother me more than it did? I was more anxious about my lack of reaction than anything.

Could this all be just because his actions alleviated my own guilty conscious? Or was the shoe going to fall off in a few days and I would lose it? Only time would tell. I just needed to focus on the plan. We were going to get married, and everything was going to work out.

When we finished eating, Irene announced that she needed a ride back to her hotel.

"I can take you," Jackson offered.

"No," Matt jumped in. "I'll take her."

The competitive nature of Matt embarrassed me. Had I never noticed before how he could act like a jealous, petulant child?

After they left, Jackson and I cleaned up the kitchen in silence.

"I'm going out for a bit," he said.

"Sure. Have a good night."

I JARRED AWAKE TO THE SOUND OF THE DOWNSTAIRS DOOR OPENING. I rolled over and looked at my alarm clock. 2:48 AM. I listened intently and heard footsteps come up the stairs.

I opened my bedroom door just in time to see Matt walking up the stairs.

"What are you still doing up?" he asked, a weird expression on his face.

I rubbed my face and yawned. "I just woke up. Are you just getting home now?"

He nodded. "Yeah."

"That must have been quite the talk with your mom."

"Yeah, time got away from us."

I smiled at him. "That's nice, babe. I'm glad you two had some time to catch up."

"Well, I better get some sleep. I have a long day tomorrow."

"Love you," I said.

Without answering, he disappeared into his bedroom.

CHAPTER TWENTY-TWO

THE NEXT MORNING, AS I FINISHED MY BREAKFAST, JACKSON CAME IN FROM one of his epic runs.

"Hi," I said. My eyes traveled over his huge legs and his messy wet hair. He looked delicious. I averted my eyes.

"Irene wants to go home today. She asked if I would drive her back, so she doesn't have to take the train."

"That's nice of you."

"Did you want to come for a drive?" he asked, his voice sounded casual.

"Uh," I paused, knowing that I really should say no. "Sure."

"Just going to shower, then we can go."

IRENE SEEMED BRIGHT AND CHIPPER WHEN WE PICKED HER UP FROM THE hotel considering how late she and Matt had talked. Jackson followed close behind, carry her suitcase like it weighed no more than a cup of coffee. He made everything look easy.

"You and Matt must have had a good talk last night," I said to her, as we walked to the truck.

She smiled. "Well, we chatted a bit on the way back to the hotel, but he said he had a big day today, so he didn't want to come up."

I stopped so short that Jackson ran into me from behind. It was kind of like being run over by a wall of muscle. Instead of knocking me over with his size, his arm snaked around my waist, and he lifted me up for two steps, carrying me with his momentum. I shuddered as his hard body pressed against my back.

"Sorry about that," his lips pressed against my ear, all rough and low. His voice sounded amused.

A ripple of something crazy shot up my spine. "My fault."

He held me a fraction longer than necessary and then released me as if nothing had happened. The entire experience left me breathless.

Irene chatted up a storm with Jackson.

Last night Matt had told me he had talked late into the night with his mom, but she just confirmed he had only dropped her off. Where had he gone? Was it weird that I had no real emotion about that? I mean, should that not bother me just a bit more than it did? I felt decidedly indifferent about the entire thing.

Had Matt gone and spent time with the same woman? Another thought that left me completely indifferent. I mentally chewed on my life, uncertain about how to proceed. What if he had needed to drive around and listen to music? He never had alone time. He was either at work or with me. I needed to stop jumping to conclusions and just trust him. We had both promised that we wanted to make this work. Now I needed to trust him and believe that he wanted a fresh start with me.

My ears perked up as I heard Irene start to grill Jackson.

"So how many years have you been in the military?"

"I have been in the navy just over ten years."

"You told Harry that you only wanted to join for a couple of years."

Jackson didn't respond.

"Harry always dreamed that you would follow in his footsteps and become a police officer."

"I like being a soldier."

She sighed. "Well, at some point you're going to have to get real about your career."

"How's that?"

"Well, what about marriage? Does your job lend itself to settling down?"

Silence.

"Are you dating anyone?"

The question dangled between them. I refrained from leaning forward to hear his response.

"Not at the moment." His voice sounded terse.

"Now don't be like that," Irene lightly scolded. "You have to settle down at some point."

Jackson rubbed the back of his neck.

"What about kids. Don't you want a family?"

"Not going to happen."

He might as well have turned around and stuck a 9-inch blade into my chest, his words cut so deep. Jackson wasn't my boyfriend. I was engaged to his pseudo-brother. A hollowness carved out into my chest, but I couldn't face the reason why.

"You just need to find yourself a nice girl."

Jackson's eyes glanced at me in the review mirror.

The conversation moved on, but I couldn't stop thinking about what I had just heard. Jackson didn't want a wife, and he didn't want babies. Jackson and I were on two different paths, and we wanted very different things. This crush of mine was getting out of control, and if I weren't careful, it would destroy everything I had worked to build with Matt. I needed to get my act together here and stop thinking about him in any capacity other than as a friend.

WE DROPPED IRENE OFF AND FOUND OURSELVES BACK ON THE ROAD. I bounced my knee while sitting beside him. We were alone. For two hours. Who was I to Jackson? I was his future sister-in-law. Nothing more, nothing less. He was gentle and protective of me, and he made me feel good about myself when he was so encouraging, but that was where it ended. I vowed to refocus my energy on Matt and our wedding. I had to.

I looked out the window and didn't even attempt to make conversation.

"You're pretty quiet," Jackson said.

"I guess," I said. I glanced over at him. He casually held the steering wheel, his sunglasses pushing back through his messy hair.

The words poured out of my mouth before I could stop them, "Why don't you want kids or marriage?"

He frowned.

"Is that too personal?"

He leaned forward to look at his side mirror, while he merged onto the highway. "My job complicates stuff."

I needed to know. I just needed to hear his words. "Why?"

He shrugged. "We're gone a lot."

I wanted to, but I couldn't seem to stop myself. "Lots of relationships deal with separation."

He glanced at me. "My job comes with a lot of uncertainty."

"What does that mean?"

He threw me a smile and shrugged. Refusing to answer.

"Why are you so elusive about your job?"

"It's just a job."

I picked up my phone and typed in "navy seal" into Google. Hundreds of articles popped up. I scrolled through some of them.

I started to read off the screen. "It's almost impossible to become a Navy SEAL and only the most elite of the elite, actually make it through the training program. Then they spend over a year training in some of the harshest environments possible."

He looked at my phone. "What are you doing?"

"I'm reading about your job. I want to know what you do." I scrolled down through another article and began to read out loud. "Combat operations take place in some of the most dangerous locations in the world....Navy SEALs remain calm while fighting terrorists, criminals, pirates, all the while sleep deprived and mentally exhausted."

I paused while my mind absorbed that. "You get into fights with terrorists?"

He rolled his shoulders. "Sometimes."

I just stared at him. Taking in his stubble, his long hair, those immense shoulders. Trying to imagine him holding a gun and shooting it. Getting shot at. He glanced at me, his expression questioning.

I pulled my eyes away from him and started to read some more to him. "SEALs operate in the shadows, approaching life-threatening combative situations via helicopter, submarine, parachute, boat, on foot, or by swimming underwater. They are masters of complicated technology, weaponry, hydrographic surveys, and charts. They specialize in explosives, camouflage, or sniper skills. SEALs have stamina, patience, and put their lives on the line during every single mission without receiving the credit they deserve."

Images flashed before my eyes of Jackson taking a running leap out of the back of some plane into a dark abyss. Scaling out of a helicopter. Coming out of the water with the weird fake grass on his head and green face paint while he approached enemies from behind with a knife. It was straight out of some Rambo movie, and it freaked me out.

I looked over at him. "Please tell me this isn't your job."

He smiled one of his devastating smiles that made my heart flip. "Don't look at me like that."

"How dangerous are these missions that you do?"

Green eyes met mine. He said in a calm voice, "It's not that bad."

At that moment I knew it was probably much worse. "It says that you put your life on the line during every single mission."

"We're trained to handle those kinds of situations."

"Situations where people are constantly trying to kill you?"

"Emily, it's just a job. It has its challenges, but it's also rewarding."

"Have you ever been shot at?"

"Once or twice."

I covered my mouth with my hand and tossed my phone on the dash. I envisioned Matt getting a phone call and then turning to tell me that Jackson was dead. My chest ached so hard I was struggling to breathe. I looked out the window and forced myself to breathe slowly. Evenly.

"Emily."

"You never told me," I accused him. "You should have told me right from the start."

"What difference would it have made?" he sounded baffled.

My arms waved in the air. "Well, maybe I wouldn't have let myself be your friend. That's the difference. Now I am, and I feel sick about this."

"So you wouldn't have become my friend?"

"Exactly," I shot back. "I would have protected myself."

A strong hand reached over and grabbed my hand. "Don't think about it."

I inhaled a deep breath. "You should come with a warning label. Dangerous job. Might get killed and leave you. Don't get too close."

"Em," he said. I tugged at my hand, but he refused to let go.

I looked out the window. "I guess I answered my question."

"What's that?"

"I can understand why women struggle with your job."

CHAPTER TWENTY-THREE

When we arrived home, Jackson and I sat at the island and ate a late lunch in silence. I pushed food over my plate. My appetite was all but gone.

I mentally lamented about how I could find out my fiancé was cheating on me and it had no emotional impact on me. But the moment I found out about how Jackson worked in a dangerous environment, I felt sick to my stomach. What if he got hurt or killed? Everyone I loved had died on me. Knowing that he continually put himself in life and death situations made me angry. I would never survive another loss. The world was a better place because Jackson was in it. It devastated me to think that he was in mortal danger because of a stupid job. It made me angry, and now I couldn't eat.

"Your car should be done tomorrow," Jackson interrupted my thoughts.

"Oh thanks," I sounded listless.

He eyeballed me and then his gaze dropped to my still full plate. "Everything okay?"

"Sure."

He leaned back. "Want to tell me what's bugging you?"

"Nothing."

He studied me for a long moment. I dropped my eyes, unable to withstand his scrutiny. I slid off my stool and started to clear my plate. He sat there watching me from beneath the brim of his baseball hat. How could I tell him that his job scared me half to death? If he knew that I was this upset about his job, he might realize that my feelings were a bit more than sisterly. I worked to hide my emotions.

"I'm fine."

"Emily."

"Matt cheated on me," I blurted out.

His expression didn't shift. He just continued to observe me.

"He told me that he fooled around with someone after the party, but he wouldn't tell me with whom."

"He told you that he slept with someone?"

I rubbed one eye. "He said that they didn't have sex, they just fooled around."

There was a tick in his jaw. "What does that mean?"

"I guess they kissed. And…"

"And what?"

"And she…" My face heated up. "She did things with her mouth."

He crossed his arms. "He told you this."

I nodded feeling oddly embarrassed. "Yeah."

Silence from him.

I started to load the dishwasher. "People make mistakes, right? I mean, I'm no angel either."

Green eyes stared at me.

I shrugged. "I think I'm just confused about some stuff."

Like the fact that people pointed guns at Jackson and tried to kill him. That his job was so dangerous, he didn't want to get married or have kids. Did that mean he thought he was going to die? How did he sleep at night? How was I ever going to sleep again at night?

I glanced up at him. His nostrils flared, but he didn't seem to be reacting at all. I shut the dishwasher and started to wipe down the counters. "Anyways."

I finished the counters and turned to walk out of the kitchen, and I almost did a face plant on his hard chest. How he had managed to move so silently around to this side of the island, I had no idea.

"Oh sorry," I said.

I tilted my head back to see if he even saw me, and his gaze, shadowed beneath the brim of his hat, was on my face. I took a step back, and he followed, stepping so close to me, he almost touched me. I took another step back, and he kept on coming. I gasped when I bumped into the island, and he stepped in so close. I thought I might faint as the heat of his body radiated around me. I trembled.

He reached out and then I squeaked as he lifted me. My ass hit the countertop, my eyes now almost level to his face. He placed a hand on either side of me on the counter, his huge arms caging me in, while he leaned forward towards me, bringing his face close to mine. Still, we didn't touch.

My eyes were wide and trapped by the intensity of his stare. I was completely still, except for my rib cage, which was working overtime to bring air into my lungs.

Slowly he leaned in close, bringing his mouth so close to mine, it was less than an inch away. His gaze pinned mine.

When time slows down, it feels like your brain is in overdrive. Thousands of thoughts flooded through my mind. This was wrong. I needed to stop. Jackson was almost kissing me. He smelled so good. He was so big. He surrounded me. I felt safe. He protected me. Nothing could hurt me. I wanted to feel him.

With tremulous lips, I slowly, tentatively moved my mouth closer to his. I could feel his breath against my lips. Just one taste. I just needed to know if the other kiss had been a complete fluke. He stood so close. I leaned up a tiny bit further. Our lips barely grazed. Our eyes met. I wanted more. I wanted to touch him. I put my hand around his neck, and my fingers slid over the thick, strong muscles covered by such smooth, warm skin. I used his solid neck as leverage as I pulled my face just a tiny bit closer. He looked into my eyes. His lips felt so soft and pliable against mine. My eyes fluttered shut against his gaze, and I moved my lips to his lips, this time a real kiss.

The moment he started kissing me back, everything went into overdrive. Two hands lightly pressure the inside of my knees, so that I widened my legs. The moment I did, he stepped in closer. His mouth tortured me, teased me, played with me. One arm came around my back, tugging me, so I was arched up against him. I gasped, my mouth opening to his, his tongue plundered me, sending my entire body into an electrifying Technicolor. His mouth over mine awakened something inside of me that I didn't recognize or understand. I felt intoxicated, dizzy, as his kiss escalated. He was all primal hot male, taking from me what he wanted. And I loved it. I moaned and clung to his neck, my fingers sliding into his thick hair. His other arm wrapped around my waist and pulled my body hard against him. I groaned as I felt the heat of his stomach through the fabric of my jeans, while he slanted his mouth over mine.

And then he lifted his head, taking his perfect lips with him. I opened my eyes, stared up into his face, my breath coming out of me in tiny little pants. I couldn't read his expression. And then he stepped back from me. I clutched the sides of the counter, unable to tear my gaze from his face. He pulled his hat down over his eyes and turned and walked out of the kitchen. I sat there frozen, as he took long strides across the room and then my body jarred as I heard the heavy sliding door open and then slam shut. Feet pounded down the steps. I heard his truck start and then drive away.

I PACED THE LENGTH OF THE KITCHEN, COMPLETELY BLOWN AWAY BY THAT exchange. I remembered the feeling of his mouth on mine, the way his firm arm yanked me hard against his torso, the way he tasted and the searing heat of everything that made him Jackson. I groaned and put my face in my hands.

Those two kisses were the most significant two moments of my sex life. Those kisses made me want many more terrible things that I should not want.

CHAPTER TWENTY-FOUR

I FINISHED CLEANING UP THE KITCHEN. I NEEDED TO FOCUS ON MY LOOMING wedding. A wedding I couldn't seem to bring myself to plan. I needed to go pick up my invitations and start mailing them out. I needed to do a cake tasting. I needed to go to a dress fitting. The caterers wanted a confirmation on the menu. I had no desire even to try and attempt to make these decisions. Instead, I just pushed everything off for another day.

I heard the sound of Jackson's truck. I froze and looked at the clock. Only 15 minutes had passed. I looked around. Should I hide in my room? Should I just pretend that he hadn't wholly devastated me with yet another kiss? Maybe we needed to talk about it.

I heard his footsteps on the stairs, and then he opened the door. It looked like he carried in his arms a dirty white stuffed animal. That dirty bit of fluff lifted its head and looked at me with fearful wide black eyes.

"What's that?" I gasped, rushing forward.

He looked down at what he carried in his arms. "I found this little one on the side of the road. I couldn't leave it."

It was a dog. Long white fur matted with blood and crusted with dirt. It looked skinny and pitiful in his arms. Big floppy ears, black eyes, and a black nose. It had a long, wide scratch down its nose. It smelled terrible.

"Oh," I said, galvanized into action. "Put the dog on the couch."

Jackson looked at me. "She's pretty dirty."

I grabbed a big white throw and laid it on top of the couch. "Come on, put her down."

Jackson gently laid the dog on the couch. It curled up into a ball and whimpered in misery.

"Is she hurt?" I asked as I crouched next to it.

Jackson moved beside me. I watched as he expertly ran his fingers gently over its legs and body. "No broken bones but she feels skinny."

I held my fingers to the dog's nose, and she timidly lifted her head up and licked my fingers.

"Oh, baby. You're such a sweetheart, aren't you?"

Jackson spoke, "I can take her to the shelter tomorrow, but I just didn't want to leave her out there."

I turned and gave him an incredulous look. "You won't be taking this dog anywhere."

"We should get it some water."

I jumped up, almost tripping over myself to get to the kitchen. I placed a bowl of water on the floor. The dog slowly crept off the couch and looked at us warily before she started to drink with great big gulps.

"Easy girl," Jackson said, as he pulled the bowl away. "You want to go slow on that."

The dog whined. What if it had internal injuries? What if it needed a doctor? I tamped down my fear. "We need to bring it to the animal hospital. Make sure she's okay."

Jackson looked at me. "Right now?"

I stood up.

"I'm going to get my purse." I stopped and looked at him. "Uh, can you drive us?"

Jackson patted the dog's head. "Looks like we are going to the hospital, buddy."

∽

THE DOG LAY IN MY LAP WHILE JACKSON DROVE. IT PANTED IN FEAR. I HAD wrapped her up in the white blanket, and she did not attempt to try and move. Her weak state worried me.

Jackson carried the dog into the hospital, and the staff showed us into an examination room. Jackson comforted the dog on the waiting table while I sat and filled out the paperwork. Not that I knew anything about the dog, but I added my phone number and address.

The vet walked in. She was tall and blond, and her hair pulled into a ponytail. She had high cheekbones and gorgeous brown eyes. "What have we here?"

"Found this one along the road," Jackson said.

She smiled up at him. "A good Samaritan. I like it."

We watched as she performed a full exam.

She took her stethoscope off and put it around her neck. "No signs of injury other than she just seems weak and severely malnourished. Do you want to drop her off at the shelter?"

I stood up. "No. I'm going to keep this dog."

Jackson gave me a wry look. "Are you sure?"

The vet gave a flirty smile. "Your girlfriend seems pretty dedicated to this one. Hope you like dogs."

I cleared my throat. "Uh, we're not dating."

Her eyes went back to Jackson's face. "Oh. Interesting."

She turned around. "I'm going to give it a few shots. Assuming that she hasn't been immunized for anything. I'm also going to prescribe some nutritiously dense food to help put some weight on. Don't restrict quantity. Let her decide how much she wants to eat. I think as soon as she has some food, she'll perk right up."

"Thanks," I said. I moved next to Jackson and put my hand on the dog's head. "Can we give her a bath?"

"I would highly recommend it," she laughed. "Please use pet shampoo. We have some special shampoo that is gentle on a dog's skin. She doesn't seem to have fleas or bites of any kind, so no need to use anything else."

"You're just the cutest little thing I have ever seen," I cooed into the dog's face. It stared up into my eyes and then licked my nose. "We're going to take such good care of you."

Jackson rubbed the back of his neck. "This dog doesn't know it yet, but it just checked into a 5-star hotel with room service."

The vet laughed. "We have an assortment of leashes and collars and other dog paraphernalia in our store. You might want to take a look on your way out."

WHILE JACKSON CUDDLED THE DOG LIKE A BABY IN HIS ARMS, I RUSHED around like a mad person in the store. I bought a dog bed, shampoo, squeaky toys, chew ropes and even a frisbee. I bought three collars, an assortment of leashes, dog food, dog treats, food bowls and a book entitled, "How to be the best dog owner in the world".

While I waited for the receptionist to bag everything up, I heard the vet speak in a low voice to Jackson. I looked over. She stared up at him and then she wrote something on the back of a card and tucked it in his shirt pocket.

Jackson swung into the truck beside me and looked over at us. "Well, no one can accuse you of doing anything half-assed."

I leaned forward, my lips on the dog's ear. "That's Jackson. He's super nice. You're going to love him."

The dog whimpered, and I could feel her tail wag against my leg.

Jackson snorted and started backing up the truck.

"So, what else did the vet say?" I asked as I cuddled my face on top of the dog's head.

"What do you mean?"

"She wrote something on a card and gave it to you. Any other tips for our baby here?"

He paused. "It was nothing."

"Well, it was something because she wrote on a card and handed it to you."

"She gave me her number."

"Like for house calls?"

"Uh, I think for other things."

My mouth dropped open, and I stared at him in amazement. "Did you ask her for her number?"

"I did not."

"That's just rude," I cried. "She's at her place of employment."

I spoke into the dog's ear. "Your vet is a shameless opportunist."

Jackson laughed. I looked up at him because I was physically unable to not look at him when he did. He was so unbelievably beautiful when he laughed. And I realized with a shock of jealousy that ripped through my body that he had every right to call the vet.

I worked to keep the jealousy out of my voice and said in a sweet voice. "Well, she's gorgeous. Are you going to call her?"

"Why are you so intent on setting me up?"

"I'm not."

"Sure seems like it."

I leaned forward and spoke into the dog's ear. "Don't listen to Jackson. He's a very bad man."

He laughed again. "Tell your dog there that I'm not going to call the vet."

"Oh?" I said airily, "Not hot enough for you?" Unable to ignore how my heart gave a squeeze that he wasn't interested.

"Nah. I just like to do the chasing."

CHAPTER TWENTY-FIVE

THE DOG WANDERED AROUND THE LOFT, SNIFFING AND SMELLING THINGS. I put a handful of food into the bowl which it downed ravenously. At Jackson's advice, we decided we'd just give her a little bit of food every hour so that she didn't gorge herself and get sick. We also did the same for water.

The dog had a sweet personality, and after she sniffed everything, she awkwardly hopped up on the couch beside me and laid her head on my lap. I lavished all the care I had within me on this stinky little dog. I was already in love. Jackson sat across from us and watched us.

"Well, are you going to name your dog?"

I pursed my lips. "She needs a good name. How about Mia?"

Jackson winced.

"What?" I asked.

"Ex-girlfriend."

I rolled my eyes. "How about Mandy?"

"Uh, Mattie might kill us."

I giggled. "Good point."

He studied the dog. "She looks like a Chloe."

I gasped. "I love that name." I looked down at the dog. "Is your name Chloe?"

Two black eyes looked up at me, and a tail wagged.

Jackson had a lazy smile on his face. "Chloe and Emily."

I stroked the dog's head. "Thank you."

"For what?"

"For giving me the best gift anyone has ever given me. I have never gotten something I loved so much from anyone."

He cleared his throat. "We should bathe her. I can smell her from here."

"I've never given a dog a bath before," I said with wide eyes. "Maybe I should YouTube it and see how it's done?"

He laughed and rubbed his eye. "I think we can handle it. Do we have a bathtub that has a shower hose?"

I nodded. "Your bathroom."

"That figures," he said, as he stood up. "Come on Chloe. Let's go."

As if she knew her name, the dog got up on shaky legs and followed behind Jackson.

"WE SHOULD'VE YOUTUBE'D THIS," JACKSON SAID THROUGH GRITTED TEETH. He was thoroughly drenched, and so was I. The only one who didn't seem to be getting any wetter or cleaner was Chloe, who apparently hated getting a bath.

She drenched us when she kicked an incredible amount of water out of the tub. Then she jumped out of the tub, causing Jackson to chase after her. She managed to outrun him and simultaneously shake water everywhere. Jackson slipped and slid after her, trying but never quite getting her in his arms. I laughed until my sides hurt. When he finally captured her in his arms, they were both panting. While he carried her back, Chloe repeatedly licked his face.

"That was like a greased pig chase," he said, looking back at the puddles of water that trailed down the hall. After that, Jackson decided to shut the bathroom door.

"Okay, time to get serious," Jackson took off his wet shirt and wet socks and stepped into the tub, jeans and all. He pulled the scrambling Chloe onto his lap and wrapped his arms around her. She instantly calmed.

I sat there on my haunches stunned. His body was a thing of beauty. All corded muscles and broad everything. And the way he tenderly cuddled Chloe to his perfect chest took my breath away.

He looked at me. "You're going to have to do the washing."

"Okay," I said blinking with nerves. I squeezed some shampoo onto Chloe and started to massage it into her fur. I alternated between using the water hose and rubbing her body. My fingers, more than once, accidentally brushed over Jackson's warm bare stomach that was nothing but smooth skin and rippling muscle. As I touched him, my insides clenched in weird ways.

He seemed oblivious to my hand brushing against him. He just shifted her to the left or the right so that I could get my hand in between him and Chloe. As I washed her belly, all I could think about was how his hard, corded stomach felt against the back of my hand. The guy radiated heat. How was it possible that someone could be this muscular? He had muscles on top of his muscles. Even though I finished washing Chloe's belly, I was having trouble pulling my hand away. So I just repeated the circular motion of my hand against her, so that I could drag the back of my hand against his abs again and again. I seemed physically unable to stop touching him. I concentrated to steady my breath. My heart pounded in my chest. I couldn't stop. I told myself to stop, but my hand kept brushing against him again and again.

"Emily," his voice was low.

My eyes slid to his face. His eyes burned hot. I swallowed. He reached out and wrapped one huge hand around the back of my neck. Slowly, he tugged me closer to him. With wide eyes, I stared up at him. My lips parted.

And then his eyes went to the door, and he dropped his hand, a second before the door swung open.

"What the hell?" Matt sounded confused as he stood looking at Jackson sitting in the tub, holding Chloe, who was doing her best to look like the most pitiful and bedraggled dog in the world. I crouched on the outside of the tub, soaked, heart racing and probably looking like I was about to combust sexually.

"We have a dog," I said, as I looked up at Matt from my knees.

He frowned. "I fucking hate dogs."

My mouth dropped open. "What?"

"God, it stinks in here. Dogs stink. And they're messy." He looked disgusted.

"Chloe is different," I said, indignant on her behalf.

Matt gave Chloe a dirty look. "So you just went out and bought a dog?"

"No. She's a homeless dog. That we saved."

"She is probably riddled with disease. No," he said with finality.

My mouth dropped open. "Matt."

"She's going back to wherever she came from," he said. "Was there any Thai left over?"

"She isn't," I said, doing nothing to disguise the stubborn tone of my voice.

Matt rubbed his forehead. "I can't even deal with this. You have no idea what kind of day I had. Is there any food?"

"In the fridge."

"Can you help me heat it up?"

I turned back to Chloe. "I can help you later. I'm not finished here."

Matt stood there for a long moment, and then the door slammed shut.

I avoided looking at Jackson.

We finished bathing Chloe, but this time, I made sure I didn't touch Jackson. I wrapped Chloe in a big fluffy white towel while Jackson stood up in the tub. His wet jeans clung to his legs. Water streamed off his chest. Our eyes met as he stepped over the edge of the tub.

I swallowed hard. I cuddled Chloe to my chest. "I'll clean your bathroom."

"You want to talk about it?"

My lips parted, but I refused to look up at him. "About what?"

"About the fact that I can't seem to keep my hands off you and you don't seem to mind one bit?"

I licked my lips, unable to meet his eyes. "No."

He stepped a bit closer to me. I stared into Chloe's wet face unable to look up.

"Jackson."

"Let me know when you're ready to talk about it."

My whole body trembled. I was wet and cold, but that wasn't what was making me shake like a leaf. "I should go change."

I turned and fumbled with the door, and escaped to my bedroom. I rubbed Chloe with the towel until she wasn't dripping anymore. My mind raced. What had he meant when he said that he couldn't keep his hands off of me? Was he trying to tell me that he wanted to kiss me?

I buried my face into Chloe's wet body, as I remembered how his stomach had felt against the back of my hand. I had practically molested him while he bathed my dog.

I looked at the ceiling. I had no idea what to think. This whole situation felt insane. I questioned why so many women were running head first towards the man. Didn't any of them see how truly terrifying he was?

I needed to go downstairs and deal with Matt and his crabby mood. Why did he hate dogs so much? He just needed to see how cute Chloe was and he would instantly change his mind. I changed into dry clothes and wrapped a new, dry towel around Chloe before I carefully carried her down the stairs.

CHAPTER TWENTY-SIX

I TUCKED A DAMP CHLOE WITH A BLANKET ONTO THE COUCH. MATT scowled while he ate leftover Thai food.

"How are you?" I walked into the kitchen.

He ignored me, reading something on his phone.

"Chloe's a cute dog. You're going to fall in love with her," I turned on the espresso machine.

Nothing. I looked over my shoulder at him. "Matt?"

He looked up at me with disgust on his face. "You need to get rid of her."

I crossed my arms. "No."

"Emily, this isn't up for discussion." He turned on his lawyer voice for this discussion. I hated his lawyer voice. It sounded arrogant and know-it-all.

I held my ground. "I agree. The idea of sending her to a shelter isn't up for discussion."

His eyes widened. "You're kidding me."

"No."

"Well, I don't want to live with a dog."

"Matt, you haven't even given her a chance. She's such a sweetheart."

"It's my final decision," he dismissed.

"You always want your way."

He looked up at me. "If my way is the right way, yeah."

"You never listen to what I want."

"Yes, I do."

"No, you don't," I yelled. I never yelled. I never raised my voice.

He looked at me in shock.

"Well listen up, Matt," my tone was sarcasm laced with hurt, "I want Chloe. And I'm keeping Chloe. If you think it is okay to make veto decisions in this relationship then I can too. And this is my final decision. I'm keeping the dog."

He stood up. "Like hell you are."

"I'm keeping the dog."

"You're going to get rid of it. This is just one of your stupid, impulsive moves. Dogs are a big commitment. You don't have it in you to commit to a dog."

My mouth gaped open. My chest rose and fell in anger. "Marriage is a commitment."

"That's different."

"No, it isn't," I said in disbelief.

"Dogs are too much work. They take up too much of your time."

"I'm keeping the dog."

He pointed his finger at me. "You're incredibly selfish. And immature."

My eyes narrowed. "I'm keeping the dog. I love that dog."

"You're supposed to love me," he bellowed. "I'm the only one you're supposed to love."

I stared at him. When it came down to it, Matt needed to be the only one that was loved. He couldn't share. And now he couldn't stand to watch me love a dog.

"I can love more than one person, Matt."

He picked up his plate and threw it. I ducked, and the plate exploded against the brick wall behind me, spraying me with food and shards of glass. I ducked my head into my arms. A wine glass sailed towards me, shattering next to me on the granite counter.

"Leave," a voice spoke from behind Matt.

I looked up. There behind Matt, towered Jackson. He looked dangerous with his corded neck, flared nostrils and green eyes that were mean slits. Jackson was gone, and a big fucking badass navy SEAL stood in my kitchen. He looked like he was ready to rip Matt's head off.

Matt took a step back. His voice sounded unsteady. "This is none of your concern."

"Get the fuck out."

Matt looked at me, giving me a death look before he grabbed his phone and keys. He kicked the dog bed on his way out, causing it to sail across the room. He slammed open the door and then was gone.

I huddled into myself.

The wine dripped down onto the floor, breaking the silence that deafened the room. I was in shock. Had Matt just thrown his dinner at my head?

My eyes lifted to Jackson. He still looked fierce. He walked towards me. I couldn't help it. I flinched when he raised his hand to my chin.

"I'm not going to hurt you," he said in a voice that was so gentle, it almost made me cry. He tilted my face. "You've been cut."

I blinked. Nothing was making sense. My brain was frozen. Unable to process what had just happened. I reached up and touched my forehead, wincing. My fingertips had blood on them.

"Come here," he said, steering me to the island. He lifted me to sit up on the countertop. I watched as he ran a clean tea towel under the water and then he was gently dabbing at my face. Only five hours earlier, in this exact spot, he had kissed me. Now he was tending my wounds from my fiancé's violence.

"Has he ever been like that before?" he asked in a very calm voice.

"No."

Green eyes stared into mine. "I think this is just a scratch. It won't scar."

I worked to breathe. Nothing in my life was making sense anymore. "I should clean up."

He put one massive hand on my knee.

Our eyes met.

"Emily."

I covered my eyes with one hand and started to cry. "I'm not ready."

That made no sense, but those are the words that came out of my mouth. He lifted a hand to cup my cheek tenderly. "Try and get some sleep, okay?"

I felt tired and sad. "Okay."

I picked up Chloe's bed from where Matt had kicked it and then I called Chloe. She stretched, jumped off the couch and followed me upstairs.

Chloe's bed remained on the floor unused. She climbed into bed and curled up to me. I lay there, my hand stroking her soft damp fur, and stared into the dark. How could I get everything back to normal? I could feel my entire world breaking and shifting, and it scared me. I needed to get Matt back on track. Things would go back to normal. They had to. We needed things to go back to the way they were.

I decided to plan the wedding. We needed to make it to that day, and everything would be fine. Matt was under so much stress at work. This whole Jackson thing wasn't helping either. The two of them had a lot of stuff to work through.

My heart pounded when I thought of Jackson. I forbid myself from thinking about him. He had no place in my life. He was a Navy SEAL who lived a dangerous life. He didn't want marriage. He didn't want kids. Jackson and I were about as compatible as a fluffy bunny and a giant wolf. Yes, he was stupidly attractive, but my excuses were over now. I needed to think of him as only my pseudo future brother-in-law. Because I was pretty sure the success of my marriage would depend on my ability to abolish Jackson from my mind.

Something woke me up. Chloe was snoring delicately in my bed. I looked at the clock. It was after 2 AM. Another noise. It was the sound of the garage door. Matt was home. I crept to my bedroom door and opened it. I peered down over the glass balcony railing. The mudroom light was on casting long shadows in the room below. I noted that Jackson had cleaned up the kitchen. I glanced over at his shut bedroom door.

I stood in the shadows and heard the heavy door slide open and then shut. Matt strolled in, not looking up. I watched as he walked to the island, and dumped his pockets. Keys and phone and change clattered on the granite.

Out of the shadows, behind Matt, materialized Jackson. I covered my mouth. He looked frightening. Like a monster ghost appearing out of thin air.

"Jesus," Matt startled, jumping back. "You scared the fuck out of me."

Jackson just stood there. Legs planted, arms crossed. "Want to explain what that was about?"

"What are you the domestic police now? Why don't you mind your own business?"

Jackson moved forward with incredible speed. Matt staggered back. A stool almost took him down, but he recovered. Jackson backed Matt up against the counter. He towered over Matt.

"Jackson," Matt sounded breathless. "It's me, Mattie."

A long pause. And then Jackson spoke in a voice that was so low that it was a growl. "I'll rip you apart until there is nothing left of you if you ever get violent with her again."

"Jackson," Matt said, sounding like he was about to argue.

Jackson grabbed Matt by the throat. Matt grabbed Jackson's hand with both of his own. Jackson lifted him up so that Matt was on his tippy toes. "This isn't up for debate, Matt. I'll fuck you up."

Matt nodded wildly. And Jackson dropped him. Matt put his hands around his neck. Jackson spoke in a normal voice. "Get some sleep. You smell like a brewery."

"Oh fuck," Matt croaked, bending over, holding his neck.

Jackson turned around and looked up towards me. Our eyes held for a long moment and then I stepped back into my room and shut the door.

I put my head against the door. Desire, lust, and awe washed over me. I looked at the ceiling trying to catch my breath. I could feel my heart in my stomach.

"This is crazy," I whispered.

Chloe raised a sleepy head and looked at me. I rushed to the bed and wrapped my arms around her neck. She smelled sweet and fresh, like a puppy.

"It's okay," I soothed her, my mouth against her fur. "Everything is going to be fine. Trust me. It's all going to work out."

CHAPTER TWENTY-SEVEN

THE NEXT MORNING, JACKSON CAME IN FROM HIS RUN WHILE CHLOE AND I ate breakfast. Chloe walked over to him, wagging her tail so hard her whole bum wagged back and forth.

"I think she likes you," I said, trying not to look at his corded stomach that I could see through his wet t-shirt.

Jackson walked into the kitchen, filled a glass up with water from the tap and chugged it. He wiped his mouth with the back of his hand. "How are you doing?"

I nodded, embarrassed on so many levels. Confessing to Jackson that Matt had cheated on me. Jackson devastating me with yet another kiss. Matt coming home and demanding we get rid of Chloe. Our fight. Jackson stepping in to protect me. I was confused on a multitude of levels. Whatever weird thing we had going on here, it had to stop. "I'm fine."

He studied me for a long moment. "Okay."

I took a deep breath. "What are you doing today?"

"I have an appointment at the hospital for an hour at 11, but after that I'm free."

I looked his body over. "Is everything okay?" Trying to figure out why he was an outpatient. He visited the hospital three times a week, but physically he seemed perfect.

Green eyes stared back at me. "Fine."

What kind of treatment could he possibly be doing at the hospital? Physically, he was as close to perfection that anyone could get. Did he have an internal injury? What if he had some disease, like cancer? Would he be able to work out like he did if he was getting treated for cancer?

He spoke again. "Your car isn't quite ready. What do you need to do?"

"Just some more wedding stuff."

He turned his head and looked out over the loft. He looked unimpressed.

Of course, he would be unimpressed. I was dragging a navy SEAL around the city to plan a wedding. Any red-blooded male would be unimpressed.

"This stuff I can do myself," I said quickly. "When my car is fixed."

His eyes narrowed on my face. "My appointment is only an hour. I'll come pick you up when I'm done."

"Jackson," I said softly. "You don't have to."

He started to walk out of the kitchen. "See you in a bit."

WE STEPPED INTO THE BAKERY THAT I HAD MADE AN APPOINTMENT WITH TO DO a cake tasting. A woman stepped forward and introduced herself as Margaret.

"So glad that you and your fiancé could come. I know you said that he was too busy so this is fantastic," she beamed up at Jackson.

My lips parted, trying to find the words to tell the woman that I had brought a different man other than my fiancé to my cake tasting but before I could find the words, Jackson reached out and shook her hand. He beamed her a smile and said, "Wouldn't miss it."

She had the same reaction any female, not six feet under would have on the receiving end of a Jackson smile. Her mouth parted slightly. She turned a pretty pink, touched her throat and giggled. "That's so sweet."

She stared stupidly up at him and his smile.

We waited.

She blushed even harder. "Oh, please come with me."

She led us to the back room. Jackson looked behind at me and winked. I responded by rolling my eyes at him. I was starting to realize that this man knew what he was doing with the opposite sex.

We both stopped when we came to the table. On five white trays, there was slice after slice of different types of cake all marked with tiny cards. Angel cake, red velvet cake, banana cake, spice cake, vanilla cake, chocolate cake. The list just went on and on.

Jackson whistled under his breath.

Margaret laughed. "We've got coffee and water. Lots of forks. And here is a sheet for you to make notes on. Just have fun."

Margaret promised to return and then we were left standing there.

I picked up the sheet and pencil and looked around. "I don't even know where to start."

"Process of elimination?"

I smiled. "You know it."

∼

THIRTY MINUTES LATER, JACKSON WAS STARING AT THE THREE PIECES OF cake left. "It's between the chocolate ganache, the black forest cake, and the German chocolate cake."

I shook my head. "I don't even want cake at the wedding anymore. If I don't eat another bite of cake in my lifetime, I'm okay."

He looked at me amused. "You're a lightweight."

"You pick."

He gave me a pointed look. "You're seriously giving up?"

"I call it a graceful defeat."

I watched as he took a tiny bite of the first cake, chewing with a seriousness of a MasterChef judge. "I think the cake is light but maybe the ganache is too sweet."

I leaned forward, spellbound. "Okay."

He tried the German chocolate cake. He looked thoughtful. "This is excellent. Dark, rich, moist."

My eyes were on his lips. He lifted his fork, and I saw his perfect white teeth as he tried the black forest cake. A flashback of those teeth nipping my bottom lip flooded my mind. I struggled to breathe.

"I like this one too," he mused.

"What do you like about it?" I asked eagerly. Lord, I loved those lips.

His eyes turned and looked directly at me. "I like cherries."

I swallowed hard. Then I turned bright red. I sputtered, "Yes, the cherry filling is a nice contrast."

I picked up my water glass and took a few gulps, trying to cool myself off. For a second there I thought he was referencing something other than the filling. I seriously needed to get my mind out of the gutter.

"So which one do you want?"

"Black Forest cake," I said, bending my head over the sheet.

Jackson opened the door, and a second later, Margaret came waltzing in. She brought us over to stand in front of a table of decorated cakes, talking to us about shapes and tiers and icing design. All I could think of was how close Jackson stood next to me. He leaned in and said into my ear very quietly. "I wasn't talking about the filling when I said I liked cherries."

My mouth dropped open. Margaret starting showing us cakes and pictures and discussing sizes and shapes. I couldn't think. My mind was swirling. Did Jackson just tell me that he liked virgins? I was a virgin! I could feel my face burning hot and red. I couldn't think.

Margaret asked me a question that didn't register.

I said, "What do you think Jackson?"

What did he mean he liked cherries? A vision of him laying me down on the bed and deflowering me washed through my mind. My stomach hurt at the thought. It would be terrifying to get naked in front of him. I felt myself flush again.

Margaret was looking at me. Had she just asked me a question? "I agree with Jackson."

Margaret tilted her head and gave me a quizzical look. Jackson gave a soft snort beside me. They started to talk again, but I wasn't paying attention.

What was going through his mind? Didn't he know that comments like that threw me completely for a loop? He might take that joking lightly, but it left me reeling with crazy, awkward thoughts about naked bodies and him doing devastatingly delicious things to my body.

This whole situation was torture. Okay. I was attracted to him, but I was all wrong for him. Not to mention that I was engaged. Engaged! To Matt.

Both Jackson and Margaret were looking at me expectedly.

"You decide Jackson," I breathed. It's not like he had propositioned me. I mean, he was just teasing me. And even if someone like Jackson wanted to do something sexy with me, he was all wrong for me. He worked a dangerous job. He was precisely the opposite of the kind of guy I needed to marry. We were incompatible on every level. So why did my heart race every time I had inappropriate thoughts about him?

How could I possibly marry someone like Matt when I didn't want to be with him like I wanted to be with Jackson?

The traitorous thought blurted into my mind, and I almost stopped breathing. Oh, my God. What was happening to me? I was engaged to Matt. I wobbled on my feet. I was a heartbeat away from having a panic attack. Why was this happening to me?

I feel trapped in my engagement.

Oh, my God. I needed to get control over this situation, or I would ruin everything. My feelings would destroy my future.

Jackson put a huge warm hand on my hip, and he tugged me closer, looking down at me like a loving fiancé would look down at his future bride. "You okay, sweetheart?"

I'm pretty sure my heart didn't know whether to stop beating entirely or to pound wildly out of my chest. For a brief second, I thought I was going to faint in his arms. The scent of cake overwhelmed my senses. Choking me. I struggled to breathe. I fanned my face. "Just a bit hot."

He ducked his head, so his face was close to mine. Green eyes looked at me with concern. "Do you need to sit down?"

I wasn't sure my legs would make it to a chair.

I whispered in complete desperation. "Please get me out of here."

Jackson put his arm around me and turned me around and started walking me towards the door. "Emily needs some fresh air."

"Oh, of course," Margaret's voice sounded so far away.

With Jackson's help, I staggered out into the sunshine. He lifted me onto the back tailgate of his truck.

"Put your head down," he said, holding my arm while I awkwardly dropped my head between my legs.

"Deep breaths," he encouraged.

I took several deep breaths and then my world started to right itself again. His legs disappeared, and I heard the truck door slam. Then he was pressing a bottle of water into my hands.

"Take a sip."

I brought my head back up and took several sips of water.

"Sorry," I said with misery. My eyes burned with tears.

A huge hand touched the back of my neck. He lifted my chin with the other hand and looked at my face.

"Emily," he said with concern. "What's going on?"

I felt a tear trickle down my cheek. "Nothing."

His thumb brushed my tear away. He stared at me with concern.

"Want to talk about it?"

I shook my head and avoided his eyes.

He sat down on the gate beside me and pulled me against him so my head nestled against the crook of his arm. I shut my eyes and concentrated on breathing.

I loved this man.

My eyes flew open. Oh, my God. I pushed myself off him. It couldn't be true. That would be just stupidity on my part. I couldn't love him. That was just insane. It was such a crazy scary thought I felt a need to escape. I scrambled off the back of the truck. "We should go."

I avoided his eyes. What if he could see my feelings in my gaze? What if he knew how I felt about him? How could this be happening to me?

"Are you sure you are okay?"

I put my hands over my face. "I'm fine."

"Emily."

A shudder went through my body at the sound of him saying my name. Really? Had I really gone and fallen in love with the most unattainable man in the world? There was no way someone like him would ever love me back.

Jackson could never find out how I felt. He was so kind to me. So caring and gentle. And I repaid him by falling in love with him? This probably happened to him all the time. Women threw themselves at him. Fell for him. I was just another casualty under his spell. My stomach felt as hard as a rock. I needed to process this.

I spun around. "We should go."

I heard the sound of his feet hitting the ground and then the slam of the truck gate being shut. "Okay. Let's go."

CHAPTER TWENTY-EIGHT

I DON'T RECOMMEND FALLING IN LOVE WITH SOMEONE OTHER THAN YOUR fiancé. It's a heartbreaking affair with no happy ending. Jackson had been nothing but a supportive and caring friend towards me, so to reward him, I spent the next four days avoiding him like he had the plague. It's kind of like being an addict. You can spend all this time indulging in your addiction, and as long as you tell yourself that you are not in over your head, you can just keep on going. The moment you get truthful and real with yourself, that self-honesty just shatters any illusions you have.

I was a goner. Way past the point of return with Jackson. I mean, the guy would walk into the room, and I could feel my heart accelerate. I was physically incapable of not looking at him when he was near. I dreamt of him, thought of him every moment, and daydreamed about a future that would never happen.

I studiously avoided him. I even went so far as to call the gallery and volunteer to come in and help with displays so that I didn't have to be home alone with him. I would catch him studying me, and it made me feel sorry for outright pushing him away, but I was so overwhelmed with my feelings for him I couldn't even deal.

Matt had stopped texting and communicating altogether. I heard him come in. Always late at night, long after I had gone to bed. Where he was going and what he was doing was anyone's guess, but I didn't have a clue how to deal with him. So I did what I always did best when things got complicated. I pretended it wasn't happening and just carried on. That was how I handled it when my parents died. That's how I handled it when my granny passed. I just sucked it up and acted like everything was fine. It was how I got through everything terrible in my life.

It was late in the afternoon, and I was sitting on the patio with Chloe listening to music on my iPod. Jackson had gone for a run. I ran upstairs to switch the laundry. I folded the towels from Jackson's bathroom. I opened the bathroom door and stepped in.

I froze. I observed the scene in slow motion. Jackson was in the shower. Steam swirled around the room. His head was back. His slicked back hair showed off the sharp angular features of his face. His eyes shut as the water pounded over his face. Massive shoulders, huge arms. Washboard stomach that tapered down to…oh, my God, his hand was on his member. And it was hard! He was masturbating. Jackson was masturbating! Frozen, I could not peel my eyes off his hand, wrapped around his aroused hardness, moving on it, up and down. I had never seen the male appendage before in my life, and I was stunned at how big it was. My breath was coming in short gasps. His hand stilled, and I dragged my eyes up to his face. Green eyes were staring at me. Dark and aroused.

The towels and my iPod dropped out of my numb hands, and the earpieces ripped out of my ears. All I could hear was my harsh breathing.

"I'm so sorry," I breathed. I backed up, hitting my head hard against the half-opened door. Holding the back of my head, I fumbled in a panic to get out. I had just violated his privacy.

"Em," he said, his voice low.

"Jackson, I'm sorry," I yanked open the door and hauled my ass out of there. I ran to my bathroom and slid down the wall, my face in my hands. I was breathing hard, even more tingly than when he kissed me. I didn't know what to do with myself.

Flashes of his body kept replaying in my mind. Jackson, in all his glory.

Aroused. Erect. It was so big. I had no idea how something like that would even fit into a woman. That wasn't even normal, was it?

Jackson was gorgeous, but Jackson naked and aroused, that was something that would ruin me for all other men. OMG. I would never be able to think of anything else when he was in the room.

Matt was never around. I didn't even care. Because I was in so deep with how I felt about Jackson, I couldn't even think straight. Did I try and end it with Matt? No. Did I try and fix things? No. Did I try and end our engagement? No. Because in my mind I was still planning on marrying Matt.

I told myself lie after lie. We were going through a rough patch. This was just wedding jitters for both of us. None of this was real. My feelings for Jackson were not real. I needed to get a grip. I needed to get my facts straight. One, Jackson was so out of my pay grade it wasn't even funny. Two, he did not want me. Most of this situation was my overactive imagination. Three, if the world was ending and for some bizarre reason we decided to cross that line, it would destroy his relationship with Matt and Irene. Four, he had a dangerous job, and he didn't want marriage, and he didn't want children. I did. Five, there was zero chance of any future between us.

Now I needed to go downstairs and act like nothing was wrong. I needed to face the music.

∽

I MADE MY WAY DOWN THE STAIRS. JACKSON WAS IN THE KITCHEN, LEANING against the counter. His hair was damp. He was wearing jeans and a t-shirt that clung to his hard chest. With his long legs crossed, he scrolled on his phone.

I sat down at the island and took a deep breath and avoided his gaze.

"I ordered some pizza," he finally said.

"Okay, thanks," my voice sounded weird.

He stepped forward and with exaggerated care, placed my iPod on the island in front of me. Neither of us spoke. I traced my finger over a pattern in the granite. Not awkward at all. I thought about his huge erect member in his big hand. I turned bright red. I covered my face with my hands and moaned.

He laughed. "Em."

"I'm very sorry about that."

"You got yourself a little-unexpected peep show."

"Jackson, stop," I pleaded. "I didn't know you were home."

"The look on your face," he baited. "It's like you've never seen anyone do that before."

My eyes, against my stern permission, flew to his face. He was staring at me with the most intense look.

"You have seen a guy jerk off before, haven't you?" he asked slowly.

I shook my head. The words were coming out of my mouth like someone had injected me with truth serum. "I haven't seen a naked guy before. At least not in real life."

Desire flickered to life in his eyes as he held my gaze. "Emily, what exactly have you done?"

I licked my lips. "Why?"

"Curious."

I told myself to think of this as a friendly sex-ed talk with an older guy friend. "I've kissed."

"And?"

I shrugged, dropping my eyes.

"Have you ever had a guy go down on you?"

My eyes flew to his face. "Like with his mouth?"

"Yes, with his mouth."

"No!"

"Have any of your little boyfriends ever coped a feel."

I looked at him suspiciously. "What kind of feel?"

"You know, maybe one of them slid their hand up your skirt and explored a bit?"

My face flamed. And something low and throbbing was happening between my legs. I was loving this conversation and hating it at the same time.

"No," my voice was barely a whisper.

He started to move. As he walked past me, he put his mouth on my ear.

I froze as sensations shot down my neck where his breath was tickling my skin.

"Ready to talk about it yet?" his voice was low.

I shook my head.

"I'm going out. Money is on the counter for the pizza."

And with that, he left.

I ate pizza by myself before dragging myself upstairs for the night.

CHAPTER TWENTY-NINE

THE NEXT MORNING, I FOUND MY CAR KEYS ON THE ISLAND. JACKSON WAS nowhere in sight which was probably for the best since things couldn't get more awkward between us. It wasn't him. It was all me. He was normal. He teased, flirted a bit, all harmless fun. I was the one ruining it with my traitorous feelings that I couldn't help but wear on my sleeve. I was ashamed about how I felt. I felt transparent around him. I wanted to spend all my time in his presence, and I also wanted to hide away from his knowing gaze.

I worked a half day at the gallery. Then I made my way to a small bistro, where I met Julie for lunch. After we ordered, she took a good look at me.

"Jesus, you look exhausted. Have you been losing weight?"

I sighed. "I don't know. I think the wedding is stressing me out." That and the fact that my fiancé and I hadn't talked in days and that he was missing in action and I didn't even care. Or maybe it was the knowledge that I had fallen in love with another man, a beautiful, unattainable man who threw me for a complete loop every single time he walked into the room.

"Do you have any big plans for your birthday?"

I shook my head. "Matt is a workaholic right now. I barely see him."

"Why don't we do a fun dinner out?"

I shook my head. That was the last thing I needed. "I don't know."

"Let me plan the entire thing. How about next Friday? That's your actual birthday," she reached across the table and squeezed my arm.

"Julie."

"I mean it. Leave it all to me. You tell Jackson since you won't give me his cell number and I'll arrange the rest. We'll go to my favorite restaurant."

I didn't want to disappoint her. "Okay."

"So," she smiled sheepishly. "Jackson didn't call."

I stared at Julie, thinking about Jackson. Julie and the vet were two attractive women who had thrown themselves at him, and he had been indifferent. The whole thing just made my stupid crush even more embarrassing.

Julie stared at me. "What's going on with you?"

I gave her a wan smile. "Nothing."

She leaned forward. "I know you. Something is going on. What is it?"

I swallowed. She was the last person I wanted to tell my problems to.

"Is it Matt?"

I shook my head and lied. "No, Matt's fine."

Her eyes narrowed. "Is it Jackson? Is he a bad house guest?"

"No!" I protested. "Jackson is a great house guest."

She leaned back and crossed her arms. "Oh, my God."

"What?" My throat tightened.

She gave a harsh laugh. "You're crushing."

My eyes went wide. "What?! No. No!"

She pointed her finger at me. "I know that look. You have some big fucking crush on Jackson."

"I don't."

Her eyes narrowed. "Does Matt know?"

I crossed my arms. "There is nothing for Matt to know because I'm not crushing. On Jackson? Please."

She shook her head. "You got it bad. I can tell."

"Julie," I said, feeling incredibly alarmed. "Don't be crazy. Don't even go there."

She gave me a knowing smile and then slapped my arm. "Oh relax, I'm just teasing you."

I heaved a sigh of relief. "Don't even tease about that kind of stuff. It isn't funny."

∾

AFTER LUNCH, I MADE MY WAY HOME. I FOUND JACKSON LYING ON THE couch, with Chloe curled up on his chest. He was reading, and she was snoring in complete contentment. I had never been so jealous of anyone in my life. I wanted to be my dog.

I kicked off my heels and flopped on the chair across from them. Jackson looked at me over his book. He looked tired. I wondered what time he had gotten home last night. Would things be weird for us after our previous conversation? Would I ever get past the fact that I had seen him naked? Flashes of him touching himself passed through my mind. I started to blush again.

"How was your day?" he asked.

"Julie took me out for lunch."

"How's Julie?" Amusement traced his voice.

"She's good. She wants to plan a little birthday dinner for me on Friday. Just a few of my friends. You're invited."

"That should be fun for you," Green eyes studied my face.

"I guess."

He raised his eyebrows in question.

I shrugged. "Parties aren't my thing. How's your day been?"

He shrugged. "Same old. I bought some groceries."

"Thanks."

"What are you doing now?"

I looked around. I still had loads of things to do for the wedding, but I couldn't seem to bring myself to do any of it. "What did you have in mind?"

"Want to take Chloe for a walk?"

∾

AFTER I CHANGED, WE STARTED OUR WALK. USUALLY, IT WAS JUST ME walking her, but Chloe seemed extra excited that Jackson was with us. She kept stopping and sticking her nose in his hand.

"Is this your usual route?" he asked, looking around.

"Yeah, I usually walk her down to the river. There's lots of grass there."

"I run down here."

We walked in compatible silence for a time.

"How are you and Matt doing?"

"I don't know. He's never around. And it seems like neither of us wants to make the first move to talk about stuff."

"You still want to get married?"

I paused for so long that Jackson looked down at me.

"I'm hoping that if we can just make it to this wedding, everything will just sort itself out."

"Is that how it works?"

I gave a short laugh. "God I hope so. We need to get past this."

"What's this?"

I looked down at my sneakers. "Things used to be easy. He was busy, but he made an effort to see me. I would do my stuff and be excited to see him. Life was easy. Now everything just seems hard."

"You seem pretty determined to get married."

I didn't want to talk about marrying Matt because it stressed me out. "I want what my parents had."

"What was that?"

"I don't know. We were a family. We were happy. Right now, I don't have any family left."

We walked in silence for a long time. "That's why you want kids. You want a family again."

"Is that so awful? To want a family?"

"No."

I sucked in my breath. "But you don't want that. You don't want a family."

"No."

Again my stupid heart impaled itself on his words.

"Well, I guess there are lots of women who don't want that either."

We stood along the riverbank and watched as Chloe moved with determination, her nose to the ground.

"If Matt told you that he didn't want children, would you still want to be with him?" His question came out of nowhere.

My heart pounded. If Matt told me he didn't want children, it would feel like a get out of jail free card. It would mean I didn't have to go through with this wedding. I slammed my mind shut on that thought, feeling immediate retribution.

I paused and looked up at him. "No. I would not want to marry him."

My words hung awkwardly between us.

He picked up a stick and threw it a ridiculous distance for Chloe. "You want kids that bad?"

I pushed both my hands through my hair. "I don't know! I'm so mixed up about everything."

"What are you mixed up about?"

Anxiety flooded my body. My stomach hurt. "Nothing."

"Okay."

I dropped to my haunches and put my arms over my head. I moaned. "I'm so fucked up."

Two strong hands grasped my wrists and gently pulled them off my head. Jackson crouched in front of me. I looked with anguish up into his face. "I don't know what I'm doing anymore."

His expression was a mixture of concern and curiosity.

I took a deep breath. "I'm a hot mess."

A smile grew on his face, and then he started to laugh. I couldn't help it. I began to laugh too.

"This isn't funny," I protested, laughing. "Nothing is working out. And instead of doing anything about my problems, I just pretend they don't exist."

Our laughter subsided, and he said with meaning. "You deserve your happy ending."

"What about you? What's your happy ending?"

"Not everyone deserves one."

I frowned. "You deserve one."

"No. I don't."

"Jackson."

He cupped my face with his large hand. "Don't let him hurt you, okay?"

My eyes were wide. I wanted to ask him why he cared. I wanted to ask him what his happy ending was? And why he didn't think he deserved one. But I didn't. Chloe came bounding over and then Jackson was rolling around and wrestling with her.

I watched from the side, wondering how my heart was going to survive saying goodbye to this man.

CHAPTER THIRTY

THE BIRTHDAY PARTY DINNER WAS A DISASTER BEFORE IT STARTED. MATT WAS scheduled to pick us up on his way home from work. No later than 6 PM. It had been over a week since I had seen him.

Now it was half past six, and there was still no sign of him. Nor had he answered any of my texts or phone calls. I paced the length of the kitchen in my heels, while Jackson sat silent, waiting for me to make up my mind.

Finally, after the second text from Julie asking where we were, I said, "I guess we should go. We're running late. Matt's just going to have to meet us there."

JACKSON DROVE. THE RESTAURANT WAS TYPICAL JULIE. ELEGANT, EXPENSIVE. Dark lighting with a French menu. We walked to a private room in the back of the restaurant. There were 15 people around the huge table, and to my dismay, most of the people were Julie's friends, not mine.

"Emily," Julie squealed, as she rushed up to me. She was wearing a beautiful slinky red dress that showed off her body to perfection.

I was enveloped in a scented hug before she turned her attention to Jackson. She clung to his arm.

"Everyone, this is Emily, and this is Jackson."

Beth walked over and lightly touched my arm.

"Happy Birthday." She pulled me into a warm hug.

"I'm so glad you are here," I said into her ear.

"I don't know anyone here, do you?"

I gave her a tight smile. "Not really."

"Where's Matt?"

I shook my head. "No idea."

Julie dragged Jackson around the table, making introductions.

"Come on, I'm sitting over here." Beth walked me to one end of the table. There were two empty seats next to her. One for me, one for Matt. Julie pulled Jackson to sit with her on the other end of the table. Beth and I chatted together while waiters circled the table, taking everyone's food order. It seemed like the entire room knew each other.

"I kind of feel like I crashed someone else's birthday party," I said under my breath.

Beth rolled her eyes. "Seriously."

The meal lasted forever. The food was good, but the service was slow. At least everyone seemed to be having a good time. I watched as Julie threw back her head with laughter and hung onto Jackson's arm. He seemed to be holding his own.

"Someone has had enough to drink," Beth said, as Julie batted her eyelashes at Jackson.

I discretely checked my phone. No texts from Matt. He had yet even to acknowledge that it was my birthday.

Everyone sang happy birthday to me. Super awkward since I was celebrating my day at a table full of strangers.

"Now it's time for champagne," Julie announced. We all waited while waiters dutifully passed out glasses of champagne to everyone.

Julie stood up. "I would like to make a toast, to my dearest friend, Emily."

I gave a smile back. I wanted to go home and crawl into bed.

"Emily, do you remember your 19th birthday?"

Oh no.

"Let's leave that one in the past," Beth sounded terse.

Julie tossed her hair and looked around the table. "But it's such a fun little tale."

I licked my lips. She wouldn't go there. Would she?

Julie touched her neck. "I guess most of you didn't know Emily when she was younger. She was such a shy timid little thing. Never had a boyfriend. And she had an enormous crush on this guy. Was he a football player?"

I swallowed. "Hockey player."

She laughed. "That's right. He was the star hockey player. You knew his class schedule by heart, didn't you?"

Jackson was watching me with a hard-to-read expression on his face.

Nerves made my hands shake. "It was just a little crush."

"Little crush? You don't do little crushes. You obsessed over him for months." She looked around the table. "For example, she knew that at 11 AM, on Tuesdays, he would be coming out of one class, so she always stationed herself at a table in the cafeteria right where he departed. And when he walked out, she would stick her nose in her books and not look up. It was adorable."

"I'm pretty sure no one cares about that," I said in a small voice. Except the entire room was listening.

"One day, and I have no idea how she managed to work up the nerve when he was walking by, she found the balls to talk to him. And she invited him out on a date." Julie put her hand on her heart. "I was so proud of my little Emily. What she didn't tell him was that she invited him out on a date on her 19th birthday."

I rubbed my forehead, avoiding Jackson's eyes. "It was a long time ago."

"She must have tried on at least 20 different outfits. I had never seen her that excited before in my life." She gave the table a sympathetic look. "He stood her up."

This was the mean Julie that I tended to avoid at all costs. For some reason, I knew the worst was yet to come.

"Julie," Beth warned.

"How long did you sit in that restaurant, waiting for him to show up?"

My face was on fire. "Not too long."

"Our little Emily has always done that. She falls for a guy from afar, and once she has a crush on someone, it's game over for her. She falls hook, line, and sinker. It's the most adorable thing you could ever see."

"So here is to Emily. The one who loves silently from afar. Cheers everyone. May this next crush of yours never find out."

I worked my throat to swallow. All eyes turned to me. My lips parted in an attempt to smile, but I felt like a hyena baring my teeth in fear.

"You can't leave us with a cliffhanger like that," someone said, from down the table.

Julie's eyes glowed while she toyed with her necklace. "I always thought that if only I had intervened on your behalf with your hockey player, you might have had better luck."

I shook my head slowly. "Julie. No."

My heart beat in my throat. I knew what was coming, but I had no idea how to stop it.

She turned and placed one hand on Jackson's shoulder. "So, I feel like it is my duty as Emily's friend to let you know that she has the most adorable crush on you."

"Holy fuck," Beth breathed beside me.

I could feel myself break into a sweat. My mouth was like sandpaper. I was so mortified. I couldn't even handle it. This was my worst nightmare. I had never wanted Jackson to know how I felt. I never wanted him to see how stupid and giddy and ridiculous I was for him. It was one of those fight or flight moments, and I wanted to flee, but my body refused. I was unable to move. So I just sat there.

Beth stood up beside me and looked around. "Well, that was just a mean bullshit story."

"It's the truth," protested Julie.

"Truth or not, it doesn't excuse you from humiliating Emily like that."

"The truth needs to be out there," Julie argued. "Considering she's engaged to his friend."

Gasps sounded around the table. I could not seem to bring myself to look at Jackson. I doubted I would ever be able to look at him again.

I stood up, feeling drunk even though I had only had half a glass of wine. I wavered on my heels. I needed to walk out of here, but I couldn't seem to move. Julie had taken a knife and split me from belly button to chin. I had been gutted, and everything private inside of me had been pulled out for the world to see. I couldn't bear to look up.

"If you would excuse me," I said politely, before leaning down to pick up my purse. I almost did a face plant as I tried to pick it up. Only my grip on the table prevented me from completely dying of embarrassment. I managed to somehow stay on my feet, despite my wobbles and then I began the long lonely walk across the room.

CHAPTER THIRTY-ONE

As I stepped outside, Beth caught up with me. "Emily. Wait. I'll drive you home."

I nodded in misery.

"I can't believe what a bitch she is," Beth seethed as we walked to her car.

I couldn't even speak. How could Julie do that to me? That was my biggest darkest secret. How could she humiliate me like that? How would I ever look Jackson in the eye again? Maybe I could move into a hotel until the wedding? Or I could tell him that she was mistaken and that I had a secret crush on someone else, but it wasn't him? Or maybe I could just get in my car with Chloe and drive, making sure never to see Jackson again. Each idea was worse than the one before.

We got into the car, and Beth looked at me, with the most sympathetic look. "Hey, are you okay?"

I started to cry and shook my head. "Why would she do that? Why would she tell him that?"

Beth rubbed my shoulder. "She was just trying to get a rise out of you. It's not like it is the truth or anything."

I raised my tear-stained face. "It's true."

Beth sat there with a stunned look on her face which just made me cry harder. "Matt and I are going through something. He's never home. We never talk. And he says he's going to be around and he never is."

"Oh sweetie," Beth rubbed my shoulder.

"I don't want to have feelings for Jackson, but he's so nice to me, and he's always encouraging me." I snorted wetly. "He makes me feel good."

Beth sighed. "Jackson would be lucky to get someone like you."

More tears squeezed out of my eyes. "You have to say that. You're my friend."

"If it makes you feel better, that guy is so sexy that I get insanely nervous when he looks at me. He just exudes all these pheromones. No one could resist him. I imagine it would be much like having Kurt Browning as your roommate."

We looked at each other and then we started laughing.

Then I started to cry again. "Everything has gone to shit. I don't know what to do with Matt, and I have just been burying my head in the sand hoping it would all go away."

"Where does Jackson fit into all of this?"

"I have these guilty thoughts about him, but I didn't know that anyone else knew. I thought I was doing a pretty good job of hiding it."

"And now Julie, the fuck-face, broadcast it to the world."

I wiped my eyes. "That was humiliating."

She started laughing. "It could have been worse."

"How?"

"Well, when you reached down for your purse…"

"My almost face plant! I know. My legs were shaking so hard."

"Not falling is a victory."

"I don't feel victorious."

She took a deep breath. "For what it's worth, Jackson had this look on his face."

"His pity for the poor stupid idiot face?"

Her eyes looked big, "No, I can't describe it. He looked stunned."

I looked out the window. "He's my friend. He's so nice to me. And now Julie ruined that. I'll never be able to look him in the eyes again."

Beth started the car. "If it makes you feel better, he's probably used to it. Everyone probably falls for him."

I shook my head. "That doesn't make me feel better."

We started to laugh again.

"What are you going to do about Matt?"

"I have no idea."

"Do you want to go get shit-faced?"

"Yes," I said. "But bad idea. I would probably end up trying to climb into Jackson's bed and completely humiliate myself. Plus I have to deal with Matt."

She drove me home and pulled in behind Matt's car. Jackson's truck wasn't there.

"Don't let fucking Julie call you tomorrow and apologize and act like nothing is wrong. This time put her on the hook for her behavior. That was unacceptable."

"Jackson said that he doesn't think she's a good friend."

Beth's eyes widened. "Finally, the voice of reason. She isn't a good friend. She's fun, but she is a mean girl."

We hugged. "Thanks, Beth."

"Sweetie, it's going to get better. Just talk to Matt, okay?"

I nodded.

I WALKED UPSTAIRS WITH A HEAVY HEART. CHLOE GREETED ME AT THE DOOR with a wagging bum and a cold nose. I bent down and wrapped my arms around her soft neck. "You're such a good dog. I love you so much."

She licked my ear. So I kissed her face.

"How was your party?" Matt's voice sounded from across the room. I looked up. He stood in the kitchen. I stood up and walked towards him.

"What happened?"

He shrugged and took a drink of his wine. "Got busy, babe."

I stood there for a long moment. He still hadn't acknowledged that it was my birthday. I had no idea how to start this conversation. He just stared at his wine.

"Matt, what's going on?"

He looked up at me, his eyes angry. "What's going on is that you're never here for me."

My mouth opened in shock. "That isn't true. I'm always here."

He gave a harsh laugh. "You keep telling yourself that."

"Is this about Chloe?"

"Julie told me all about your crush on Jackson."

I stood there completely still. "Excuse me?"

"Oh yeah, she let me in on your big secret."

"I think she's exaggerating."

He snorted. "You think you have a chance with a guy like that?"

"You're totally out of line here, Matt. Jackson is your friend."

"Exactly. Did you just hear yourself? Jackson is my fucking friend."

My heart pounded. "Nothing has happened."

"Yes but the difference is you have wanted something to happen, didn't you?"

"When were you talking to Julie?"

"Don't change the subject."

"There is no subject to change."

"Don't lie to me, Emily. You have the hots for Jackson. Admit it."

I stood there in dismay. "This has been blown out of proportion."

"Admit it," he snarled.

"I'm not the one who left the party and fooled around with some stranger."

He looked at the ceiling. "How did I know that you would never be able to let that go."

"It's the truth. And I don't think you should get mad about something so stupid when you did worse."

He gave me a sick smile. "It wasn't a stranger."

I shook my head. I didn't want to hear what he had to say. "Matt."

"It was Julie, and it wasn't just once either. This has been going on for a while."

I gasped.

"Oh don't give me that look. Is there any difference between you harboring all these secret lustful feelings for Jackson and me doing something with your best friend?"

He had a point. I tried to think my way through this situation. "I didn't act on my feelings. That's the difference."

He laughed. "I don't have feelings for Julie. She was just some warm body that meant absolutely nothing to me. But you have feelings for Jackson. In my books, that's way worse."

I crossed my arms over my stomach. "It's not like Jackson has feelings back. We haven't crossed any lines."

Except he kissed me. Twice. And almost kissed me a third time.

"You haven't crossed any lines," he laughed. "That's rich. Like someone like Jackson would ever want to come within a hundred feet of your line."

I knew he was right. On all accounts. He was fucking mean about it, but it was the truth. My crush, my stupid feelings, it was a worse betrayal than anything else. "I'm sorry."

"Too fucking late." He picked up his keys.

"Where are you going?" I started to feel panicked. "Please Matt, don't leave."

"Don't fucking touch me," he said, holding his hands up.

"Don't do this. We need to talk."

He turned around and paused for a fraction of a second and then he started laughing. "Oh, this is fucking rich."

I turned around. Jackson was standing in the doorway, holding my leftover birthday cake. I wanted to bury my face in my hands. Matt walked out, and as he passed Jackson, he said, "I don't fucking want her. Even all her money doesn't make this worth it."

Jackson stood staring at Matt.

Matt tossed his keys up in the air. "She's all yours. Not that you fucking want her."

My shame was complete.

CHAPTER THIRTY-TWO

WE BOTH LISTENED TO THE SOUND OF MATT'S CAR ROAR TO A START.
Jackson looked at me. I cleared my throat, trying to assess just how
awkward this was going to be.

"How much of that fight did you hear?"

"Enough," he said. I watched as he walked towards me and then set the
cake on the counter. Mortified doesn't even begin to cover how I felt. My
mortification level was so high, that I could barely breathe.

I couldn't look at him.

"Well then," I said staring at my feet, "I think I'm going to go to bed.
Thanks for coming tonight and I apologize for how awkward this must
have been for you."

I started to walk past him. He grabbed my hand and pulled me to stop
in front of him. I couldn't look at his face, so I just stared straight ahead at
his enormous chest.

He reached down and very gently lifted my chin so that I stared up at
his face. He looked concerned. "What's going on with you and Matt?"

The greatest irony in this entire night was that I was more embarrassed and concerned about Jackson finding out about my feelings than I
was about the fact that my fiancé admitted to cheating on me with my
bitch friend before walking out on me.

"Nothing good," I said truthfully, my eyes dropping back down to his chest. I couldn't bear to see pity or compassion in his eyes.

"Is it over between you two?"

"I think so."

"Are you okay?"

"I don't know."

He didn't say anything. I only wanted to go upstairs and crawl into bed.

"I'm sorry for embarrassing you. Tonight was bad."

I looked up at his face. Green eyes held my gaze.

"I'm going to bed." I moved past him.

I WALKED UPSTAIRS AND HAD THE LONGEST SHOWER OF MY LIFE, WISHING that the water could wash away tonight. I pulled on a pair of panties and a tank top. I was just about to climb into bed when I heard a soft knock on the door. I grabbed a throw blanket off my bed and wrapped it around my body.

I opened the door. Jackson stood in the dark hallway. He was wearing a pair of grey drawstring shorts and no shirt. His features were hard to see in the dim light, but he seemed impossibly big. We stood looking at each other for a long moment. My stupid heart was beating a thousand miles a minute.

"You can't go to bed without opening my birthday present."

Tears stung my eyes. "What?"

He pulled a flat perfectly wrapped gift from behind his back. "Happy Birthday."

With trembling fingers, I took it from his hand. "What is it?"

"You have to open it to find out."

I unwrapped a book entitled "Wet dog: A comedy for you, a horror story for your dog. Don't let them read in the dark."

It was a photo book of hundreds of dogs taking baths.

I started to laugh and fought to not burst into tears. "Thank you. This is so perfect."

"I thought you might appreciate the humor."

"I love it so much." I clasped the book tightly to my chest. I couldn't drag my eyes off the floor. "Jackson...I'm sorry. Tonight was..."

My voice trailed off. He stood in front of me, patiently waiting.

I took a deep breath. "I'm sorry about tonight. I hope what you heard doesn't wreck our friendship."

"He said you were all mine."

"What?" My head jerked up so I could see his face. His pupils were so big, and his green eyes looked dark.

I gasped as he reached out and tugged me against the warm skin of his bare chest. His hand reached into my hair, and he pulled my head back. His mouth came over mine. Rough. Possessive. Taking more than giving. I moaned, and the book and blanket fell to my feet as I put my arms around his neck. He picked me up. I wrapped my legs around his waist, and he pinned me against the wall as his mouth did a slow assault on mine. I felt his hands on my bottom, and he hauled me up, grinding himself against me. I gasped as his mouth trailed down over my neck, hitting every nerve along the way.

He lifted his head and looked at me. "Tell me to stop."

I thought my heart would pound right out of my chest. I didn't want him to stop. I didn't understand what was happening, but I didn't want it to end.

"Again." My fingers wrapped in his hair, and I pulled his mouth down to mine again. He rewarded me with another mind-blowing kiss. The entire Universe spun.

I felt him walking, and then I was being lowered down onto his bed.

"Emily," he breathed. He was lying between my legs but held himself above me with his arms. He looked down at me, his eyes running over my face.

A terrible thought crashed in, piercing my brain.

"Is this because you feel sorry for me?"

He looked a bit shocked, and then a slow smile crossed his face. "Sweetheart, where the fuck do you get these ideas?"

I swallowed. I was having trouble breathing. "I just think that maybe you are trying to make me feel better because you're so nice to me."

"I told you, I'm not a nice guy," he growled, dipping his head down and sucking on my neck until I was arching up against his mouth.

He lifted his head and looked down at me. I felt a warm hand on my stomach and then it was sliding up beneath my tank top. I gasped when his huge hand gently teased my breast, rolling my nipple between his fingers. I had never felt sensations like that. I felt strange sparks shoot down my body.

He watched my face as he slowly pushed my tank top up so that both my breasts were exposed. I couldn't believe I was lying in Jackson's bed and he was touching me. Kissing me. With my chest exposed.

I cried out with shock when his mouth latched onto my breast. He sucked me hard while his other hand moved to my other breast.

"Jackson," I gasped, arching up against his mouth. What was happening? Crazy feelings were flooding my entire body.

"Tell me to stop," he moved his mouth to my other breast. I bit my lip and tossed my head as he sucked and played with my nipple in his mouth. I had never felt anything like that before in my life. I never wanted it to end.

He lifted his head and looked down at me. "I just want one taste, and then I promise I'll stop."

"What?" I struggled to keep up with what was happening. One of his hands tugged my panties down over my hips and pulled them away from my body. I raised my head, dizzy with desire, as I saw him drop to the end of the bed, his face between my legs. It took a moment for me to process what he was about to do.

"No," I gasped, terrified of him tasting me. Terrified of his face so close to my most private place. I tried to close my legs as two huge hands wrapped around my thighs, and then I was being yanked down the bed, so his mouth was right above me.

He looked up at me.

"Please," he asked, as his firm grip slowly pushed my legs apart, so I was open and exposed to him.

"I'm scared," I whispered to him.

"Let me do this please," his voice was low. "If you don't like it, I'll stop."

I wanted so bad to please him and was terrified that I would not. "Okay."

I felt his mouth descend on me. His mouth was warm and wet. Pure sensation overwhelmed me as I felt his mouth begin to devour me.

"Oh God," I said, as my hands gripped the sheets, as glorious sensations rushed through me. His mouth was torture, tormenting me to the point that I felt feverish, completely desperate and drugged. I could not get enough, yet I was drowning in feeling, my entire body was tightening towards something I didn't understand.

He didn't let up on his perfect torture. I jerked against the unrelenting speed and precision of his tongue. I couldn't breathe. I couldn't think. I heard begging and realized it was me, saying please over and over again. His tongue was wicked. Coaxing, demanding, licking, tormenting me to the point of madness. My legs were spread wide of my own volition, and then my fingers were yanking on his hair holding his mouth tighter against me. My hips bucked. I panted so desperately against the escalating pressure that was building inside of me. White light flashed across the back of my eyelids, and my whole body jolted as my orgasm slammed into me, causing my hips to arch off the bed, pushing myself hard against his mouth as I stiffened and then a long guttural moan ripped from me. Rolling magnificent sensations coursed through my body, leaving me lightheaded as I collapsed back on the bed, my arm flung over my face.

CHAPTER THIRTY-THREE

I PANTED AS I LAY THERE. HIS MOUTH DROPPED SLOW KISSES UP MY THIGH.

"God that was a turn on," his voice was thick. I looked down at him between my legs. His green eyes so dilated that they looked black. "I want to do that again."

The whole bed spun slowly.

"What's happening?" I gasped, still struggling to pull air into my lungs.

I heard him laugh. He moved up the bed and then lifted me. I found myself lying on top of Jackson's chest. I lifted myself up with my arms so that I could look down at his face. Two large hands pushed into my hair. Green eyes smiled lazily up at me.

"Fuck, you are so pure and innocent."

I blushed, feeling so vulnerable.

His smiled broadened. "I can't seem to keep my hands off of you."

I blinked at him, trying to read his words. I couldn't believe that he actually couldn't keep his hands off me. "You don't mean that."

He studied my face, amused. "Why don't you think I mean that?"

I frowned. "Because you are you. And I'm me."

He tilted his head, a beautiful smile played on his lips. He dropped his hands to my tank top and slowly tugged it over my head. "You don't think I want you?"

My eyes slid shut, and I moaned as his hands slid down my chest and two sets of fingers rolled my nipples.

"Emily, all I want is you. I can't get enough of you. Your taste, the sounds you make. God, the way you smell. You drive me fucking crazy. I lose my mind around you."

My eyes opened onto his face. "What?"

He tugged on my hair, pulling my mouth down to his. He spoke against my mouth. "The things I want to do to you. I can barely control myself."

And then he lifted his mouth to mine. My mouth opened to his as he slowly, gently explored my mouth with his. I moaned and planted my hands on either side of his head, as his tongue played with mine. He sucked my bottom lip into his mouth, and I felt his teeth scrape the sensitive skin. His mouth traced along my jaw and he nipped at the sensitive lobe of my ear.

Hands roughly yanked at my bottom, pulled me up against the length of his body. I felt something hard and hot straining against his shorts. It pressed against my bare stomach.

"Do you feel how hard I am for you, Emily?" His breath was hot against my neck. "Do you know what I want to do to you? This is real. There is nothing fake about what I want."

His words caused shivers down my spine. My heart pounded. I turned my head and buried my face against his neck. How I had come to be lying completely naked on top of Jackson was beyond me, but I didn't want it to stop. His hips raised up, lifting me, and then he was pushing his shorts down. I snuggled back against him, and my eyes opened wide when I felt his hot naked member straining against the bare skin of my stomach. His fingers slid into my hair, and then he was devastating me again with another one of his kisses. I moaned as his experienced tongue explored my mouth, making the entire world spin again.

My head jerked up when I felt his fingers slide between my legs.

"Let me touch you," he said. "Let me show you how good I can make you feel."

My eyes went wide as I felt a finger glide down the length of me. My hips gave an uncontrolled jerk upward. Something crazy was happening inside of me. I lifted my head, uncertain of the sensations that were assaulting me.

"You're so soft," he said, as his finger traced around the edge of my opening. My breath was coming out in harsh gasps. He held my gaze as he slowly pushed one finger inside of me. I opened my mouth and moaned as his finger languorously moved inside of me. My head arched back as sensations flooded over me. His touch created the most intense longing within me. His touch was impossible. Everything blended. My hips jerked, I moaned, and blood rushed to my head. Heat curled down my spine.

"Jackson," I moaned.

And then he was yanking my legs so that I was kneeling on either side of him, while simultaneously pushing me up, so I was sitting astride him. Two strong hands pulled my hips forward. His huge member was hard and flat against his stomach. My apex was pressing down on the base of his huge erection. He tugged on my knees and slid me up against the length of him. I bit my lip as sensations flooded me.

His obvious arousal gave me courage. "Can I touch it?"

He grabbed my hand and guided it down. My hand curled around his girth. It was bigger and heavier than I imagined. It was hard, and yet the skin was so soft. It felt like satin. I bent over and carefully inspected it with my fingers. My eyes raised to his face. "It's not like I expected."

He sounded amused. "And what did you expect?"

I continued to explore with my fingertips. "I don't know. It's so much nicer."

A smile touched his lips. Green eyes watched my face.

"Do you think it would fit?"

His hips pushed up against me, driving his length tighter between my legs. "It'll fit."

"It just seems so big."

He shut his eyes and gave a short laugh. "Trust me. It'll fit."

I continued to draw my fingers up and down the length of him. "How do I do this?"

His eyes opened. He swallowed again. "Are you sure?"

I nodded. There was nothing more I wanted than to lose my virginity to this man. Future be damned. I knew that there was no future between us. I knew that he couldn't promise me a relationship, but I trusted him. And I wanted my first time to be with him.

"Lift up your hips," he instructed. I went up on my knees, and he grasped his length so that it was standing up straight. He was breathing harder as he guided it between my legs.

I gasped in shock as I felt the head of him butt up against my entrance. His fingers moved to slide over me. Teasing me. Another hand moved up to play with one of my breasts. My thighs trembled, my breath was jerking in and out. The feeling of his fingers playing with me was making me crazy. I could feel the silky warmth of him pressing up against me, creating the most incredible sensation.

"Jackson," I whispered, suddenly so unsure of what to do.

His hands moved to my hips, and then he was pulling me slowly down onto him. I felt his hugeness slowly start to penetrate me. His eyes met mine, his face one of intense concentration.

"Oh Jesus," I said in awe. It felt big and invasive, slowly stretching me around him.

"Emily?" his voice was a question.

I nodded.

He pulled me down a bit further, with excruciating slowness. I could feel him throbbing inside of me. And then he stopped. I hovered over him, my thighs trembling so hard. My whole body was starting to shake.

He lifted his body, so he was sitting up, while his hands still held me poised over him. His mouth pressed against mine. "Put your arms around my neck."

My hands wrapped around his neck.

"This is going to hurt a bit," he said as he wrapped his arms around my waist. Then he thrust up with his hips, driving the rest of himself into me.

I cried into his mouth, arching. My body was a complicated mess of throbbing, pulsing desire and sharp biting pain. He flipped me over onto my back, and he was still buried deep inside of me, pinning me to the bed.

"Fuck," he said harshly, breathing hard against my neck. My legs trembled. My breath was coming out of me in little tiny gasps. The sheer size of him inside of me was a shock. I felt myself convulse around him. I whimpered as I jerked in an attempt to relieve the pressure of him filling me.

He pushed himself up, so he was looking down at me. "Are you okay?"

I stared up at the concern on his face. I took a deep yoga breath and forced myself to relax a bit, adjusting to the massive size of him within me.

"That's it," he watched me, his face a mask of concentration.

He shifted his hips slightly, and I felt him press deeper into me. It felt foreign, and the slight friction made my eyes go wide. It was like when his fingers were inside of me only about a thousand times more intense.

He was watching my face. He did it again. This time it felt so good, I bit my lip and moaned.

"You like that? You like it when I move inside of you?"

"Yeah," I gasped. He was so huge and so powerfully male. It scared me and thrilled me at the same time.

My entire body shuddered as he lifted his hips and slowly pulled himself back out of me, creating the most intense sensations. His fingers grabbed my hair, and he pulled my head back, so my neck was arched. And then he was slowly thrusting back into me.

I groaned out loud as the most intense friction vibrated inside of me.

"You feel so fucking incredible," his voice was low. His entire body was shaking with the effort to control himself.

I moaned as he dipped his head and feasted on my hard nipple. A ripple coursed through my body and I felt myself clench around him. His other hand reached up and pinched my other nipple, tugging at it, causing me to cry out as sensations caused me to twitch around him.

"I want you so bad," he breathed.

I felt the intensity grow as he pulled out and then slowly pushed himself back in. He was so huge. Stretching me. Sending the most insane ripples of pleasure up my spine.

"You intoxicate me. I'm obsessed with you," he breathed as he slowly pushed himself higher into me.

"Jackson," I gasped, as I felt him swell and surge bigger inside of me. I needed him to move. Faster, like his fingers, when they moved inside of me at such a breathtaking pace.

I dug my feet into the bed and pushed up my hips, causing him to sink even further into me. My fingers clawed down his back. Something dark and dangerous awakened in me. I needed more. I pushed my hips up and down in a frantic, uncoordinated jerk.

"Oh fuck," he groaned and then he was moving. I cried out, feeling the strength of him as he thrust again and again up into me. I felt him grab my arms and pin them above my head. His face was above me, and his breath was harsh.

My greed was insatiable. I could not get enough. The ache in me built to a fevered pitch, and I was frantic with need. I could not get enough of him as he impaled me, plundered me, filled me and fucked me. My heart was racing. My vision was going white. I couldn't catch my breath. I was bucking up against him, and my voice was crying out every time he thrust into me. I could feel my orgasm building so hard, so fast and then a thin scream ripped out of me, as my entire body convulsed and writhed. I felt myself clench around him like a vice grip and then he was driving me up the bed, with magnificent savage mad thrusts, and I was floating and arching and still crying out, and then he shouted and with a final devastating crush buried himself deep into me.

CHAPTER THIRTY-FOUR

HE WAS STILL HARD AND INSIDE OF ME. WE BOTH WORKED TO BREATH. Jackson lifted his head and looked down at me. He brushed the hair off my face and studied me.

"Are you okay?"

I stared up at him. My heart filled with so many things. Love, desire, joy, happiness. I was more than okay. I was deliriously happy. I lifted my hands and pushed them through his thick hair. "Yes."

His green eyes scrutinized me. "You sure?"

"Can we do that again?"

A smile grew across his face, his straight white teeth flashed. "I might need a minute."

I watched him wince slightly and then he pulled out of me. He rolled off me, dropping onto his back beside me. My entire body was a mass of tingling sensations. My core throbbed. My legs trembled. Every part of my body felt alive.

I could not believe that I had just done that. I had just lost my virginity. My granny had always said that sex was special, and I should save it for the right person, but she had failed to mention that it would be the most intense, most incredible experience of my life.

"What are you thinking?" his voice cut through my thoughts.

I turned my head to meet his green eyes. My lips parted at the sheer beauty of this man. I had saved myself for someone special. Jackson was the most special person I knew, and I had no regrets that I had given myself to him.

"I think my granny would have loved you," I said, blushing when I realized that he probably didn't want to talk about my granny only moments after having sex.

He rolled over on his side and brought his hand up to my face, using the tips of his fingers to brush some hair off my face. "Oh yeah? Why do you think that?"

I chewed on my bottom lip. "You're a very strong person. I mean, you're mentally tough. So was my granny. When my parents died, she was as devastated as I was, but she just gathered me up and took care of me. I was a real mess, but she was strong."

His fingertips traced down to my collarbone. "You were 16?"

"15."

"You were just a kid."

Our eyes met. I swallowed. "I wasn't very strong. I was a complete mess after that."

"Emily," he said softly. "You survived something terrible. It takes a really strong person to survive something like that."

"She used to tell me the same thing."

"You miss her."

"Every day."

"Do you have any other family?"

I shook my head. "Both my parents were only children. All my grandparents are gone. It's just me left. I'm the last one left."

"Who helped you when your granny left?"

I swallowed and shook my head, giving him a smaller smile. "She did."

He studied me for a long moment. "Tell me."

"She was diagnosed with cancer in my third year of University. And she asked me to move back home with her. She made an 8-page list of everything she thought I needed to know before she left."

His smile was beautiful. "Like what?"

"Everything from how to manage my finances, how to cut fresh flowers to put in a vase, how to iron a blouse, how to properly set the table," I gave a short laugh. "We had so much fun. She made everything so much fun. We laughed together so much that year."

His eyes traveled over my face.

"She also planned every detail of her funeral, from what she wanted to wear to what music she wanted to play. She died four days after I graduated. It was like she had timed it, so it didn't disrupt my exams."

I smiled at him, feeling stupid that not only was I talking about my granny, but I was also now going on about her death. Wow. Sexy pillow talk. But the words kept coming out of my mouth.

"Every day for a month after she died, she had a handwritten letter for me."

"Wow."

"I was a bigger mess after she left than when my parents died."

He picked up one of my hands and gently kissed it. "You're strong like her."

I shook my head. "Not really, but some people tell me that I have her eyes."

"Surviving is a sign of incredible strength, Emily."

Said the man who had survived much, much worse than me as a tiny child. "Is that why you're so strong?"

He went completely still for a long moment. I reached up and cupped his face with my hand, knowing that I didn't want to push him on anything.

He nuzzled his lips into the palm of my hand and gave it a soft kiss. His gaze met mine. "Want some birthday cake?"

I started to laugh. "What?"

"We have half a birthday cake downstairs," his eyes looked at the clock. "And we still have thirty minutes of birthday left."

I giggled. "Yeah. I totally want birthday cake."

He rolled over and tossed a t-shirt of his at my head. "You can wear that."

The green t-shirt I pulled over my head enveloped me in his delicious smell. It was so big it came down to my knees. I watched as he pulled his grey shorts up over his hips.

"Come on birthday girl."

In the hallway, I picked up the picture book off the floor of the wet dogs.

We made our way down to the kitchen. Jackson pulled the cake out of the fridge and cut a piece so big that he had to put it on a dinner plate. He pulled out one fork, and we sat at the island. I flipped through the book, laughing over the hilarious photos of wet dogs, while he routinely fed me bites of cake.

"Look at this one."

"Are you sure that's a dog? It looks more like a drowned rat."

"Look at the ears on this dog."

"I wonder if they're coming out with a second edition, Wet owners giving their dog a bath."

I laughed. "Next time we'll be pros."

"Next time we can go for coffee while Chloe gets dropped off at the groomers."

I glanced up at him, loving the way the word "we" so easily rolled off his tongue. I knew that there was no "we". I knew that this was a temporary fantasy world in which he disappeared in seven weeks. I also knew that I had no place in his future and he had no place in mine.

He was watching me. "Why are you sad?"

I smiled and shook my head. "I'm not."

"I could see the emotion cross your face. What are you thinking?"

I was thinking that I had finally found the kind of love that my granny used to talk about. The type of love that threw you off a bridge without wings, but at the last moment, he swoops beneath you and catches you in his arms. The kind of love that was so big, so real and so alive, it seemed to fill every single cell in your body. And unlike other people, my love had an expiration date on it. It was fleeting and would only last less than two months before it would disappear. I already missed him. This was real. This was happening. And it would never last. Like the day my granny told me she was dying, I felt the same sense of panic over the idea of saying goodbye to this man.

I shook my head. "Nothing."

"Liar."

"More cake please," I said, watching as he loaded the fork and fed me a bite. He watched me chew and then reached out and used his thumb to brush it across my bottom lip.

"Icing," he said, before sticking his thumb in his mouth.

We stared at each other for a long moment and then I launched myself at him. He hauled me up into his lap so that my legs wrapped around his waist. His mouth devoured me. Left me breathless.

And then, I was suddenly being hauled up and tossed over his shoulder.

"Jackson," I gasped laughing.

He was running up the stairs, taking them two at a time. And then he flipped me back on the bed and made short work of kicking off his shorts. His arousal was huge, hard and intimidatingly big. I gave a half scream-laugh when he pounced on the bed, landing on all fours, on either side of me. He reminded me of some crazy wild jungle animal about to devour his prey.

He looked down at me with an intensity that made my entire body shiver.

"You scared?" he growled in a low voice.

"No," I said, my breath catching. Loving every dangerous second.

"You would be," he said, as he dipped his head down and nuzzled my neck roughly. "If you knew what I was going to do to you."

A loud pounding of someone knocking on the door sounded from below followed by the frantic barking of Chloe. I blinked as Jackson moved with speed off the bed and pulled on his shorts.

"Who would knock at this time of night?" I couldn't keep the fear out of my voice.

His eyes traveled down my body, "Don't move. I'll be right back."

I sat up in bed as Jackson disappeared down to the door. I heard the loft door slide open and then the sound of voices. I listened, my heart pounding. I couldn't hear words, but I listened to the tone. Something bad happened.

A moment later, Jackson pushed into the room. He took a deep breath. "Get dressed. Matt's been in a car accident."

"What? Who was that?"

He pulled a t-shirt over his head. "The police."

I scrambled off the bed, unsure what was happening. I found my underwear on the floor beside the bed. My entire body was trembling. "What did they say? Is he okay?"

Jackson stopped moving and turned to look at me. "They said it wasn't good. They told us that we needed to get to the hospital as quickly as possible."

CHAPTER THIRTY-FIVE

AT THE HOSPITAL, I WAITED ON A HARD CHAIR IN THE LOUNGE. MY STOMACH turned uneasily at the overpowering smell of antiseptic. I huddled, watching as Jackson talked to the cops and an ER doctor in the hallway. What had happened? All we were told so far was that Matt was in surgery.

I watched as Jackson ran his fingers through his hair, nodded and then turned and walked towards me. He sat down on the chair beside me and leaned forward, so his arms rested on his knees. He turned his head so his serious green eyes could meet mine.

My voice shook. "What happened?"

"It was a single-vehicle accident. Matt was drunk. He lost control of his car going over a bridge, and he flipped the vehicle upside down into the water."

My hands flew up to cover my mouth.

"Some Samaritan who was jogging saw the entire thing happen. That guy just happened to be a water rescue diver."

I couldn't breathe, much less speak.

"When they pulled Matt out of the car, he wasn't breathing. They did CPR on him for close to 35 minutes until the ambulance managed to start his heart again. They say he's lucky to be alive."

My breath was coming in and out of my chest in little gasps. "Is he going to be okay?"

He shook his head. "They don't know at this point."

The blood drained out of my face. "Oh no."

He watched my face. "They just brought Matt into surgery. I need to go get Irene."

I worked to bring oxygen into my lungs. My heart ached for the woman who was going to wale up to the worst news a person can hear.

"Emily, I don't want to leave you here alone, but I can't tell her this on the phone and then ask her to get here by herself."

I shook my head. "No. You have to go."

He wrapped a huge arm around me and hugged me close so that he could kiss my forehead. "I want you to call Beth. You shouldn't be here alone."

"I will."

He paused. "You can't tell Irene that you and Matt broke up."

"What? You want me to lie?"

His expression was gentle. "You can let Matt tell her when he wakes up. But right now, Irene will feel helpless and alone. And she needs you to be there, right beside her. Let her lean on you, as his fiancé."

My eyes searched his face. "I'm a terrible liar."

He cupped my face with his hand. "I know you are. That's one of the things I adore about you most."

His thumb wiped a tear from my cheek. "Are you going to be okay here?"

I squared my shoulders and nodded. "I am. Just go get Irene."

He stood up and then hesitated. I stood up, and he turned to envelop me in a strong hug. I felt his strength seep into my body. I breathed in his scent. And then he stepped back and was gone.

BETH SHOWED UP IN RECORD TIME. WE DIDN'T SPEAK. WE JUST SAT huddled together in the family waiting room for something to happen. We waited for the doctors to tell us that Matt had made it through surgery okay. Or for Irene and Jackson to show up. For some news. Beth went to get coffee for us, but other than that, she never left my side.

I sat, my knees up and my head on my knees. I felt numb. So much had happened in the last 24 hours, it didn't even feel real.

"Are you okay?" Beth asked me for the hundredth time.

I looked over at her. "Should we call Julie?"

Her look was questioning borderline incredulous. "Julie?"

I licked my lips. "Matt was sleeping with her."

Her eyes were like saucers. "What?"

"Matt and I talked after the party, and I guess she had told him about my feelings for Jackson. Matt was livid."

She blinked. "He was livid? He was sleeping with Julie, and he was upset that you liked Jackson because he treats you like a human being?"

I breathed in through my nose. "Matt broke it off with me. He told me that the money wasn't worth the effort of being with me."

"Oh Em. Are you okay?"

I dropped my head back, so I was looking up at the ceiling. "So, then after he left, Jackson gave me this birthday gift, and it was so perfect and thoughtful and then the next thing I knew we were having crazy wild sex."

Her mouth dropped wide open. "You slept with Jackson?"

My eyes felt hot and dry. "I don't know why they call it sleeping with someone. We did no sleeping."

The look on her face looked beyond shocked and then she gave a half laugh of disbelief. "Holy shit."

"And then the police showed up, and here we are."

"Holy fuck," she said. She stared at me for a long moment. "How are you doing?"

I shrugged. "I feel weird. I can't wrap my mind around anything that has happened."

"That's because you lived a lifetime in one night."

I sucked air into my lungs. "I feel like a fraud sitting here pretending to be Matt's fiancé."

"No shit," she said, her eyes wide. "But you need to pretend otherwise they'll kick us out of here and not give us any information."

"Right," I nodded. "Okay."

A COUPLE OF HOURS LATER, A MAN WALKED TOWARDS US WEARING BLUE scrubs and a long scrub gown that flapped behind his legs as he walked. My heart was in my throat as he walked up to me.

"Are you Matt's fiancé?"

I stood and opened my mouth, but no words came out.

Beth moved to stand next to me. "She is."

The doctor had kind brown eyes. "Matt is currently undergoing brain surgery to stop a brain bleed."

I stared up at him. My body felt frozen. "Is that from the accident?"

"Matt wasn't wearing his seatbelt at the time of his accident. Typical of motor vehicle accidents, he hit the front of his head on the windshield. That's where the brain bleed is."

"Are you the surgeon?" I asked, my tongue felt thick and stupid.

"I'm one of four surgeons working on Matt."

"So, he's still in surgery?"

"We found a mass in Matt's brain in the frontal lobe. The accident damaged it during the accident, and that's what we are working on right now."

"What do you mean when you say mass?"

"We did a biopsy. The mass is a benign tumor growing in the front of his brain. Right above his hairline."

"Matt has a tumor? In his brain?" I couldn't even keep up with this conversation. I felt like I was on an episode of Grey's Anatomy.

"Some blood vessels that feed that mass are bleeding. So we would like your permission to try and remove the mass."

I brought my hand up to my head, trying to keep up with this conversation. Why were they asking me? Why wouldn't they just do it?

"You need permission?"

He nodded. "We need permission. The surgery comes with its own set of risks."

"What kind of risks?"

"The frontal lobe is responsible for a lot of important functions. If we remove a mass of that size, risks could include problems with speech, memory, muscle weakness, balance issues, vision issues, coordination issues."

"And if you don't remove it?"

"There is a chance we won't get the bleeding under control which could result in a stroke, brain swelling or even a coma."

I stared up at this man. "What are you going to do?"

He gave me an apologetic smile. "As his fiancé, the decision is up to you."

I turned and looked at Beth. Her eyes were wide.

I looked back up at the doctor. "What do you think I should do?"

"We think it's riskier to leave the tumor in Matt's brain. We want to remove it. Despite the risks."

"Do it," my voice sounded so far away. "Take it out."

CHAPTER THIRTY-SIX

"THE DOCTOR WOULD LIKE TO TALK TO YOU," A FEMALE VOICE JARRED ME out of my restless sleep. I opened my eyes. I was curled up in a hard chair. Irene looked as dazed as I felt. The only person who seemed normal was Jackson, who nursed a coffee.

The nurse ushered us into a family room that had two worn couches and a couple of boxes of Kleenex on the side tables. We didn't speak.

The doctor walked into the room and carried a file.

"Matt made it through the surgery with flying colors," he said, sitting down across from us.

"Oh thank God," Irene clutched her chest.

"He sustained a significant head injury. We managed to remove the mass in his frontal lobe successfully. There's a small amount of swelling which we're monitoring so we currently have him in a medically induced coma. This is so he remains out of pain, and it gives his body the best chance to heal."

We sat in stunned silence.

"He's being moved to the ICU. We won't know the extent of his injuries until he wakes up, but we're doing everything we can to keep him comfortable."

"When can I see him?" Irene asked.

"Give the nurses in the ICU a few hours to get him settled. After that, we will be allowing the family to go in and see him for five minutes at a time. At this point, the best course of action for Matt is rest."

Tears streamed down her face. "We don't know how this happened. The police say that he was drinking and driving. That doesn't sound like my son."

The doctor cleared his throat. "Did any of you notice any significant changes in Matt's behavior over the last few weeks or months leading up to his accident?"

"What kind of changes?" Jackson asked.

"Irritability or aggression? Mood swings. A lack of inhibition, perhaps?"

I swallowed. Thinking about how Matt had been a complete madman in the last two months. "Yes."

Irene swung around and looked at me. Her eyes searched my face.

The doctor continued. "The benign mass that we found in Matt's head was putting significant pressure on the surrounding tissues of his frontal lobe. The frontal lobe is the part of the brain that's responsible for reasoning, language, impulse control, emotions, judgment, social or sexual behavior. The fact that he was engaged in such high-risk behavior with drinking and driving could very well be a result of the tumor pressing on his brain. It took away his ability to monitor his actions reasonably."

The entire room shrank. My blood ran cold. This explained so much. How Matt had changed from a high strung lawyer to a completely crazy person who drank too much, never called, engaged in promiscuous behavior and acted out with violence when he got upset.

My stomach felt sick.

"But you think he'll make a complete recovery?" Irene pressed.

"I don't want to undermine the extent of Matt's brain injury. He could experience motor or speech issues, memory issues, there is a grocery list of things that he could struggle with, but before I scare you, we just won't know until he wakes up. Right now we're working to ensure he doesn't develop an infection or undue swelling in his brain. After he wakes up, we'll be better able to assess further complications."

The three of us sat there. No one spoke.

He gave us a tired smile. "Matt's a fit young man. His body is strong. His heart rate and blood pressure are good. We're cautiously optimistic about his recovery."

He left the room while we tried to process what he had just told us.

Irene looked at me. "What kind of changes did you see in Matt?"

"What?"

She looked angry. "You told the doctor that you witnessed behavioral changes in Matt. I want to know what you saw."

I huddled in my chair. "Matt was always busy at his job, but the last couple of months, he was never home. Usually he would text or call, but lately, he wasn't even doing that."

"What else?"

I swallowed hard, avoiding Jackson's gaze. "When he was around, he was often angry or moody, but I thought that was just because he was stressed out from work. I noticed that he was drinking more too."

"You should have done something about it," her voice accused.

My head jerked up. Her arms crossed and her face was white and pinched. "Why didn't you make him see a doctor? This could have been avoided."

"Irene," Jackson said gently.

She stood up. "No. I wasn't there, but Emily was. She should have noticed these big personality changes in Matt and then made him see a doctor. This accident could have been avoided if we had found the tumor earlier. But she didn't."

"Irene, that isn't fair to Emily," Jackson said with a sympathetic look on his face. "I was there, too."

She pointed a finger at me. "You could have prevented this. This is your fault."

Then she burst into tears and walked out of the room.

I covered my face with my hands.

"She's just upset," Jackson said. "She's afraid, and she's taking it out on you. This isn't your fault."

I shook my head. "I noticed the changes. She's right. I should have done something. Instead of addressing it or even talking to him about it, I stuck my head in the sand."

"We all saw Matt change. His Mom, me, everyone was baffled by his behavior, but not one of us thought he was sick."

"Instead of helping him, instead of addressing it with him, I let it escalate to the point that I cheated on him!"

His jaw clenched. "I was there, and if I recall, he cheated on you first and then dumped you. You can't own this. This isn't your fault."

My eyes lifted to meet his green ones. How could I absolve myself from this? I had loved Matt until he had gotten sick and been a bad partner. Then I had just let him go off and be destructive and harmful to himself and others so that I could pursue Jackson. I allowed myself to fall in love with Jackson and flung that in Matt's face so that he dumped me in a fit of rage and not an hour later, I was in bed with Jackson. I didn't deserve Matt or Jackson.

I shook my head. "Irene is right. I could've prevented this."

"Emily."

I dropped my eyes from his beautiful face.

～

DAYS SLOWLY TICKED BY. THEY ALLOWED US TO SEE MATT FOR ONLY FIVE minutes at a time. We alternated between sitting beside his bed and waiting in the waiting room. I didn't speak. To anyone. In turn, Jackson forced us to go home to rest, eat and shower but there was always one of us at the hospital.

Irene and I made up. She apologized for her outburst. I apologized for not doing more to help Matt. We were on speaking terms, but instead of turning to each there for support, we just endured our feelings of fear and pain by ourselves.

My entire body, wracked with guilt, resulted in a tight chest and an upset stomach. My throat felt like it was going to close in on me. I wasn't hungry, but I was exhausted all the time. All I wanted to do was sleep a hundred years, but instead, we spent all our time sitting, trying to stay awake in that awful little waiting room. Even if Irene had apologized, she was right. I had been there watching Matt morph into someone I didn't recognize seemingly overnight. And his rash and outrageous behavior had caused the accident. I think we all felt guilty about missing the symptoms. But there was no excuse for what I did with Jackson. I had allowed myself to develop monstrous feelings for Jackson and the first chance I got, I had slept with him. If that didn't make me a horrible person, I don't know what did.

CHAPTER THIRTY-SEVEN

I DROVE WITH JACKSON BACK TO THE HOSPITAL AFTER MANAGING TO GET A couple of hours of rest. With my shower and a fresh change of clothes, I almost felt human. We pulled into the hospital parking lot that felt way too familiar. How strange that in six days this hospital and surrounding area had become our new reality.

Jackson turned off the truck and looked over at me.

"Emily, how are you doing?"

I stared unseeing out the front of the windshield. "I'm fine."

"Be honest with me. Don't bullshit me."

I turned and looked at him. "You want to know how I feel? I feel guilty for being the worst partner in the world."

"You don't have anything to feel guilty about."

"I cheated on him."

"You can't cheat on someone after they dump you. He had just admitted to sleeping with your friend and then he told you, in front of me, that it was over between the two of you."

"That wasn't his fault. That was his weird brain tumor's fault. What's my excuse?" my eyes filled with tears. "What's my excuse for sleeping with you?"

"You tell me."

I looked at him in disbelief, and my voice was incredulous. "What?"

"Why did you sleep with me?"

"Just because I have feelings for you does not justify me cheating on Matt."

He went completely still. "What feelings?"

I gave a half laugh that sounded more like a sob. "Don't act like this is a surprise to you. Everyone knew. Julie all but announced it to the world."

"That was real?"

Oh shit. I froze.

Jackson looked stunned. "You have feelings for me?"

Humiliation washed over me. I ripped open the door of the truck and started to run across the parking lot. I thought my feelings were transparent enough for the entire world to see. How was this news? I was in love with Jackson. What did he think I was feeling? Did he think that we had only ended up in bed because I was feeling a bit revengeful? How could I have felt so much for him, felt so special around him and shared my body with him and he didn't even realize how I felt?

A hand grabbed my arm and spun me around. He was breathing hard, looking down at me.

"What?" I yelled.

"Why are you running?" he sounded pissed.

"Just forget I said anything."

"I'm not just going to forget that."

"You have to," I was shouting. "I want a redo."

"You don't get a fucking redo on that." He shouted back.

We eyeballed each other. My breath was coming through my nose harsh and fast. I broke my gaze away first, unable to maintain eye contact with the intensity that was vibrating out of him. I started to back away from him. "It doesn't matter now."

He reached out and grabbed me, pulling me back. "Stop."

I lifted up both hands. "This isn't something you need to fix, Jackson. You were there when everything in my life was going to shit. And frankly, I don't think anyone could blame me because anyone would fall for you."

"I'm not trying to fix you. I'm trying to understand." His voice sounded strained.

"I love you," I said between gritted teeth. "What's so hard to understand about that?"

His head jerked back as if I had slapped him. I could see the panic cross his eyes. Since I had known Jackson, this was the first time I felt him losing his grip on his emotions.

I let out a pent-up breath. I needed to let the poor bastard off the hook from his weird sense of responsibility that he carried around for everyone.

"Jackson, you and I want different things. All I want is to feel safe and have a family. Those are my two goals. You live this dangerous life, and you don't want a wife or kids. I always knew nothing could come of us."

"What are you saying?"

"I'm saying that you don't have to worry that I have any expectations from you. We can't take back what happened, and I'll always feel a lot of guilt about that, but I don't expect anything from you."

His head jerked, and his jaw tightened. "So what? You're just going to go back to Matt?"

I drew my breath and then released it. I had no answer to that. Would I ever be able to be with Matt after knowing what it was like to be with Jackson? I was in love with this huge man that stood before me. There was no denying it, but it was evident that he did not share the same feelings.

A jarring sound interrupted us. It was Jackson's cell phone.

We stood there for a long moment until finally, he brought the phone to his ear.

He answered and then listened. "Okay."

He hung up and looked at me with resignation on his face. "Matt just woke up."

Oh fuck. It was time to face the music.

"Okay."

We started walking towards the hospital doors. I took deep, shuddery breaths, trying in vain to compose myself. We got on the elevator, and I could feel the emotions rippling through him. What those feelings were, I had no clue. Did it matter now? The damage was done. We had crossed a line that was so big it was impossible to come back from. Now we needed to deal with the fallout of our actions.

THE DOCTOR PULLED THE THREE OF US INTO THE SAME SMALL ROOM.

"Well, we have some great news. Matt has woken up. We have taken him off the ventilator. His voice is raspy because his vocal cords are still tender and sore, but he's talking, and his speech patterns seem to be fine. He knows who he is. He knows his name."

Irene sagged back into the couch. "Oh thank God."

"But it appears that Matt is experiencing some retrograde amnesia."

"What does that mean," Irene's voice trembled.

"It seems like Matt has lost a significant chunk of time from his memory."

"He can't remember?"

"Sometimes memory comes back after a traumatic brain injury, and sometimes it doesn't. Time will tell. But at this point, Matt has no recollection of the past five months of his life."

Irene and I both gasped.

Jackson spoke. "Does he know what happened to him?"

"We told him he was in a single vehicle accident and he knows he has lost a significant chunk of time in his memory. The most important thing right now is that we don't upset him. Keeping him as calm and relaxed as possible is how we can best take care of him."

"When can we see him?" Irene vibrated beside me.

The doctor glanced over at me. I hadn't yet spoken a word. I hadn't even moved a muscle. "He's asking for Emily."

I swallowed hard. I had no idea how to deal with this situation. So much had happened in the last five months.

The doctor stood up. "We don't want to tire him out, so we're going to keep the visits to five minutes per person for now. Just speak calmly and softly to him. Reassure him if you can."

Without looking at either Jackson or Irene, I followed the doctor to Matt's bedside. Matt's blue eyes looked up at me. He looked pale and weak lying on the bed surrounded by tubes.

"Matt," I stood at the foot of the bed. My entire body shook.

His smile was real. "Emily."

"You gave us quite the scare," my voice was soft.

"Come here," his voice rasped. Like he had a terrible cold.

I walked over to the side of the bed, and he grabbed my hand. "Your hair is so long."

I gave him a sad smile. "I was growing it out for the wedding."

"They told me it's May. My last memory is of going back to work after Christmas."

"Do you remember anything after that?" I asked cautiously.

He frowned and stared up at me. "Nothing."

I nodded and sat gingerly on the chair beside his bed. "Your mom is here. She's practically beside herself."

He studied my face. "You look thinner. Are you okay?"

I blinked rapidly. "It's been pretty scary."

He grabbed my hand, and with that, I started to cry again. I sat there smiling at him while giant tears rolled down my face. This was the old Matt. The man I had agreed to marry. The raging lunatic was gone.

"Emily," he said softly. "I'm sorry for scaring you."

I dashed the tears from my face. My throat felt so tight I couldn't speak. I nodded.

He shut his eyes and smiled. "I can't wait to marry you, Emily. In my head, we've only been engaged a couple of weeks, and here our wedding is coming up in a couple of months."

A sob escaped my throat. Matt had managed to go back in time. The rest of us remained stuck in the present. I had no idea how to deal with this. I only knew I wasn't supposed to upset him. "Yeah."

He opened his eyes. "Did we plan something good? I know how anxious you were about planning the wedding. I hope I took enough time to help you get everything ready."

A memory of Jackson helping me pick invitations. Doing the cake tasting. Teasing me about my giant wedding binder. More tears squeezed out of my eyes. "It's pretty much ready, but Matt, we can delay the wedding while you recover."

He squeezed my hand. "No way. I can't wait to marry you. No way are we delaying anything."

I swallowed my tears and gave him a watery smile. My poor confused heart was squeezed so tight, that I wasn't sure it was still beating. "We can talk about that later. I think Jackson and your mom want to see you and the doctor said we aren't allowed to tire you out."

His eyes went wide, and his body went still. "What did you just say?"

I shook my head. "We're supposed to only take five minutes each."

"What do you mean Jackson is here? Is he here because of the accident?" Matt's eyes were big.

I forgot that Matt would not remember inviting Jackson to live with us. All of that had been erased. "Jackson's been living with us for a couple of months. You invited him to live with us."

A weird expression crossed his face. "I would've never done that. Never."

My lips parted. "Matt."

He looked distraught. He tried to raise his head. "You've got to get him to leave, Emily. He can't be here."

The nurse bustled in. "Matt, you're going to have to calm down. Your heart rate is too high."

He pushed her hand away. "Emily. Promise me you will make him leave."

My lips parted in shock.

"Matt," the nurse was speaking in a loud voice. "You need to calm down Matt. If you don't calm down, we're going to have to sedate you."

"Promise me," he shouted. "Emily. Promise me."

I stood up feeling completely panicked. "I promise."

The nurse pushed a needle into his IV line and then Matt's head rolled back and then he was entirely out of it.

She looked at me with accusation in her voice. "Matt can't be upset like this. I had to sedate him."

"I didn't know," I said tearfully.

"Whatever you talked about, you must not talk about it with him again. Is that clear?"

I nodded and fled the room.

CHAPTER THIRTY-EIGHT

"Well, there's no question, Jackson's going to have to leave," Irene said to me. We stood outside of the ICU. Jackson wasn't around.

I stared at her in disbelief. "Excuse me?"

She crossed her arms with a resolute air. "What's the problem?"

I felt stunned at the lack of loyalty towards Jackson. "The problem is that Jackson has been our rock for the past week. He has catered to both of our needs, holding us up emotionally. He drove two hours in the middle of the night to come and get you after Matt's accident. And now you're going to toss him aside because Matt got a bit emotional?"

She lifted her chin. "My son's health is in danger. No one is going to jeopardize his recovery. Not even Jackson."

"Jackson is part of this family. You can't ask him to leave."

A stubborn look crossed her face that reminded me all too much of Matt. "Yes I can and I will."

"You're letting your emotions cloud your judgment."

She looked me right in the eye. "I think you're letting your emotions for Jackson cloud your judgment."

Low blow, even for Irene. I spoke slowly, trying to choose my words carefully. "You can't hurt one son because you want to heal your other son."

Her nostrils flared. "Matt is the only son I have in this hospital. He's my only priority."

I felt so much anger and hurt on behalf of Jackson, I couldn't even speak. "You're wrong on every single level."

"She's right," Jackson's low voice spoke from beside us. He stood there with a tray of coffees for us. His expression was impossible to read. "I'll go."

My heart cracked when I looked at Jackson. He had emotionally stepped back so far behind a wall, all that was left behind was a man completely devoid of emotion.

"No," I said sharply. "This is wrong."

Jackson handed Irene the tray of coffees, and then he reached forward and kissed her on the forehead. "I want Matt to get better as much as you do. He and I will have to work on our relationship when he's feeling stronger."

Irene's cheeks burned pink. She was unable to meet either of our eyes. "I'm going to check on Matt."

We stood there until the whoosh of the heavy door shut behind her.

"I hate her," I said with venom in my voice. "And right now I hate Matt."

Something flickered in Jackson's eyes. "Emily. You need to be there for them."

But who would be there for me? I tried not to beg without avail, "Don't go. Please don't go."

Green eyes looked down at my face. "Can you take care of both of them for me?"

I shook my head, fighting tears. "They don't deserve your care or your love."

"No," he said gently. "It's the other way around."

My face crumpled. I felt so much hurt on Jackson's behalf that I almost couldn't breathe. How much rejection and pain had this man experienced in his life that he believed he didn't deserve their love. "Where will you go?"

"I'll be around. I have to finish my outpatient treatment."

"You're going to be staying in New York?" My heart started to beat again.

His gaze fixated on something beyond my head. "I have another seven weeks here."

I worked to swallow, my thoughts immediately going to my granny's penthouse. "You need a place to stay. You can stay at my other place."

His eyes swung back to my face. He rocked on his heels. "Not necessary."

I started to dig through my purse for my keys frantically. "It is a full-sized penthouse with a pool and the most incredible gym. There are six bedrooms and a kitchen. Fully furnished, a nice big patio. There's even cleaning staff that comes once a week. I'll let them know you're coming. Martha can stock the kitchen. It'll be no problem."

He rubbed the back of his neck. "Emily. I don't need to stay there. I can find my own place."

I pulled the keys out and my face lifted to his. I wanted him to stay there. Even if I couldn't be near him, it would bring me a measure of comfort knowing where he was. At least for the next seven weeks.

It was incredibly manipulative, but I pulled the one string that I knew would do the trick. "It'd make me feel safe, and it would bring me comfort to know where you are. In case I need you."

Green eyes studied my face for a long moment. And then he gave me a curt nod. "Text me the address."

CHAPTER THIRTY-NINE

AFTER BEING READ THE RIOT ACT FROM MATT'S DOCTOR, IRENE AND I FELL into an uneasy truce. No one mentioned Jackson, and his presence had all but been erased. I, on the other hand, felt such a loss at his departure, I thought my heart was going to split.

That first night when we came home and found his room cleared out and his keys on the island, I almost burst into tears. I called Martha, and she had assured me that the penthouse was ready before he arrived.

One day bled into another. I drove Irene to the hospital, and we took turns visiting with Matt. Mostly he slept. I stole away, a couple of times during the day, to drive back to the loft and take Chloe out for potty breaks. I hated how alone the loft felt without Jackson.

Incredibly gracious and understanding, the gallery assured me that I didn't need to return until everything was back to normal.

It was a surreal experience talking with Matt. He remembered nothing. The doctors warned me that I should not discuss Matt's negative behavior prior to the accident. They told both Irene and I that we needed to keep him calm. When he was back on his feet, we could share some of the events that had occurred. As it was, we still hadn't told him that he had been drinking and driving without a seatbelt.

I missed Jackson to the point of pain. There were a hundred times where I almost drove to the penthouse to see him, but I refrained from doing so. What exactly would I say to him? Jackson and I had no future. We had developed a friendship, but we had ruined it when we crossed that line that we couldn't uncross. Now he knew the true extent of my feelings.

My face burned with shame as I recalled the look of panic and shock on his face when I had confessed to him that I loved him. Trust me. He didn't want to see me. I was the crush that had taken things too far. I had done the unthinkable by falling for him and then telling him how I felt. He probably thanked his lucky stars that he had made an escape when he did.

Matt was a further complication. He was so innocent and happy when he saw me. He had no idea about the destruction and devastation of the past few months. All he knew was that we had gotten engaged and we were about to get married. He asked me question after question about the wedding and continually assured me that he would be on his feet and ready to walk down the aisle with me. I, on the other hand, was having more than cold feet. It felt like my entire body was encased in ice. I felt nothing. Nothing for Matt. Nothing for the wedding. It felt like I was stuck in some weird limbo that I could not get out of. So, like every other time in my life, I pretended. I pretended everything was okay.

IRENE AND I DROVE TO THE HOSPITAL.

"Look at all the blossoms on the trees," Irene said, peering out the window. "It seems to have become spring almost overnight."

"Yes," I said. "It's come early this year."

"You're going to have such beautiful weather for your wedding. It's only six weeks away."

I took a deep breath. "Do you think that's a good idea?"

She looked at me sharply. "What are you talking about?"

I chewed on my bottom lip. "Well, I don't want to push Matt. He can barely walk."

"The wedding is the only thing he talks about. He needs this. That's his goal for recovery. You can't take that away from him."

I needed to tell him that we had ended our relationship. When would he be strong enough to face that he had cheated on me and then I had cheated on him? We were running out of time. "It's just coming so fast. I don't even know if I can get everything ready."

She practically ground her teeth. "Then hire a damn wedding planner. But you aren't delaying it. Can you imagine the kind of setback that could create for him emotionally?"

I swallowed. "Okay. It was just a suggestion."

"You need to start thinking about Matt. Marriage is more about giving and less about taking. You'd be smart to remember that."

I took a deep breath. I could do this.

Later that day, I stood in the lineup of the hospital cafeteria. My phone buzzed.

Jackson: How's Matt doing?

I stared at the text and thought that my heart would pound through my chest.

Me: He's getting stronger. Still struggling to walk but he's eating and sleeping well. The doctors are pleased with his progress

Jackson: Does he remember anything?

Me: Not yet

Jackson: How are you doing?

Uh, let's see. I feel trapped. I was caught in some surreal world where I pretended everything was fine when it wasn't. The only person who knew the truth about what had happened had left. And my heart was bleeding on my sleeve for someone who didn't love me back and didn't want to be with me.

Me: I'm fine. How about you?

Jackson: I'm fine

I wanted to tell Jackson that I missed him every hour of every day. That life was dreary and grey without him, and nothing had been right since he had left. I wanted to beg him to come back. That I needed him. That he was my rock and that I felt like I was falling apart without him in my life. But I had already freaked him out once with my heartfelt emotions. I didn't need to go there again.

Me: The doctors don't want us to talk about the last five months

Jackson: So Matt doesn't know what he did to you?

Me: No. Nor what I did to him

Jackson: Does he still think you are engaged?

Me: Yes

I sat staring at my phone willing it to buzz again with a text, but nothing else came. I sat there until the coffees went cold, but he never texted back.

THREE MORE DAYS PASSED WHEN ANOTHER TEXT CAME THROUGH.

Jackson: I think I just scared the living fuck out of your house cleaner

Me: Martha? What happened?

Jackson: She was vacuuming. I was just coming in from a run. She didn't hear me come in and when she turned around and saw me standing there, she started screaming at me in Spanish

For the first time in what felt like weeks, I started to laugh.

Me: ha ha ha. Poor Martha. Is she okay?

Jackson: She's fine. She insisted on making me pancakes

A huge smile ripped across my face.

Me: She worked for my granny for 37 years

Jackson: She told me. And you were right

Me: About what?

Jackson: You do have your granny's eyes

I clutched the phone to my chest. Tears threatened to spill over.

Me: You want to see Chloe sometime? She misses you

A long pause ensued. I wasn't sure if he was even going to respond.

Jackson: Probably not a good idea

A tear, this time, did spill over my cheek.

Me: Okay. Let me know if you change your mind

CHAPTER FORTY

ANOTHER TWO WEEKS PASSED. I TALKED TO THE DOCTOR IN PRIVATE, explaining that I wasn't engaged to Matt and asked him when I could talk to Matt about our reality. The doctor understood the situation and was even sympathetic to my case, but he warned me that upsetting Matt, which might increase his blood pressure, could cause irreparable damage. Matt's blood vessels in his brain were still healing, and he cautioned me to hang onto my secrets for a while longer.

The staff moved Matt out of ICU and onto a general ward. He started to walk with assistance. He couldn't walk far, but with the help of the physiotherapist, he moved his legs on his volition. Matt returned to being the witty, easy going, intelligent guy that I had agreed to marry.

It frightened me how easy it was to just slide back into our old routines. I mean, would it be so bad to marry Matt? I may not love him in that heart-pounding kind of love that I had for Jackson, but Matt was a good man, and he would be an incredible father. And it wasn't like I was choosing between two men. Jackson had made it abundantly clear that he wasn't interested in me in a romantic way.

When Matt had been a raging lunatic and acted deranged, I had been willing to proceed with this marriage. Now he was sweet, sensitive and kind, but I couldn't imagine moving forward.

I waited in his room while he walked around the ward.

He frowned when he saw me. "What are you doing here?"

"Visiting you," I said lightly.

"Isn't today Tuesday?" he looked perplexed.

"It is."

"You have your wedding dress fitting today," he said, wincing as he sat back down on the side of the bed. His arm that was holding onto the IV pole was trembling.

Oh shit. I completely had forgotten about that.

"Matt," I said gently, "I don't need to do that today. I'm going to call and cancel."

His gaze flew up to my face. "Emily. Come on. You told me that you and Beth are meeting at the bridal store for your final fittings and then you're going out for dinner."

"I don't feel like it," I said with a sigh.

He swung his legs with effort back into his bed. "You need this. You've been sitting beside my bed forever. Come on. Get dressed and get out there. You deserve a break. Take a night off with Beth."

I stared dubiously at him. "What about you?"

He shrugged and smirked. "Well, I'll eat a delicious dinner on a blue plastic tray and then I might get adventurous and watch some TV with my mom. I think there might be a rerun of Law and Order tonight."

I didn't give a shit about my wedding dress fitting but the thought of spending some time with Beth sounded appealing. "Are you sure?"

He winked at me. "I'm sick of you. Get out of here."

Two hours later, I stood in the bridal store with Beth. I stood on the podium while the seamstress yanked at my dress.

"What have you been eating?" she grunted.

I looked down at the beautiful white wedding dress. "Why?"

She stood up and yanked at the embroidered bodice. "Getting tight in the boobs and too loose in the waist."

"I think it's fine."

"Must be fixed," she said in her thick accent. "Stay there, and I'll be right back."

In the mirror, I looked like a bride. I owned the most beautiful wedding dress in the world, but I felt sick to my stomach. I was marrying the wrong man.

My hands flew to my face. And there it was. I didn't want to marry Matt. Tears started streaming down my face.

"You know, I never really thought pink was my color but I think this particular pink makes me look very dewy and fresh," Beth walked into the room and checked herself out in the mirror. When I didn't answer, her eyes met mine in the reflection.

She spun around. "Emily."

"I'm fine."

She rushed towards me. "You're fine? Is that why you're standing here crying?"

The seamstress came bustling back in and stopped at the look on my face. "Tears are normal for the bride. Trust me."

That only made me cry harder. What was I doing? I couldn't marry Matt. Matt was wonderful, but Jackson owned my heart. How could I lay beside Matt on our wedding night when I would only be thinking of another man? It wasn't fair to Matt, and it wasn't fair to me.

"I can't do this," I managed to speak.

Seamstress shook her head. "That's okay. I have new measurements. You come back soon, and your dress will be perfect."

An hour later, Beth and I sat in a booth at the back of some dimly lit bar. We wanted privacy, and I needed to talk.

"I thought things were going well for you and Matt," Beth asked cautiously.

"They are. He's a changed man."

"But you love Jackson."

I nodded in misery. "I feel like an idiot but yeah. I do."

She twisted the coaster around in her hands. "Maybe you just need to tell Jackson how you feel?"

I lifted my wet eyes to her. "Already did that. Right there in a big dramatic fashion in the hospital parking lot, I confessed my undying love to him."

Her gaze went big. "What did he say?"

I shook my head. "He looked cornered. Sort of like a wild animal that was trying to gnaw off his leg out of a trap."

She started to laugh. "It can't have been that bad."

"I might have been downplaying just how bad it was. Sheer panic and fear. It was written all over his face."

She reached her hand out and covered mine. "I'm sorry."

"I want safe. I want security. I want someone who's going to come home every night. I want to raise a little family. I want those boring family vacations that everyone complains about. And Jackson is the exact opposite of all of that. He lives a dangerous life. He doesn't want commitment. He doesn't want kids. Even if I got him, he would emotionally destroy me. I couldn't live with that kind of fear and uncertainty in my life."

Beth gave me a funny look. "Can I ask what you love about him then?"

I swallowed hard. "That's the irony. He makes me feel safe."

"Well that's a good thing, isn't it?" she argued.

I wiped my nose with the back of my sleeve. I was a disaster doing the ugly cry in public, and I couldn't even stop myself. "Who am I to him? He came to New York for some mysterious treatment and somehow Matt, not this Matt, but the wild Matt wanted to reconcile with him."

"What happened between them?"

"I have no idea. But whatever it was, it wasn't good."

"And they never did reconcile."

"It was like Matt wanted him there but then couldn't deal with him being there. And Jackson was just waiting, like me, for Matt to show up every once in awhile. So Jackson and I spent time together."

Beth gave me a sympathetic look. "And you fell for him."

More tears fell. "It was like the perfect storm. The more aggressive Matt acted, the more protective Jackson got. And the safer I felt. It was like that situation played into all of our needs."

"And then you two slept together."

I looked at my hands. "I don't think it meant the same thing to him as it did to me."

"It was your first time," her voice was sympathetic, "of course it meant something to you."

"It definitely wasn't his first time."

We both looked at each other and then at the same time, we started to laugh. I laughed until I cried. Beth had her face on the table, and her shoulders were shaking so hard. When we both came up for air, we both had tears in our eyes.

"Shit," she said. "I mean, out of all the guys, you had to pick him? Seriously!"

I wailed. "I don't even know how that happened."

"How was…"

Really good," I interrupted. Flashes of Jackson, naked, devastating me with another kiss. Touching me. Lifting me up. Moving on top of me. It was a movie that played over regularly in my mind. Once started, it was hard to stop.

Beth leaned forward, her elbows on the table, her hands covering her mouth. "Julie would have a shit fit if she ever found out."

A wet snort came out. "Fuck her. She fucked Matt. Repeatedly."

"Matt doesn't know?"

I shook my head. "No. How easily did he get off? He had the affair. I get the secret."

She rolled her eyes. "That sucks."

"I can't marry Matt. I need to break this off with him."

"When are you going to do that?"

I shrugged. "When the doctor says I'm allowed to upset him?"

"But before the wedding, right?"

"Helpful advice."

"Hey, with your luck, he'll be going straight from the hospital to the church."

I pointed at her. "Don't even jinx me like that."

"Are you going to be okay?"

I took a deep breath. "Yeah. I think I have spent so much time living in fear of being alone that maybe I just need to embrace it and accept that I might need to be alone for awhile. But I'd rather be alone than be with the wrong guy just because I'm afraid to be alone."

We sat there in silence for a long moment.

"You ever hear from him?"

I shrugged. "Just a couple texts here and there."

"So are you going to keep up the charade until Matt is better? Do you think you'll have a change of heart?"

I shook my head. "No. I know I won't. I don't want to marry Matt."

CHAPTER FORTY-ONE

THREE DAYS LATER, I SAT IN MATT'S ROOM WHILE HE ATE DINNER.

"Want some green Jello?" he asked with a smile.

I smiled back and shook my head. "All yours."

"I managed to walk around the ward three times this afternoon."

"That's so good," I smiled. I remember how Matt used to go for hour-long runs just to burn off his excess energy. How times had changed.

"I'm a bit concerned about my mom," he looked over at me. "I think the commute from the hospital to the loft is taking a toll on her."

I didn't argue. Irene looked more exhausted every day. "It's been a tough go."

He ran his tongue over his teeth. "Do you still have your granny's condo?"

"Yes."

"I know it's a lot to ask, but do you think she could stay there for awhile? If I recall, the condo is only a couple of minutes from here. She could leave anytime she wanted and go for a nap or a swim. You know how much she loves swimming." Matt gave me a beguiling smile.

I couldn't bring myself to meet Matt's eyes. "Well, someone is staying there right now."

"Who?" He frowned. "You didn't rent it, did you?"

I cleared my throat and then scratched my eyebrow. "I offered for Jackson to stay there."

His head jerked back. "Excuse me?"

I swallowed, trying to bring some saliva into my dry mouth. "Irene didn't want him around because he upset you. But Jackson is getting treatment at the military hospital. I didn't think anyone would even care. It isn't like we're seeing him."

He shook his head. "No."

"Matt. You don't remember a lot, but you wanted Jackson to come and live with us. You insisted."

"I never would have done that."

"Well, it wasn't me. You pushed for him to live with us, and you should know he was pretty great to both of us when he lived with us."

"He isn't welcome in our lives. I want you to ask him to leave."

I felt my entire posture go rigid. "I'm not asking him to leave. He's been through enough."

He gave a harsh laugh. "He's been through enough? You're really going to say that to me?"

"You don't know everything."

"Oh yeah? Are you going to throw my amnesia in my face every time we disagree?"

"That isn't even fair but letting him camp out in a place we never use, isn't a big deal."

"Emily, if you knew what I knew, you wouldn't say that."

"Well, I'm not going to kick him out. I'll pay for a hotel for Irene if she wants to go lie down during the day, but you can't ask me to ask him to leave."

"I'm not asking," Matt glared at me. "I'm telling you."

I looked at him in complete bafflement. "What exactly happened between the two of you?"

He shook his head. "Just get rid of him. There's no room for him in our lives."

"I will not."

"You're going to choose my dad's charity case over your fiancé?" He sounded loud and rude.

My legs shook as I stood up.

"You're leaving? Really? That's your solution? To run away from this talk?"

"I can't marry someone who keeps secrets from me, Matt."

"That doesn't even make sense," he yelled.

"I'm not entering into this marriage with a lot of secrets," I repeated. "So think about that."

"What's all this commotion," Irene said from the door.

"Ask your son," I hitched my purse over my shoulder, "I'm going home."

I WALKED DOWN THE HALLWAY, MY EYES BLINDED WITH TEARS. THIS WAS A nightmare that would not end.

"Emily!" a voice called from behind me. "Emily!"

I stopped in my tracks, but I didn't turn around. I waited until Irene caught up.

"What do you think you are doing," she hissed at me. "How dare you upset him like that?"

"He's not reasonable."

"He's sick."

"He can't tell me to kick Jackson out of my granny's place. Jackson's doing what you asked. He's kept his distance from all of us. Why can't Matt leave him alone?"

"Matt needs to heal and doesn't need this drama."

I shook my head. "You were all for this drama a couple of months ago when it looked like they were reconciling."

"If Matt doesn't want to have anything to do with Jackson, that's his prerogative. We aren't going to push him on that."

"I'm not asking for Matt to talk to Jackson, but someone had to be there for Jackson when his so-called family turned their backs on him."

"That's uncalled for."

"If the truth fits."

She pointed her finger at me. "Matt is going to be your husband. You need to learn to stand by him."

I threw my head back and laughed. "That's rich."

"I'm very disappointed in you, Emily. I thought you were cut from better cloth."

My tone was ice. "I think we've all been experiencing a lot of stress lately, so I'm going to let that comment slide. There's a hotel across the street. I'm going to pay for a room for you there because I think you look tired and you could use the extra rest and perhaps we all could use some space."

Her skin flushed darkly. I turned and walked rapidly away from her.

I DIDN'T CRY UNTIL I GOT TO MY CAR. MY HEART BROKE FOR JACKSON. THE man had done nothing but bestow undue patience and kindness towards Matt, Irene and myself. Every time I turned around, he had been there for us. Especially me. And now the only two people that he could call family in this world turned their backs on him. I cried for the little boy who had such a rough start to this world, who had grown up to be one of the most incredible men I had met in my life. Why couldn't they see that about him? Why were they so horrible to him? It broke my heart to see him shunned by the two people who should love him.

TEN MINUTES LATER, I STOOD AT MY GRANNY'S PENTHOUSE, KNOCKING AT the door even though I had my own key.

The door swung open. Jackson stood there. He wore a pair of faded jeans, and his hair was damp. My mouth went dry as my eyes traveled over his naked muscular torso.

"Hey," his expression was guarded.

I felt suddenly, ridiculously, nervous. "Hey. Sorry to bother you."

He swung the door wide open. "Come on in."

I followed him inside. Seeing a half-naked Jackson in my granny's penthouse felt like two worlds colliding. I felt a mixture of such loneliness and sorrow, loss and love that I wanted to throw myself on the familiar marble floor and weep with desperation.

He glanced over his shoulder and turned around when he saw the expression on my face. "You okay?"

I swallowed, momentarily unable to speak. "It's just hard to be here."

With you.

Something tender flickered in his eyes. "I bet."

"I should go," I said, spinning around and moving towards the door.

I opened it, but a big hand came up beside my head and pushed the door shut. His voice was deep and low in my opposite ear, "Where are you going?"

A shudder the size of a California earthquake rippled down my spine. Desire, emotion, everything both good and bad quaked through my body. I could feel the heat of him through my t-shirt. His fresh, clean scent filled my nostrils. I felt like an addict who had stayed sober for a couple of weeks and now was face to face with my drug of choice.

I stood there for the longest of moments, completely still, trying to work up my courage to just walk away. My erratic breath sounded for us to hear.

His big, warm hand lightly pushed hair off my neck.

"Emily."

The sound of my name on his lips was the tipping point. I spun around, and then he lifted me up into his strong arms. My legs wrapped around his waist and my back simultaneously hit the door. His mouth slanted over mine, kissing me as I've never been kissed before. I clung to his neck and moaned as his tongue did wicked, wonderful, perfect things to my mouth.

A big hand wrapped around my hair, tugging my head back. I cried out as his mouth slid down a delicate nerve in my neck, causing an electric shock to shoot down my back. Another big hand grabbed my butt and yanked me hard against him, grinding me hard against his hips. I felt his arousal pushing against my apex.

"This isn't why I came here," I moaned, as I pushed my hands through his thick hair, pulling his mouth closer to my neck.

"Tell me why you're here," his voice was muffled against my neck.

"I don't know," I moaned, my eyes wide open and staring at the high ceiling of the entrance. "I couldn't stay away."

He lifted his head, and two green eyes stared into my own. The look he gave me was so honest and real that it made me want to burst into tears. I felt like I had been living a lie for the last couple of weeks and finally, I was able to breathe and be myself.

A large hand came up and pushed the hair off my face. "Are you okay?"

I fought not to cry. I shook my head.

"Want to talk?"

I shook my head again. "I need to go."

Some emotion I couldn't decipher flitted across his gaze so fast I wasn't sure I had seen anything at all. He slowly lowered me down onto my trembling legs.

"I'm sorry," I said, and this time I did start crying. My entire face crumpled up. God this man must be so tired of my tears.

"Emily talk to me," his voice was unfeigned. He held my hand and looked at me with such concern, it only made me cry harder. Sobbing, I wrenched my hand out of his before turning and disappearing out the door.

CHAPTER FORTY-TWO

CHLOE AND I WALKED HOME FROM THE RIVER. ON HER LEASH, SHE SNIFFED the grass. I thought about the disaster my life had become. Why had I shown up last night at the penthouse? I showed up there out of empathy and sadness for Jackson but seeing him had done something to me. I had no control around the man. He felt like oxygen to my starved brain and heart.

I shook my head. I hated myself for going there. I hated myself even more for leaving. Now I avoided Irene and Matt. I ignored half a dozen texts and two phone calls from them, and now I was avoiding the hospital. I needed to face the music at some point, but I felt so tired. I wanted to lie in bed and sleep my problems away.

Problems that wouldn't go away. Jackson would leave New York in four short weeks to go back to his life. Once I broke things off from Matt, it was safe to say that I would never see either of them again. The past few weeks without Jackson had reminded me of the weeks after my granny had died. Grey and barren. I glimpsed how my future unfolded in front of me. I wasn't sure if I'd be able to withstand the crush of how lonely it would be.

I didn't see him. One minute I was wrapped in my thoughts, and then he stood there. I stopped walking. I took in his appearance. The man looked rough. Angry. He was dressed in dirty jeans and an old black jean jacket. His black hair slicked off his harsh features. His dark eyes were cold as he took me in.

"You out for a walk?" he stepped forward and knelt over Chloe. He held her face too hard as she worked to back away from his touch.

I pulled her leash and tried to step around him.

His grip was like steel on my arm. "Where do you think you're going?"

"My husband is waiting for me," my voice faltered over my lie. Terrible thoughts ran through my mind as I tried to remember all the steps from my defense class.

He gave a harsh laugh and grabbed me hard. "I don't think so."

I dropped Chloe's leash and used both arms to push against his chest. "What are you doing?"

"You look like a nice piece of tight ass," his eyes raked over my body. "Not like those whores I'm usually with."

My eyes darted around, as I tried to find another human being in the area. There was no one. The place was deserted. Chloe was gone. She had taken off at an alarming rate back to the loft. Tears blurred my eyes. I made a move to run but he yanked me back so hard I lost my balance.

"Leave me alone," I said through clenched teeth.

His hand connected with my cheek with such force I saw stars. And then his hand came back the other way, hitting my face so forcefully it knocked me off my feet. Gravel dug into my hands as I turned and tried to crawl away. I felt his grip on my hips as I kicked and screamed. I had visions of this man hurting me, raping me, killing me.

"That's it," he yanked me hard. "I love it when they fight. Nothing turns me on more."

My arms and my hands beat him, trying to scratch, claw, connect with something. He tossed me so hard to the ground that the breath knocked out of me. I lay there on my side, struggled to get air into my lungs, but my rib cage refused, and I wheezed and gasped, unable to breathe I was so winded.

He knelt over me and then he ripped my shirt open. Dirty hands pushed up beneath my bra, and cold fingers pinched and dug into my breasts. I managed to rake my nails down over the length of his face before he back-handed me. Pain exploded in my head. I tasted blood. Tears blurred my vision. I heard him laugh and then his dirty hands tore at my pants. Fighting my belt, greedy, yanking at it so hard, my hips lifted off the ground.

A surge of fear went through me. Was this happening to me? I tried to lift my knees. I tried to buck him off, but the weight of him on my thighs was too heavy.

"Nooo," I screamed, crying so hard I couldn't bring oxygen into my lungs. I heard Chloe barking in the distance.

"That's it, baby," he grunted, as he yanked my pants down to my hips. I watched through blurred eyes as he trailed one dirty hand over my chest and then he slowly, started to undo the belt on his pants.

"No," I whimpered, trying to push up. His hands came to my throat, choking me. My hands went around his neck, fighting him. I couldn't breathe. I was suffocating. He was going to kill me. I was going to die at the hands of a madman. I thought I would have a heart attack before he managed to choke the life out of me. I didn't want to die like this. I didn't want to be murdered on the side of the road with no one around, no one wondering where I was. Who would take care of Chloe? I would never see Jackson again. I clawed at his face, but to no avail. His ugly features swam before my eyes. I could feel myself begin to black out. I cursed his face in my mind. I cursed this animal that was going to take away my last chance to see Jackson again.

And then he was gone.

I rolled over on my stomach, coughing and gasping in pain as I tried to pull air into my lungs. I pushed myself to a kneeling position. I needed to run. I needed to get away. What if he came back? My pants were on my hips. I staggered to my feet, pulling up my pants. I was crying and shaking, completely in shock. I became conscious of the sound of someone getting hit. Repeatedly. I swung around, and Jackson knelt over him and repeat-edly pounded his fists into the guy's face.

"Jackson," I wailed, my voice sounding thin and reedy.

He stopped and looked up at me. His face was a mask of rage. His eyes had murder in them. Blood splatter covered his face. He was breathing like a crazy man. I bent over and howled in pain and fear.

He rushed towards me. I collapsed into his arms, sobbing and clinging to his hoodie. He had his hands on my chin as he took in my bloody face. I tasted the bitter iron of my blood dripping down my lip. I used the back of my hand to wipe my mouth. Tears poured from my eyes, and I hurt so much I thought I was going to blackout.

"Oh baby," he soothed. "Sweetheart."

"I want to go home," I sobbed, trying to hold my ripped shirt together. I looked around in horror. Was this happening to me? What was happening to me?

He peeled off his sweatshirt and then ever so gently helped me lift my arms so that I could slide it over my head. He looked down at my face and said in a low voice, "I'm going to kill that piece of shit."

I sobbed so hard I could barely breathe. "No, please. I just want to go home."

He lifted me up. My arms went around his thick neck, and I wrapped my legs around his waist. He started to walk. We stopped when he stepped over the unconscious body of the man who had attacked me. And then he reached down, and with one hand, grabbed the man by the collar and started to drag him behind him.

We walked like that for the three blocks back to the loft. My face buried in his neck while I bled all over his shirt. I could hear the sound of the man's body being dragged carelessly along the gravel road.

We got to the loft, and Jackson just dropped the guy, letting his limp head bounce on the ground.

"Is he dead?" I asked, my voice muffled against Jackson's neck.

"No."

He carried me up the stairs and put me gently on the couch. I curled my knees up to my chest. "You need to call the police."

"After I tend to you."

"Call them first," I begged, terrified that the man would wake up. Come up here. Hurt us.

Jackson stood up and pulled out his phone. Chloe bound up onto the couch beside me and tilted her head at me. She looked at me with concern on her face.

I reached out and gently touched her nose. I vaguely heard Jackson talking. Words like assault and perpetrator. Our address. And then he tossed the phone down and crouched in front of me.

"Let me see your face," he pulled my hand gently from my eye. His fingers palpitated my face. I winced.

"I don't think anything is broken," he said, "But you have a bloody nose." He left for a moment and then returned with a cold cloth in his hands. I shut my eyes as he dabbed the cloth over my skin.

My eyes met his. "Why are you here?"

"I couldn't stay away," he said, his face a mask of concentration as he wiped my lip.

"How did you know?" I began to cry again.

"I got here, and you and Chloe were gone. I thought I would find you on your route. I started walking, and Chloe saw me and came towards me. Barking. Her leash trailing behind her. I heard you scream."

I stared into his eyes, tears gushing down my face. "You saved me."

The sound of a siren peeled from blocks away. Getting closer and closer.

"Wait here," he stood up and disappeared downstairs. I heard the sound of car doors slamming and then voices. Heavy footsteps on the stairs and then a female cop stood looking at me. She spoke into the radio on her shoulder. Then she walked towards me.

"My name is Constable Jenkins. Do you need an ambulance?"

I shook my head. I burrowed deeper into Jackson's sweatshirt. Where was he? I wanted him to come back upstairs.

She sat down and gave me a long look. "Want to tell me what happened?"

In a choked voice, I relayed what had happened.

"Where is Jackson?" I begged her, my eyes glued to the door.

"If by Jackson you mean the guy who's breathing fire and looks like he wants to kill someone, he's giving his statement to the police outside."

I heard the slow rise and fall of an ambulance siren as it approached the property.

"I don't need an ambulance," I repeated.

"The guy who assaulted you does."

I put my face in my hands. "I just want to go have a shower."

"We'd like to take you to the hospital. To check you over and run some tests."

CHAPTER FORTY-THREE

I SAT HUDDLED ON THE BED IN THE EMERGENCY ROOM. A POLICE OFFICER asked me if they could take some evidence. They swabbed my hands and my nails. A female officer asked if I needed a rape kit. I violently shook my head.

They asked Jackson to talk to the police in another room. A female doctor came in.

"How are you doing?"

"My face hurts."

She flashed her penlight in my eyes and then lay me back and palpitated my stomach. I winced.

"Is that tender?"

"I don't remember him punching me in the stomach."

"We're going to do a urine test for blood in the urine, okay? So you need to pee in a little cup, but I promise you if it comes back negative, you can go home. I don't think you have a concussion."

"Okay."

I feared that Jackson had murdered the other guy and would get arrested.

"Is the man who assaulted me going to die?"

She took a deep breath. "No, the person who worked him over did an excellent job of pulverizing him to the point that he will be drinking out of a straw for the next few months, but he won't die."

I let out a harsh breath. The relief was so intense that stars swam before my eyes.

"Hey," she reached over and squeezed my arm. "They say that the man is suspected of hurting a lot of women. He's going to go to jail for a long time. You don't have to worry about him, okay?"

She handed me a cup, directed me to the washroom and told me to hang tight.

In the washroom, I studied my face. My nose trailed crusty blood. My upper lip was swollen. My cheekbones had started to swell and bruise. I sported bruises on my neck where he had choked me. I peed in the cup, left it in the little window box, and then washed my face and my hands.

I walked back to my bed and shut the curtains. I took off my hospital gown. My bra and shirt had disappeared as evidence, so I pulled Jackson's hoodie back over my body. It hung down to my knees. It smelled faintly of him. I put my knees up on the bed and lay my head on my knees. I needed to go home.

Jackson's voice sounded from outside the curtain. He came in. Our eyes met.

I worked my throat. His sympathetic look made me want to burst into tears.

"Thank you for saving me," I said in a tiny voice.

"I should have killed that asshole," he walked over to the bed. I moved my feet, and he sat down on the side. He picked up my hand. I looked at his knuckles. They were swollen and bloody.

"Your hands, Jackson!"

He shrugged and stared at me. "Do you want me to call Matt?"

The only person I wanted to be around right now was Jackson. "No."

We stared at each other. I tried, but I couldn't read the expression in his eyes.

The words tumbled out of my mouth, "I wasn't paying attention. I didn't have my phone. I didn't even see him. I was in my own little world.

One minute I was daydreaming and then the next minute he attacked me. All my defenses, all my training was useless."

He squeezed my hand. "Emily, you are 5-foot-nothing, and you barely weigh 100 pounds. The guy outweighed you by at least a hundred pounds. Only a bullet between his eyes could have stopped him."

"You stopped him."

He swallowed. "I saw Chloe running towards me and then I heard you scream. I swear my heart stopped. When I saw that asshole on you, I fucking lost my mind."

He stared straight ahead. I could see the rage and frustration on his face. "If you hadn't stopped me I would've killed him."

I looked at his huge hand, holding mine. "They say that he hurt a lot of women."

"Emily."

I looked up into his green eyes. "Please tell me what he's done."

He fought to control his emotions. "They say they have tied his finger-prints to the rape and murder of nine women."

I had a flash of that man and the cold rage in his eyes. When that man attacked me, I knew he would kill me.

"He strangled them."

"Yes."

"Will you please hold me?"

He moved down the bed and then lifted me against his chest. I shut my eyes and clung to him. How was I going to live without this man? I had absolutely no idea. I felt Jackson's big arms wrap around me. This was the one place that I felt safe.

I shut my eyes. I wanted to go home.

Voices sounded outside the curtain. Two men talked quietly in front of my curtain.

"Hey, Doug, what are you here for?"

"Domestic gone bad. You?"

"Paperwork on an attempted assault. You'll never guess who they caught."

"Who?"

"The throat slayer."

I stiffened and raised my head. Alert and listening.

"No shit! Some lady finally have a 45 in her purse?"

"No, get this. Some woman is attacked. Her dog runs back to her place, and her friend goes looking for her. The guy is a fucking Navy SEAL."

"You're shitting me."

"So this SEAL fucking destroys this guy. The girl says she saw him only hitting her assailant's face, but both his arms were broken, fifteen bones broken in his hands, nine of his ribs. His nose was broken in eight places. His jaw was broken in six places. There was nothing left of his face. Then Navy SEAL guy carries the woman back to her place, and he dragged this guy behind him like the piece of garbage he is. Doctors said his pants were down and they'll be picking gravel out of his dick for weeks."

"No shit." The guy laughed.

"The Navy SEAL dude? Had a couple scrapes on his knuckles."

"Any charges against him?"

"Not even close. The chief of police came down and shook his hand. Thanked him for his civic duty."

"How's the girl?"

"She got lucky. No rape. Just beat up. We're going to Ducky's later to celebrate. If I can find the SEAL dude, I'm going to invite him."

"Count me in. See you later."

"You bet."

I turned and looked up at Jackson. Green eyes looked down at me. I struggled to articulate my thoughts. The curtain whipped open, and the doctor observed the two of us lying on the bed together with Jackson's arms wrapped around me.

"So are you the boyfriend?"

He shook his head.

"I have to talk to your friend here for a moment, and then you can take her home."

Jackson lifted me up, sat me on the bed and with one last look at me, disappeared around the corner. She watched him walk away, and then she shut the curtains.

"We got your urine sample back. No blood in the urine," she pushed her glasses off her face.

I nodded. "Okay."

"But we do have high levels of hCG," she looked at me like I should know what this meant.

I shrugged.

"Human chorionic gonadotropin, also known as hCG, is a hormone produced by the placenta after implantation."

My mouth parted. Thinking. "Placenta?"

"You're pregnant."

I felt dizzy. She caught me and helped me place my head between my legs. Her soft hand rubbed my back. "I take it this is a shock."

I stared at the floor between my legs. "There must be some mistake."

"We ran the test twice. They were both definitive. I take it this isn't planned?"

I sat up and blinked. "I'm supposed to get married in four weeks, and my fiancé thinks I'm a virgin."

Her mouth parted. "Okay. That's a complication."

"How pregnant am I?"

"When was your last period?"

I thought back. "About six weeks ago?"

"The first day of pregnancy is counted from the first day of your last period. So that would make you approximately six weeks pregnant."

I shook my head. "But I had a light period two weeks ago."

"That was probably just some spotting. That's a fairly common occurrence."

I concentrated on breathing. "Is the baby okay?"

"Some abdominal pain is normal. Your organs are shifting, your uterus is expanding, and all those ligaments are stretching," she said. "I suspected you were pregnant, but I wanted to rule out other things in light of your attack. If you experience any bleeding, come back."

I couldn't wrap my brain around this. I was pregnant. With Jackson's baby. Jackson, the guy who was emphatic that he didn't want children.

"So is the guy I just kicked out of here the dad?"

I stared at her. "How did you know?"

"Lucky guess," she said wryly.

I dropped my face into my hands. "Oh, my God."

She rubbed my back again. "Listen. You've had an insane day. Go home, get some rest. Drink plenty of water. No alcohol or drugs. As soon as you can, get in to see your regular doctor. And you should go on some prenatal vitamins as soon as possible."

CHAPTER FORTY-FOUR

JACKSON DROVE ME BACK TO THE LOFT. I HUDDLED IN THE PASSENGER SEAT, unable to speak. He glanced at me frequently, but I couldn't meet his eyes. I tried to wrap my mind around everything, but my mind was blank.

When we reached the loft, he got out of the truck and walked around to my side. He opened the door, and I reached out my arms to him. He picked me up and carried me up into the loft. He continued to carry me up to my bedroom. And then we stood in my bathroom.

He didn't say a word to me, just turned on the shower. I started to cry. With an unbelievably gentle touch, he helped me pull his sweatshirt over my head. I kicked off my clothes, and then I stepped beneath the warm spray.

Heavy emotions continued to roll over me. And then he was behind me, his huge arms wrapped around me from behind. I turned around and clung to him, sobbing my heart out. He didn't say a word, he just held me to his chest.

When I could cry no more, he took a bar of soap and a cloth and gently washed my body. I stood there like a rag doll, unmoving as he washed every inch of me. He washed my hair. Holding my neck as he tilted my head back to rinse.

I opened my eyes and looked up at him. He had taken off his shirt, but he still wore his jeans. He inspected my face. When his eyes dropped to my bruised neck, I could see his nostrils flare in anger.

Our eyes met. This man had saved me from imminent death. I owed him my life.

"Thank you," I whispered.

He swallowed and reached behind me, turning the water off.

Much like the time I had barfed, he dried me off. And then he picked me up and carried me to sit on my bed.

I allowed him to pull a t-shirt over my head and then held onto his shoulder while he helped me step into a pair of panties. He whipped back the covers off the bed, and I climbed in. I curled up on my side and stared up at him.

"Can I get you something to drink?" his voice sounded low.

I shook my head. I wanted to ask him to get in and hold me, but I was afraid that he would say no.

He nodded and stepped back.

I lifted my head, my voice full of fear. "Are you leaving?"

"I'm not going anywhere."

I relaxed again. I couldn't seem to keep my eyes open. "I feel so tired."

"You're coming off adrenaline. Just try and sleep. You'll feel better once you sleep."

"Don't leave me," the words sounded jumbled to my ears.

His voice sounded so far away. "I couldn't if I tried."

I JERKED AWAKE. THE ROOM WAS BLACK. I SAT UP, DISORIENTED. MY EYES adjusted to the lack of light. Jackson sat on a chair, his long legs crossed, his feet up on the edge of the bed. His arms were crossed, and he stared back at me. His features looked dark and angular in the dim light.

"How long have I been asleep?" my voice croaked.

He checked his military watch. "About six hours."

I swallowed, my mouth dry. "Have you been sitting here with me the entire time?"

"Pretty much."

I flopped back on my pillow and stared up at the ceiling. He had sat and guarded me while I slept. How was I not supposed to love this man? He made the task impossible.

I was pregnant. The thought jarred through my mind.

I sat straight back up, my heart pounding hard. Holy fuck. Had that been a dream? Had the doctor told me that I was having a baby?

I looked over at Jackson. "Was I at the hospital?"

He stood up abruptly and walked over to put his big, warm, hand on my forehead. "You don't remember?"

It wasn't a dream. I had visited the emergency room. I peed in a cup. And the woman doctor had told me that I was pregnant.

"I do remember. I'm just fuzzy on the details."

He sat on the edge of the bed and looked at me. "You were in shock."

I swallowed hard and stared at this huge man. A part of him was growing inside of me in the version of a tiny baby. I felt my heart start to pound. A cold wave washed over my skin, and I felt a bit light-headed.

I dropped my face into my hands and struggled not to blurt out my news. His warm hand wrapped around the back of my neck. I was in love with Jackson. He didn't want children. And I was engaged to Matt who was lying in the hospital recovering from a brain injury. My wedding, which I had yet to cancel, charged towards me at an alarming rate. Jackson would leave in a few short weeks. And I was pregnant with the wrong man's child.

"I feel sick," I said, my voice muffled.

"Emily, we need to feed you. Your blood sugar levels are probably really low."

"It's not that," I said from beneath my hands.

"What is it?"

I shook my head.

He got off the bed, and then he sorted through my dresser drawers. He returned with a big sweater and a pair of soft yoga pants. I stood up, and under his watchful eye, I pulled them on.

"You go on down," I said. "I'll be just a minute."

"You sure?"

I nodded. Not only did I need to pee, but I needed to gain control over the wild words that threatened to blurt out of my mouth.

I LOOKED IN THE MIRROR OF THE BATHROOM. IN THE LIGHT, MY BRUISES were more pronounced than they had been at the hospital. Especially the ones around my neck.

My eyes looked wide and a bit wild. I was pregnant. A baby was growing inside of me. Jackson's baby. I put my face in a towel and muffled a scream. I wanted a family, but not like this. I didn't want to trap the love of my life into something that he didn't want. Every single time I had asked Jackson about kids he had been resolute that he did not want them.

I tried to imagine his reaction if I walked downstairs and told him what the doctor had told me. I had a terrible vision of him turning around and walking out of the loft. I would be left here alone. By myself.

My nostrils flared in fear. I feared to be alone right now. I needed to keep my mouth shut. At least a little bit longer. At least until tomorrow. Tonight Jackson would be here for me. I needed him. I needed his safe presence. I would still be pregnant tomorrow. I would tell him then. Surely one day wouldn't make a difference.

HE STARTED TO COOK AN OMELET. I SLID ONTO ONE OF THE STOOLS AROUND the island and watched him. His jeans were dry. I remembered him standing behind me in the shower with his jeans.

"Did you use the dryer?"

He looked over his shoulder at me, an amused expression on his face. "Is that okay?"

My head bobbed. "Totally okay."

He chopped up a salad and then drizzled my favorite dressing on it before sliding it in front of me with a fork.

"Aren't you eating?"

"Already ate."

My appetite was ravenous. I couldn't get that salad into my mouth fast enough. He put the omelet in front of me and then sat across from me.

"Have you been eating enough?" he watched me eat.

"Yeah, why?"

"You look like you've lost some weight."

"It's been busy."

He looked around. "Where is Irene staying?"

I swallowed. "She's checked into the hotel across from the hospital. She was finding the commute back and forth too strenuous."

I didn't mention that since she had turned her back on Jackson, our relationship had been on the frosty side.

His big arms crossed over his hard chest. He nodded. "What else?"

I glanced up at him. "What do you mean?"

"Is everything okay with you and Matt?"

My eyes dropped to my plate. "I needed some space."

"Your phone has been dinging all day."

I breathed in hard through my nostrils. "We had a fight, and I was avoiding him and Irene. And then today happened."

"You should text him and let him know you are okay."

I shrugged. "Maybe."

I didn't want to think about Matt or Irene. Those two people had consumed every moment of my life for weeks. They had taken over my small world. I just needed a break from them both.

A yawn overtook me.

He stood up and held out his hand. "Time to go back to bed."

I let him lead me back upstairs. "I don't know why I'm still tired."

He watched as I pulled off some clothes and then climbed back into bed. I stared up at him. My heart ached so much. He looked down at me. I was afraid that he would leave.

"Can you lie down with me?" my voice sounded small.

For one long moment, I thought he would refuse. Then he grabbed his t-shirt and pulled it over his head. "Move over."

I scooted over, and I watched as he kicked off his jeans. Then he climbed into bed beside me.

"Roll over," his voice was low.

I curled up on my side, my back to him. A giant arm snaked around my waist, and then he tugged me back against him, so my back was flush against his warm torso. He curved his huge body against mine, so I was lying in a warm Jackson cocoon.

I sighed and snuggled my head into the pillow. He pushed my hair away from my neck and then I felt his hot breath against my skin.

"Did you lock the door?" I mumbled.

"You're safe. You can sleep."

And with those words in my ears, I drifted into a dark, peaceful abyss.

CHAPTER FORTY-FIVE

THE HARSH LIGHT OF DAY HURT MY EYES. I WOKE ALONE IN BED. Disoriented, I sat up. Memories of the day before washed over me. Getting attacked. Pregnant. Being taken care of by Jackson. Falling asleep in his arms.

I staggered my stiff body to the bathroom and peered in the mirror. Hot and puffy eyes looked back at me. The swelling around my lip had subsided, but the bruises on my neck seemed more pronounced. I looked closer. I could almost see fingerprints on my neck. I shuddered. If Jackson hadn't saved me, I would've been murdered yesterday.

Today I needed to end it with Matt, and I needed to come clean with Jackson about the baby. I dropped my face into my hands. I dreaded both tasks.

I showered and made my way downstairs. A bowl of cut fruit waited on the island. A note from Jackson stated that he had taken Chloe for a walk. My phone rested next to the note.

Twenty text messages from Matt. He was sorry. He wanted to talk. Was I okay?

I stared into space for a long moment. I had no desire to see Matt or Irene today.

I texted him back.

Me: Sorry. I should've texted you yesterday. I just needed some space.

Matt: Please come see me today. I need to talk to you.

Me: Okay

I heard two sets of footsteps on the stairs. The door clattered as it slid open. Chloe ran towards me at full tilt.

"Chloe," I said, feeling joy. She planted both of her front paws on my legs, smiling her dog smile while I rubbed her face.

Jackson walked towards us. He assessed me.

I assessed him back. He looked serious and pensive.

"How are you feeling?"

I nodded. "Good."

The truth was I was slightly queasy, but I did feel well rested.

He nodded and walked into the kitchen. I spun around in my seat and watched as he poured himself a glass of water.

"You want to talk about yesterday?"

I shook my head. "Not yet."

"At some point, you're going to need to."

I couldn't talk about it until I could think about it. And right now it was buried so deep in my brain behind all the other things I didn't want to think about. I was barely conscious of it being there.

"Not today."

He sipped his drink and watched as I picked up my fork and slowly ate my fruit. The silence between us hung heavy. I could tell that something was up.

"You're leaving," I blurted out, voicing my greatest fear.

"I have to fly back to Virginia for a couple of days. There's an arbitration that I'm required to attend."

My heart hardened into a chunk of ice. He was leaving.

"For your job?"

"Yes."

"Are you coming back?"

"I still have my outpatient program to finish."

I blinked at the frustration in his voice. "Jackson, why are you an outpatient? Are you sick?"

He snorted. "It's just a bullshit mandatory process."

I sensed that today was not the day that I should bring up the baby. Giddy relief washed over that. I could avoid that conversation for another day. "You don't seem that impressed."

"It's part of my obligatory COA that I need to do before they let me back into operations."

"You have to do this before they let you work?"

He crossed his thick arms. "Yup."

I had no idea what that meant or why it was happening, but I sensed that he was at the end of his patience on the matter. "When do you get back?"

He switched gears. "Are you going to see Matt today?"

I shrugged.

"How's he doing?"

"Well, he's able to walk for at least 5 minutes at a time. He hasn't been sleeping all that good, but I'm told that's part of his brain being hurt. The doctor said it would get better with time. He's lost weight, but his appetite is good."

"Has his memory come back?"

"Not yet."

"So he remembers nothing of the past five months?"

"No. He's really sensitive about his memory loss which the doctors also said is normal. The doctor told me not to talk about our broken engagement because they don't want him to become agitated or upset."

"So he doesn't remember cheating on you or breaking up with you."

"No."

"Does that mean he thinks you are still engaged?"

I chewed on my lip. "Yes."

Silence hung between us.

His voice sounded low and ridiculously gentle. "How are you doing with all of this?"

"It's weird to pretend that nothing has happened and not talk about it."

He didn't speak.

I tried again. "It doesn't feel real but…"

"But you can't get honest about it because you aren't supposed to."

"Yes."

He looked around the loft. "You should move into your granny's place while I'm gone. I don't like you being out here alone when I'm gone."

He would only be here for a few more weeks, and then he would be gone for good. "Okay."

"My flight leaves in four hours. Why don't you pack up and I'll help you move your bags."

JACKSON TOOK OUT THE GARBAGE AND LOADED CHLOE'S STUFF INTO MY CAR, while I put together a bag for myself. It would be weird to be back at the penthouse, but I looked forward to it. That place felt more like home than the loft did. After my granny had died, I couldn't bear to be there, but now it might comfort me while Jackson was gone.

Jackson followed so close behind my car, I could only see the enormous grill of his truck in my review mirror. How much patience did he require to follow so slowly behind me? That was the difference between us. I did a three-point check before I changed lanes. I was cautious and held my steering wheel at two and ten. He barely kept his hands on the steering wheel, much less his eyes on the road. He drove his truck like a bat out of hell. Jackson thumbed danger in the face. I lived to stay safe. I found his courage wildly intoxicating.

He carried my bags up to the penthouse and then I sat on the couch and waited for him to pack his bags.

He reappeared a few moments later, and my heart stuttered in my chest. He looked like a soldier with his grey and white military fatigues. A faded military grade baseball cap was pulled low over his eyes. He seemed impossibly tough.

My heart slammed into my chest. Fear seized my throat, making it tough for me to speak. "Are you going to fight?"

He snorted in amusement. "I wish. My flight is military. No civilian dress on those flights."

I let out a big pent-up breath. "Oh."

He picked up his black duffle bag that I knew from experience weighed more than I did. A terrible feeling that he wouldn't return crushed my chest.

"You're coming back right?" I sounded like a lovesick teenager in angst. But I couldn't stop myself from asking.

"I'll be back on Friday."

I stood up and anxiously wiped my hands on my pants. I wanted to launch myself at him, but instead, I stood there and memorized every inch of him. The way his long hair licked up beneath his hat. His big black watch that wrapped around his thick wrist. The shape of his eyes that were shaded by his hat. The hard angular planes of his face. The thickness of his corded neck. The man was absolutely massive.

My hand pressed against my stomach. And this giant of a man had planted his seed inside of me. I broke out in a sweat and swayed on my feet. I was about as petite as one could get. I had a faint thought that this baby might kill me coming out if it took after it's father.

His eyes narrowed. "Are you okay?"

"Oh, yeah. Totally." I lied through my teeth.

He frowned and looked at me.

I worked to school my expression. "Have a good flight."

We stared at each other. Finally, he nodded curtly and then turned and was gone.

CHAPTER FORTY-SIX

I was walking towards Matt's room when Irene appeared out of nowhere and grabbed my arm.

"Where were you?"

Even though I had done my best to cover the bruises with makeup, I instinctively touched my neck.

"Hi, Irene."

Her eyes bore into me. "Thanks to you, Matt had two difficult nights. What did I tell you about not upsetting him?"

I swallowed the fear down my throat. I had spent an entire hour practicing telling Matt that we could no longer get married. If he couldn't handle me going missing for a day and a half, how would he take this news?

"The doctors are worried about the blood vessels in his brain. Remember that," she hissed.

I hated this. How long would I be trapped in this charade?

I folded. "I promise I won't upset him."

In his room, Matt flirted with a cute nurse.

"Hey, there's my girl," his smile brightened when I walked into the room.

I pasted a smile on my face. "Hey there."

By some unspoken consent, Matt and I did not broach the subject of Jackson or the penthouse. Nor did I mention that I had gotten attacked the day before. I certainly didn't mention that I had moved into the penthouse. Instead, we chatted about non-events, like how his roommate had gone home, and how the fire alarm had gone off twice yesterday. He also mused that he thought we should add ten people to the guest list for our wedding.

EACH NIGHT I RETURNED ALONE TO THE PENTHOUSE. TO MAKE MYSELF FEEL better, I alternated between lying on top of both Jackson's bed and my granny's. I practiced countless renditions of telling Matt that it was over and telling Jackson that I was pregnant with his child. I barfed two mornings in a row. I made an appointment to see my GP, and the rest of the time I sat listlessly on the patio lost in my thoughts.

The shock of being pregnant wore off and the reality set in. Every conversation that Jackson had told me that he didn't want children, I replayed in my head. I looked for any faint clue that he might have been on the fence about the subject and came back to the conclusion that he was certain that he did not want kids. He did not want a family. He did not want a wife.

Financially, the baby and I would have no problems, but the more I contemplated being a single mom, the more scared I got. How was I going to cope? How would I make all those scary decisions myself? I could barely take care of myself, so why did I think I could take care of a child?

I was sure that Jackson would want nothing to do with us. And I was even more certain that the moment he found out, he would disappear. It was an understatement to say that I dreaded telling him.

I told no one. Instead, I went back, day after day, to the hospital and pretended that I was the happy and blissful fiancée of Matt. I chatted about the wedding with him. Watched TV with him in the big chair beside his bed. I wheeled him down to the cafeteria for lunch one day and dinner the next. The rest of the time I mentally counted down to Friday, the day that Jackson would return.

ON FRIDAY, I SPENT AN INORDINATE AMOUNT OF TIME ON MY HAIR AND make-up. I even put on a skirt. Jackson hadn't indicated when his flight was, so I procrastinated going to the hospital hoping that he would show up before I left.

Finally, mid-afternoon, I headed to the hospital. Matt's door was propped open, and I could hear laughter. Matt and Irene. Tension left my shoulders. If both of them were in a good mood, it would mean that we'd have a good day.

I stepped into the room and stopped short. Jackson sat on the chair beside Matt's bed, and Irene perched on the end of Matt's bed. Matt, unaware of my arrival, laughed at something.

Only Jackson saw me. His gaze flicked to me, but he smiled at Matt's story. I swallowed as I noticed the faded jeans that hugged his hips so perfectly and a basic grey t-shirt stretched over his chest. I think my heart was trying to pound out of my chest.

Had I stepped into some alternative universe? How was it possible that Jackson was included back into the family fold when they had shunned him a couple of weeks ago?

Matt turned his head, and his smile was huge. "Emily."

My face felt frozen in shock. "Hi."

Irene avoided my glance, but Jackson pinned me with his green gaze.

"I had the most amazing idea," Matt said, waving me over. "You're going to love it."

"Don't keep me in suspense."

"I know you're stressing about walking up the aisle by yourself and then I had the most brilliant idea. I asked Jackson, and he agreed."

I gave Matt a double take. "He agreed to what?"

"Jackson agreed to walk you down the aisle."

I stared dumbly at the group. My first instinct was to flee. I physically had to restrain myself from backing out of the room. "He did?"

"I, for one, think it's a brilliant idea. Nothing would thrill me more," Irene jumped in.

I turned my stupid expression to her. "You do?"

"Look at her face, look how much I surprised her," Matt laughed. "This is priceless."

My numb lips barely moved. "How did this come about?"

"I texted Jackson and asked him. He immediately wrote back and said yes. And the rest is history. Did you know that he was in Virginia this week?"

My throat worked convulsively to swallow. "You don't say."

I looked at Jackson, and he stared back at me, his expression blank.

"Come on. We've been waiting for you to show up. We want to go down to the cafeteria to grab dinner."

Irene rushed to get the wheelchair while Matt unsteadily got to his feet. Jackson stood up, and Matt reached out to grab his arm. With his recent weight loss, Matt looked diminutive next to Jackson's huge frame.

I watched as Jackson wheeled Matt down to the cafeteria. It was a weird de ja vu moment. Matt talked a mile a minute, and Jackson listened silently. Matt laughed as Jackson dipped the wheelchair back and tilted it, so he was riding on only one wheel.

"Want to tell me what happened?" I asked Irene, who walked beside me.

"I have no idea what you are talking about."

We finished dinner. Irene returned to the hotel and Jackson, Matt and I watched a rerun of Law and Order. My mind spun in a hundred different directions.

Irene had kicked Jackson out of the hospital and said that he wasn't part of their family. Matt had demanded that I kick Jackson out of the penthouse and told me that he was not welcome in our lives. Now they both rolled out the red carpet for him. What baffled me, even more, was that Jackson was open to such overtures. Why would he let them treat him so poorly? It made no sense. Jackson didn't tolerate bullshit. Yet, he willingly participated in this insincere family drama. The more I thought about it, the more pissed I got.

Irene and Matt acted so selfishly. And Jackson just took it. Is this how they treated him when he was a kid? Had he been on the receiving end of such hot and cold treatment his entire life? I almost couldn't contain my rage. I wanted to hurt Matt, but I wanted to hurt Irene more. My heart ached for Jackson who Matt privately referred to as "the charity case." No wonder Jackson didn't want a family. He had the worst luck of any person when it came to families. Even the family who supposedly rescued him abused him on some level. It took all my emotional control to sit there and not lose my shit.

The nurse came in and told us that visiting hours were over.

"Jack, can you make sure my girl here gets to her car safe? I would do it myself, but I'm pretty sure if something happened she would need to protect me, not the other way around," Matt joked.

The joke fell flat in light of what had happened only a week earlier, but Jackson took the request seriously. "You bet."

I walked to the door without looking back at Matt.

"Hey," he called after me, probably wondering why I wasn't saying a proper good night.

I ignored his call and started to walk rapidly down the wide hospital corridor.

JACKSON CAUGHT UP WITH ME AND WALKED EASILY BESIDE ME. WE RODE THE elevator in silence, and when the door slid open I took off towards the big sliding glass doors, not caring if he kept up with me or not. Why would he let Irene and Matt treat him like a second-class citizen? He acted like everything was normal, but that was the farthest thing from the truth. I needed to get away from him. Clear my head. I couldn't speak to him about it right now. I knew whatever would come out would be all wrong.

"Are you parked in the parking lot?"

"The overflow lot, but I can walk there myself."

"Show me."

We walked out into the fresh night air. I was so angry, I couldn't speak.

"Something you want to say?"

"No," I said tersely.

He walked me to my car and without saying a word I got in and started my car. I didn't offer to drive him back to his truck. In fact, I didn't even give him a second glance as I peeled out of the lot. I needed to get away from everyone. I needed time to think and calm down. I certainly didn't need him following me home.

I WAS TWO BLOCKS AWAY WHEN SUDDENLY A BIG ASS GRILL SHOWED UP IN MY review mirror.

"You've got to be kidding me," I yelled at no one in particular. I debated trying to lose him but realized that with my inability to change lanes without shoulder checking, there was no way I would ever manage that. Instead, I hunched over my steering wheel seething at the injustice that Irene and Matt bestowed on Jackson.

CHAPTER FORTY-SEVEN

I PULLED INTO MY PARKING STALL IN THE PARKADE OF THE PENTHOUSE. I jumped out of my car and started rapidly walking towards the elevator, not waiting for Jackson who was still in the process of parking his truck. With luck, I would be already on my way upstairs by the time he got to the elevator.

I got halfway across the parkade when I heard his door slam.

"Something bugging you?" His voice sounded so relaxed and easygoing, I thought my blood would start boiling. I spun around on my heels and stomped back to him. I walked right up to him and glared up at his face.

"You're walking me down the aisle?" I spat up at him. "Really? Matt just snaps his fingers, and you come crawling?"

His eyes widened with interest. "A couple of weeks ago you were pissed when they wanted me gone. I thought you would be happy they included me at your wedding."

"Are you upset that I haven't broken it off with Matt yet?"

"I don't need to know what your plans are. I've nothing to do with that. You can do whatever you want."

I flinched. I will admit. That stung but I needed to bring him back to the point of the fact that Matt and Irene were cruel. Did he not see that?

I put my hand on my hip. I looked at him with disbelief. "Don't you see what they're doing? Why are you putting up with their shit?"

He shrugged. "They're family."

"They don't act like family."

We eyeballed each other for a long moment. I felt so frustrated I turned on my heels and started to walk away.

"Family deserves loyalty."

In two seconds flat, I was back in his face. "Neither of them deserve your loyalty."

Another long moment ticked between us.

"I'm not loyal to someone because of how they treat me. I'm loyal because of the person I am."

I went completely still. The image of a young boy, at the mercy of a violent drunk, flashed before my eyes. Ted had smashed his bones, terrorized him and abused him in ways no child should ever be abused. That child's loyalty to Ted had been breathtaking.

Waves of pain washed over me so intensely that I almost couldn't breathe.

"It's not right," I squeezed out of my constricted throat.

"Why are you so upset about this?" he sounded mystified.

"Because you deserve so much better," I yelled at him. "Because it hurts me to see others hurt you."

"A bullet hurts. Violence hurts." He ran his hand through his hair in frustration. "This is nothing."

"If this is nothing than why does it feel like my heart is breaking," I yelled. I pushed past him. I couldn't let this man see me cry again. If I cried in front of him one more time, he would never talk to me again.

He moved so quick. He spun me around. His mouth came down on mine. Hot. Savage. Wild. I moaned into his mouth and wrapped my arms around his thick neck. Why did it feel like every time he touched me, I was coming in from the cold? My hands grabbed fingers full of his hair. He immobilized me against the truck. His mouth. It was everywhere. On my neck. On my shoulder. My lips. I couldn't think I was so turned on. All I could do was hang on and feel.

He lifted me up and my legs automatically wrapped around his waist while his mouth continued to assault me. My skirt bunched up around my waist. His glorious hard body, his excitement, and his arousal only fueled my own.

He shifted beneath me, and then the rasp of his zipper. His hard fullness butted up against the thin fabric of my underwear. He reached one hand between my legs and with a strong tug my panties tore from my hips.

One powerful thrust buried him into me. Beautiful sensations coursed through my entire body. He stood there and breathed hard against my neck. I was pinned, literally pinned, up against the truck, impaled on him.

He raised his head. His eyes locked with my own as he spoke, "I wish I wanted what you wanted."

I panted. Dizzy. Out of my mind with lust. He grabbed the back of my hair and pulled my head back roughly. I stared back at him in a daze.

"I want you to have everything you ever dreamed of. Do you understand?"

I didn't. I didn't understand what he said to me. None of this made sense. He stared at me, anger and desire written all over his face. And then, finally, he thrust into me. Hard. Up against his big black truck. It felt so incredible, so fulfilling that I could only hang on and moan.

Like everything Jackson, he moved with power and endurance. My entire body got tighter and tighter. I fought my orgasm, but I could only hang on so long. I let out a long, peeled cry. He stilled and watched my face as my entire body shuddered in ecstasy around him. We remained there for a long moment, both of us breathing hard. His hardness still buried in me.

"I don't want a family or commitment," he said against my lips, without kissing me. "But Matt does."

His words stabbed me in the heart.

"Jackson."

"You should marry him," he said, without expression on his face. "He's a good guy."

He was still rock hard and hadn't yet come. He pulled out of me and lifted me down onto shaking legs. I brushed my skirt down, needing a moment to compose myself. The moment had come. I needed to tell him that he was going to be a father. I took a deep breath.

"Please let me talk to you."

He looked at me for a long moment, and then he said in a clear voice. "I'm not what you want, and I'm not someone you can fix."

My mouth dropped open. I watched as he climbed into his truck. Without looking at me, he backed up and then peeled away.

ON SHAKING LEGS, I WALKED UP TO THE PENTHOUSE. IN MY HEART, I KNEW that he would not come back here. Jackson was gone.

The sense of loss crushed me so hard that it felt like someone had died. Numb, I sat on the couch in the dark for hours and willed him to walk through the door. But he didn't. Eventually, I staggered to his guest room and crawled into his bed. I could faintly smell him in the bed, and the familiar scent overwhelmed me on every level. Clutching his pillow around my waist, I wanted to, but I couldn't cry.

Jackson wasn't coming back. There was a black hole in my chest. This feeling destroyed me more than when my parents had been murdered. This darkness and pain pierced sharper than when my granny had died. I wasn't sure I would survive the night. How was it possible that a human being could endure this much loss?

Jackson. I knew from the moment my heart had turned towards this man that this would only end in devastation, but I had been powerless to stop myself. Like a plant that faces towards the sun, I had been unable to resist him. I had thought that I knew what losing him would be like. I had attempted to mentally and emotionally prepare myself. I had thought that the small amount of time I had been given with him would be worth the pain in the long run. I had never been more wrong about anything in my life.

He was wrong for me on so many levels, but my heart wanted what my heart wanted. And now, stupidly, my heart would never be the same again.

I debated calling him and telling him about the baby, but his words stopped me. He didn't want what I wanted. He had been clear in letting me know that it was over between us. I needed to accept this and move forward.

CHAPTER FORTY-EIGHT

For three days, I stayed away from the hospital. I didn't take calls. I didn't answer texts. I dragged myself through the motions of sustaining my life by eating and sleeping and keeping Chloe alive, but that was all I was able to manage. I slept for hours at a time, and the rest of my waking time I just sat.

Everything up to this point caught up with me. Everything stressful and bad had been pushed to the background because Jackson had been there to cushion the fall. He had countered everything with his strength and his protective nature, and somehow nothing had been insurmountable. Now, I stood alone and faced an impending hurricane, but my house had disappeared on me. Without Jackson in the background, I felt exposed and unsure of myself.

I determined I needed to come clean to Matt. I needed to end our engagement. I wanted to be brave and tell him that it was over for good. But there never seemed to be a good time to have that talk. So we pretended that everything was fine. My heart hurt so much that my instinct was to hide that pain. In doing so, I carried on like everything was fine. I wanted to be truthful, but the effort was so monumental, I instead busied my mind with the final details of the wedding.

It shocked me how easy it was to pretend. Each moment that ticked away brought us closer to our wedding day.

Thoughts, weird bad thoughts, repeated in my mind. Could I marry Matt? Jackson had ripped my heart out of my chest, so I felt numb. Did it matter one way or another if I married Matt? On an emotional level, I couldn't determine if it would be better for me to marry Matt or to end it.

What if I told Matt that he and I had slept together? He had no memory of the last five months. This baby could be passed off as his.

These dark thoughts gripped my mind as I teetered back and forth like a spinning top. Things had at one time been good between Matt and me. Maybe we could have our happy ending after all? Lots of women had pretended that one man's baby was another man's. Was it that bad? Matt would love this child, and this child would have a father. Was that the preferable action than to condemn this child to a lifetime with only me to parent it through life? Was I qualified to parent another human being? Look at the mess my life was in. Would one small lie make that much of a difference in the big picture of things?

It didn't help that Matt was the master of pretending. He knew that I was struggling, but he glossed over my vacant moods and numb state. If I was going to start this marriage with a lie, who better to start it with than a man who didn't want my truth?

I knew that Matt wanted the finer things in life. I had a lot of money. I could offer him that life, the vacations and all the trappings that he desired. In exchange, I would give my child a father.

Sometimes, I came to grips with my insane thoughts and returned to the fact that I needed to just end this charade, but no matter how much I tried, I could not find the strength within me to speak the truth.

There was a small, traitorous part of me that hoped that while Matt was still in my life, there was a chance I would see Jackson. Maybe he would show up at the hospital? Perhaps I would run into him outside in the parking lot? How pathetic that I would delay the inevitable for just one more glimpse of him. One more conversation. One more moment.

I couldn't accept that I would never see Jackson again. If I married Matt, at least I would be fed small tidbits about Jackson's life. As crazy as it was, that was almost the best reason I had to marry Matt.

THEN I RAN OUT OF TIME.

CHAPTER FORTY-NINE

I STOOD IN THE ROOM IN THE BACK OF THE CHURCH AND STARED IN THE mirror. My red hair was piled up on the top of my head. My sleeveless wedding dress's tight embroidered bodice nipped at my waist, and the skirt billowed out in an expanse of tulle to the floor. It was too tight. I guess that's what happens when you're ten weeks pregnant. Your wedding dress becomes a straight jacket on your rib cage. I took a deep breath and hated how I was unable to expand my lungs to full capacity.

"You look like a princess," Beth breathed from beside me.

We stared at our reflections in the mirror. I looked so serious. So young and uncertain. How had I ended up here? Had my indecisiveness and my inability to speak my mind brought me to this point? I felt wracked with uncertainty.

The problem was I felt numb. I could feel nothing. My entire being was whitewashed, and there was no color, no feeling, no sense of what was right and what was wrong.

"Do you think I should marry Matt?" I asked Beth.

The champagne flute hovered halfway to her lips. Our eyes met in the mirror.

"Is that a rhetorical question?"

"It's a real question."

I watched as she drained the entire glass. "Oh, God."

I waited as she poured herself another glass. And then downed that one.

She squared her shoulders and looked at me. "You can't hold what I say against me if you don't do what I think you should do."

I nodded.

"I think marrying Matt is the biggest mistake you could make in your life. And I think from the moment you say 'I do' to the moment you get your inevitable divorce, you are going to regret it every day of your life."

"Oh."

She poured herself a third glass. "You promised me that you wouldn't hold that against me."

"I won't."

"And I'll be there for you every single day if you decide to go through with this."

"Thanks."

"And if you do marry him and you end up deliriously happy you won't hold this conversation against me."

"I won't."

There was a knock at the door. Was that Jackson? My heart almost stopped.

The usher wanted to let us know that all the guests were seated. Matt was ready to take his place at the front.

Beth looked at me, and I widened my eyes at her.

Beth spoke. "Tell them that the bride needs five more minutes."

He nodded and shut the door behind him.

"Do you think Jackson is here?" My hands shook so hard my bouquet fluttered.

"You want me to go check?"

I nodded, grateful that she didn't mention my obsession with Jackson when I should focus on Matt.

"I'll be right back," she slipped out of the room.

∾

THE DOOR OPENED. THE ENTIRE ROOM SHRUNK AND THE WORLD TOOK ON color again. Jackson shut the door behind him. He stared at me, and I stared back. His black suit faultlessly hugged his huge form. I realized I had never actually seen him without some version of a beard on his face. The effects of his shaven face were stunning. He had the most beautiful jawline I had ever seen, and his cheekbones were so angular they looked like they could cut glass. I melted beneath his intense stare. His eyes roamed over me, taking in my hair, my dress, my trembling lips.

I realized at that moment, the only reason I hadn't called off the wedding was I needed to see this man one last time. I loved him to the point of being heartsick. How could I feel so much for him and he felt nothing back? How was it possible that love this big, this real, this intense could be so one-sided?

His jaw tightened. "You look perfect."

I worked my throat, trying to find something to say, but I could only stare back at him.

Moments ticked by.

He cleared his throat. "I got my papers. I'm being released from the outpatient program, and they're sending me for training in a couple of weeks. I'll probably be gone by the time you and Matt get back from your honeymoon."

I dropped onto a crouch and put my face in my hands. His words stabbed into my heart. I wanted to curl up in a ball and never get up.

"Are you okay?" he crouched down beside me.

"Why are you telling me this?" I looked up at his face. My heart was breaking in two.

"I wasn't sure if I would have a chance to say goodbye to you."

My eyes squeezed shut. I took several big breaths. "I don't want to say goodbye."

"Emily."

A sharp rap on the door and then Beth stuck her head in. "They're about to cue the music."

She glanced at Jackson and me and then backed out.

"You ready?" his voice was low.

My mind raced. This was a monumental mistake. He pulled me to my feet. I looked up at his face and willed him to look at me. I needed to see what he was thinking. I wanted to know what he was feeling. One flicker of emotion in his gaze and I would pick up my skirts and run to the doors.

He avoided my gaze and instead offered me his arm.

My shaking hand clung to the solid muscle of his forearm. This man had somehow become my rock. When I let go of him, I would simply wash away.

We stood at the entrance of the sanctuary. The music changed to Canon in D, and then there was a soft rumble as a hundred people stood up and turned to look at me. Matt stood at the front of the church beside the minister.

My legs shook so hard that I almost couldn't walk. I clung to Jackson, and slowly we started up a thousand mile long aisle. We walked and walked, and like a bad dream, we never seemed to reach the front.

I can do this, I told myself. Just get through this.

At the front, Jackson proffered his hand and helped me up the steps. I got to the second top step and looked back into his face. I saw a flicker of something in his expression. He dropped my hand, but my fingers clung to his. He was my lifeline. My protector. The person I loved. The father of my child. I didn't want to let go of him. I felt his grip re-tighten around my hand.

The audience shifted behind us. Whispering started. Matt cleared his throat, and then he stepped down towards me and offered me his hand. I looked at it and then looked back at Jackson's face. Green eyes watched me.

I looked back at Matt and shook my head.

Matt whispered. "Sweetheart, come on. Let go of poor Jackson. You're embarrassing him."

Tears pricked the back of my eyes. I started to let go of my lifeline, but Jackson's hand tightened around mine. Our eyes met again.

I swallowed, staring at the man I loved. Unable to look at the man I was supposed to marry.

Matt stepped down beside me, and his grip tightened like a vice around my wrist. "Come."

"I can't marry you, Matt."

Matt gave me a beguiling smile, his tone soothed. "Emily, come on."

I shook my head.

Matt's grip on my wrist tightened, and he tugged at me. Like he could physically drag me.

Jackson moved to stand beside me. "She said no."

Matt stepped up to Jackson's face and hissed. "What the fuck are you doing?"

"She said no," Jackson repeated quietly, still holding onto my hand.

People in the audience talked openly. The music continued to play.

"Is there a problem," the minister crept forward and looked between the three of us.

"Emily has some wedding jitters," Matt said between clenched teeth. "We just need to get her to let go of Jackson and then we'll be on our way."

The minister walked around to my side and spoke quietly, "Are you nervous? Do you need a few minutes?"

I looked up at the minster's kind face. His warm brown eyes gave me the most sympathetic look imaginable.

Matt leaned in and hissed, "Emily, you're embarrassing yourself and me. All of our friends and coworkers are watching."

The minister put his hands up. "Calm, please, let's remain calm. We want to handle this in a very calm fashion."

"I don't want to marry you," I said in a small voice.

We watched as Matt walked away. He grabbed the edge of the table and did some deep breathing. He turned and then a flower vase sailed towards my head. Jackson's arm reached in front of me and deflected the vase. It hit the side of the pulpit spraying water, flowers and glass in every direction. The audience gasped.

Matt picked up a silver offering plate, and it moved like a frisbee, but at the last moment, it veered off and hit the minister in the head. The minister looked at me, his eyes wide. He brought his hand up to his forehead and then looked at his hand. There was blood on his fingers. He moaned, and staggered off the side and sat down on the steps. I stood transfixed as someone from the audience ran up to him.

"You're not doing this to me," Matt announced, pointing his finger at me.

I stood there. Jackson still held my hand.

"You're such a frigid little bitch. No one but me is ever going to want to marry you," he ranted, as he picked up a hymnal and fired it towards me. Jackson reached and deflected that, too.

Jackson's voice was low. "Matt shut up."

Matt charged towards us, and he hauled back and punched Jackson in the face. Someone in the audience screamed. Jackson's head snapped back as Matt's fist connected with his face, but he didn't react. His hand still held my own.

Matt wound up to hit Jackson again, and I couldn't take it anymore. It had to stop.

"I'm pregnant."

Matt and Jackson looked at me with equally stunned expressions on their faces.

"I'm pregnant," I repeated.

You could feel the entire audience freeze. Canon in D continued to play softly in the background.

No one breathed. Except for Matt who was breathing so hard he was panting. "Well, that's impossible since you and I have never slept together."

"I'm truly sorry."

"Who's the father?" he asked, his voice was low, full of rage.

I swallowed and just stood there.

"Who the fuck is the father?" he screamed.

They both looked at me.

"Jackson."

Green eyes widened. Matt's mouth dropped open.

Then he pointed at me. "Fuck you."

He pointed at Jackson. "And fuck you, too. You're dead to me."

He looked out around the audience and said in a loud voice. "My fiancée is a stupid slut who got herself knocked up with my brother. My alleged brother. Who's just some white trash asshole that my parents brought home one day like a fucking stray dog."

Matt gave an exaggerated bow and then walked out the side door.

Jackson didn't move. I looked up at him.

My lips parted. "Say something."

He dropped my hand.

"No," I whispered.

His gaze looked my face over, and his expression was unreadable. His lip was bleeding. His eyes were blank. He turned and walked down the aisle.

The stunned congregation looked on.

The music started winding down and then went completely silent.

And then he was gone.

100 pairs of eyes swung back to me. I stood there frozen, in a trance. And then I did the only thing that a sane person can do in that situation. I picked up my skirts, and I ran.

NOTE FROM ODETTE

DEAR READER,

Thank you so much for reading my book. It means the world to me. I'm not expert at military, but I researched like a mad person. Any errors, please forgive me. I did my best. I have the most deep profound respect for the men and women who serve their country. Thank you to them all.

Sorry for the cliff hanger!! You have no idea how much I fought with this ending. I worked so hard to make this only one book, but Jackson was persistent. He wanted his story told. And that is how the conclusion of this duet was born.

Do you know how much power you have as a reader? Great reviews, for an indie author like me, are so incredibly valuable. If you enjoyed this book, please consider leaving a review.

A huge thanks to Parker Huntington, Grace Cheng, Sonia Mendes, CJ Hunt and the fabulous women of GVWA. I couldn't do what I do without their help and support.

And a profound thanks to my readers who make this amazing career possible. I appreciate each and everyone of you!

. . .

Love,
 Odette Stone

ODETTE STONE

NAVY SEAL ROMANCE BOOKS

My Fiancé's Brother: Book 1 (The Navy SEAL Series)

My Fiancé's Brother: Book 2 (The Navy SEAL Series)

My Fake Fiancé: Book 3, Stand alone (The Navy SEAL Series)

My Donut Princess: Book 4, Free Novella (The Navy SEAL Series)

SPORTS HOCKEY ROMANCE BOOKS

Puck Me Secretly, Book 1 (Vancouver Wolves Hockey Romance)

Home Game, Book 2 (Vancouver Wolves Hockey Romance)

Hook My Heart, Free Novella (Vancouver Wolves Hockey Romance)

ABOUT ODETTE

Odette Stone lives in Vancouver, Canada. Writing is her passion but when you can pull her away from her stories she loves to read, drink coffee, go for long walks and is particularly fond of action or suspense movies.

Made in the USA
Monee, IL
07 January 2020